Cliff Hangers:
Anna

A Cliff Ford Mystery

TERRY TOLER

Cliff Hangers: Anna
Published by: BeHoldings, LLC

Copyright @2021, **BeHoldings, LLC**
Terry Toler
All Rights Reserved

Book Cover: BeHoldings Publishing
Editor: Jeanne Leach
Contributing Editor: Donna Kos

For information email: terry@terrytoler.com.

Our books can be purchased in bulk for promotional, educational, and business use. Please contact your bookseller or the BeHoldings Publishing Sales department at:sales@terrytoler.com

For booking information email: booking@terrytoler.com.

First U.S. Edition: October, 2021
ISBN 978-1-954710-06-1

OTHER BOOKS BY TERRY TOLER

Fiction

The Longest Day
The Reformation of Mars
The Late, Great Planet Jupiter
The Great Wall of Ven-Us
Saturn: The Eden Experiment
The Mercury Protocols
Save The Girls
The Ingenue
Saving Sara
Save The Queen
No Girl Left Behind
The Launch
The Blue Rose
Body Count
Save Me Twice
Cliff Hangers: Anna

Non-Fiction

How to Make More Than a Million Dollars
The Heart Attacked
Seven Years of Promise
Mission Possible
Marriage Made in Heaven
21 Days to Physical Healing
21 Days to Spiritual Fitness
21 Days to Divine Health
21 Days to a Great Marriage
21 Days to Financial Freedom
21 Days to Sharing Your Faith
21 Days to Mission Possible
7 Days to Emotional Freedom

Uncommon Finances
Uncommon Health
Uncommon Marriage
The Jesus Diet
Suddenly Free
Feeling Free

For more information on these books and other resources check out TerryToler.com.

Thank you for purchasing this novel from best-selling
author Terry Toler. As an additional thank you, Terry wants to give
you a free gift.

Sign up for:

Updates
New Releases
Announcements
At terrytoler.com

We'll send you the first three chapters of The Launch,
a Jamie Austen novella, free of charge. The one that started
the Spy Stories and Eden Stories Franchises.

1

This wasn't the first time I had to go to the morgue and wouldn't be the last.

Before I did, I needed a double shot. The *Hipster Coffee Cafe* was my go-to place. Six days a week. Except on Sunday. When I took a day of rest from the calories, sugar, and caffeine.

As usual, the place was packed. It took nearly ten minutes to get to the front of the line. When I did, the familiar smile was one of the reasons I hadn't missed a morning in months.

"Good morning, Cliff," the barista behind the counter said.

My name was Cliff Ford. I was thirty-four. Homicide detective. I'd been with the Chicago PD for eight years. Risen through the ranks on a fast track to senior detective. I worked the south side of Chicago so there was no shortage of murders to investigate.

Across the counter was a twenty-eight-year-old woman who looked like she wasn't a day over forty. She'd taken my order more times than I would ever admit to anyone. I didn't actually know her age. I was only guessing. From my experience, nowadays twenty-eight-year-old women could look forty or eighteen.

Except for the crooked teeth, the girl was above average in the looks department. She had a ring on her finger, so she was obviously married, though I'd never asked.

"I'll have the usual," I said to her, while pulling out a few small bills from my wallet.

"Someday, you're going to surprise me and order something different, Cliff."

I gave her a sly grin. "I doubt it. I'm a creature of habit."

"We'll have it right out," she said, returning the friendly grin, although she kept her mouth tightly closed when she smiled to hide what was obviously an insecurity.

The banter made me feel normal. The empty bed I woke up in every morning depressed me. Reminded me of the loss and the old routine I'd never get back. The coffeemaker on the kitchen counter sat there collecting dust. I hadn't touched it in over a year. Not since the day I'd made the last cup of coffee I'd ever make for my wife.

The coffee shop was like a safe haven for me. The girl and the stiff drink gave me a new morning routine. Something to look forward to. That's why I came to *Hipsters*. Also, why I never deviated from my routine. If I did, I was afraid I'd feel lost. Like I did for several months until I found the place.

Unfortunately, the line was pushing in against me, so I stepped to the side. Katy, the crooked-smile girl, gave me a nod as if she was acknowledging that we wouldn't get a chance to talk that morning. There'd been a few mornings when we talked for two or three minutes before a customer interrupted us. Those days were the best ones. Even though they were short, I left the coffee shop feeling like the void was filled. If only for a few hours. Sort of like the caffeine, which also wore off around the same time.

In short order, my coffee smoothie was ready. Apparent by the gesture of the man behind the counter who held my drink high in the air while looking in my direction.

"Thanks, Jed," I said to him. I was on a first name basis with everyone in the bar. It's how I kept my sanity. Made me feel like I had a life. Apart from my job, this was the extent of my social interaction. If you could call it that.

I looked around for a place to sit. Standing room only except for one chair in the corner.

Perfect.

I liked to have my back to the wall. Facing out. So no one could sneak up on me. As if they would in a local coffee shop. Out of habit,

I touched the gun on my hip for the first of what would be at least a dozen times before lunch. Concealed by my suit jacket that hung down over it.

A woman sat in the other seat across from the empty chair. Silky black hair. Her back was to me. As I got closer, I could tell she was typing on a laptop.

"Is this seat taken?" I asked hesitantly. It didn't seem like it was.

She shook her head no without looking up from the computer screen. Though I thought I heard a sigh, like she didn't want to be bothered with company. No problem. I wasn't much of a conversationalist. Since my wife died, I hadn't had a conversation with a woman who wasn't a colleague that lasted longer than five minutes.

When I sat, I doubt I could've said anything anyway without stammering. The woman took my breath away. Amber eyes. Black bangs that hung down to the side and over deep, jet-black eyebrows. Thin lips. Sturdy jaw with high cheekbones. A slight flowery smell lingered over the table.

Why did I feel guilty?

The last thing I expected that morning was to meet a girl. Then I realized we hadn't actually met. I'd spoken four words. She'd spoken none. Unless you included the rude sigh which spoke volumes.

The continued silence gave me an opportunity to observe her.

Maybe she was Puerto Rican.

My inquisitive detective nature kicked in. It came with the trade. I'd tried to tamp it down in the past, but unsuccessfully. If nothing else, it gave me a chance to hone my skills. At least that was my justification for the mental gymnastics.

The woman had toned arms. *A Pilates instructor?* Maybe.

Runner? Probably.

Swimmer?

No.

Her hair was too full and rich. Chlorine-damaged hair had a distinct look.

Kick boxer? A real possibility.

Although I couldn't see her legs under the table, I assumed her legs were as toned as her arms. I could tell she was wearing a form-fitting dress. Black. Likely wearing black high heeled pumps. Or sneakers. She'd change into her dress shoes when she got to work.

Black haired girl had that air of someone who had martial arts training.

I was proficient as well. Maybe I could ask about that. Somehow work it into the conversation.

When she reached for her coffee, I remembered my drink and took a big gulp to match her movement.

I tried hard not to stare. The woman was gorgeous.

"It's busy today," I said, referring to the long line that was now out the door.

She looked up and twisted her lips, obviously bothered by the intrusion. "I'll tell you the same thing I told the other three guys. I don't give out my number to strangers."

"Good policy. You can't be too careful in this world."

She looked back down and resumed typing. Now I felt uncomfortable and squirmed in my seat and looked for an opportunity to make a quick exit without it appearing like I'd been shot down.

I also felt a touch of anger. No reason for the hostility.

"I don't remember asking for your number, though," I said, as I tried to regain a little bit of dignity.

That caused her to look up for a second time. "I didn't mean to be rude. I'm just working."

Was that an apology? A lame one, at best.

"No problemo. I'll finish my drink and keep my mouth shut."

Problemo?

What an idiot. Not only was it a stupid thing to say, but it might be considered racist in this politically correct world we suddenly lived in. We were in Chicago where political correctness flourished.

I kept kicking myself over the comment. The Dominican girl didn't have an accent. So why did I imitate one?

Not Dominican, but somewhere in that vicinity.

4

More awkward silence.

Actually, I welcomed silence. Truthfully, I was thinking I should leave before I said something else stupid.

The morgue awaited.

I should figure out a way to work that into the conversation.

The thought brought a smile to my face.

I could opine on the murder capital of the world, Chicago. I'd lived there my whole life. A good place or bad place to be a homicide detective, depending on your perspective. Good because there was never a shortage of work. Bad for the same reason.

After another big sip of my smoothie, I turned my focus back to figuring out where she was from. I'd changed my mind and decided she was from a different island in the same region. I couldn't stop the introspection. Profiling and pigeon-holing people was what I did for a living. Unfortunately, it carried over into my personal life more often than not.

Say something.

I needed to speak again to let her know I wasn't a complete fool. "My name is Cliff Ford, by the way."

I would have offered my hand, but she kept typing.

"Anna," she said without looking up. I thought I caught a flash of deception in her voice.

Another thing I was trained at. Spotting liars. I could tell a person was lying by facial expressions and by the tone of his or her voice. That skill served me well when I was investigating murders. Something I couldn't just turn off in a personal conversation.

We just met.

Why would she be lying to me?

I decided to give Anna the benefit of the doubt. She clearly didn't want to give out her number or her real name to a complete stranger.

Understandable.

Awkward silence for another two minutes.

We both took more sips of our drinks than normal. She now seemed nervous as well.

The caffeine gave me a jolt. My drink was a smoothie they made special just for me. Chilled coffee. One frozen banana. Almond milk. Rolled oats. A heaping spoonful of peanut butter. With chocolate sprinkles on top. And an extra shot of caffeine.

Not that I needed the extra juice. I was already a high-strung adrenaline junkie. My metabolism kept my BMI under ten. That and my intense daily workouts which I did every afternoon after work. The extra caffeine made me feel invincible. Which I sometimes needed in my line of work. Like when I busted a door down not knowing how many guns were on the other side of it.

My *Turn Me into a Maniac* smoothie, as I called it, was almost gone in what would be record time. I had to consciously keep my hand from shaking as I took another drink. A deep breath was a lame attempt to slow my heart rate down. Between the girl and the caffeine, I felt like someone had sent an electric charge through my body.

I decided I needed to finish my drink and get out of there. I'd take it with me, but I was on my motorcycle. Carrying it wasn't an option. Neither was throwing it away. I wouldn't give Venezuelan girl the satisfaction. Like she had somehow won.

Won what?

Why did it feel so awkward? Sitting there not talking to each other seemed weird. Abruptly getting up seemed weirder.

The typing slowed down, so it appeared she had wrapped up whatever she was doing. Maybe she'd get up and leave first and relieve me of the torture. I couldn't let her. I had to know where she was from. My mind now vacillated between South and Central America as her point of origin.

Anna didn't leave.

"Do you come here often, Cliff?" she asked, after she closed the laptop.

"Now that sounds like a pickup line to me," I quipped. "Before you go any further, you should know that I don't give out my number to strangers either."

I made sure the grin on my face let her know I was kidding.

"Touché," she said, and let out a chuckle and then a mesmerizing grin.

After that, I couldn't make myself leave even if I had the strength in my legs to stand up. For twenty minutes we talked. I grilled her with questions. Like I was a detective on a case. Turns out she was from Miami. Parents were from Cuba. I couldn't believe I'd gotten that so wrong.

Then I realized she might've lied again. My guard was down so I wasn't looking for signs of deception.

Anna didn't seem to mind the rapid-fire questions, although she always added a question to her answer. She had her own agenda and kept analyzing me like she was a counselor. Or psychiatrist. Both of us appeared to avoid discussing our jobs.

I knew my reason why. Some girls thought being a homicide detective was cool. Exciting. Mysterious. Others thought it was creepy. My wife was in the latter category. I was afraid to mention it to Anna. I wondered why she was avoiding telling me what she did for a living. My guess was that she knew a woman shrink was a turn-off to most guys.

My sister had said on more than one occasion that I should see one. Maybe this qualified as a session. The thought almost made me laugh out loud. I'd mention it when she called, which could be at any time since she called me every day to see how I was doing.

"What's so funny?" Anna asked, as I quickly wiped away whatever grin had been on my face.

"Nothing. I was just thinking about someone."

"Girlfriend?"

I shook my head no. I instinctively reached for my ring finger. I'd only taken it off for the first time two weeks ago. At my sister's insistence. Now I wished I still had it on. It'd be a perfect excuse to get out of the rest of the conversation.

"Sister," I quickly added. "She'd be happy with me right now."

"Why's that?"

"She says I need to get out more and not be so afraid to talk to women."

"You don't seem to be having any trouble talking to me."

I shrugged my shoulders.

Anna had no idea that my stomach was churning, and anxiety was swirling around inside of me like a jetty. I was trained to maintain a poker face at all times. Those skills were being tested at that very moment. Fortunately, Anna kept the conversation going. If she was still nervous, she was hiding it well.

"Although, I feel like I've just been through an interrogation," Anna added. "Your style is to ask a lot of questions, isn't it?"

"Sorry about that. I'm a detective. That's what I do for a living." I left out the homicide part.

"That explains it."

"Hey. You asked a lot of questions too. You like to put people in categories. Are you a psychiatrist?"

"High school guidance counselor."

Did I just see deception for a second time?

High school guidance counselors didn't wear tight dresses. I looked over at the clock on the wall. Coming up on quarter to nine. School was already in session. Wouldn't a guidance counselor have to be there at first bell?

Stop it!

Why did I distrust what she was telling me? Analyzing and parsing every word that came out of the mouth of a suspect or witness was one thing. Grilling a pretty girl in a coffee shop was bordering on insanity.

As if she sensed my confusion, Anna said, "I should be going." She looked down at her watch. "I'm going to be late. My first kids start to show up at nine."

Now she seemed like the one in a hurry to get out of there.

She stood and I did as well. Which I immediately regretted. Although chivalrous, it seemed like I was trying too hard.

I held out my hand, and she shook it. Firmly. The girl definitely worked out. I could see her full body now. Her dress went down further than I first thought. Almost to her knees. Form fitting, but not as tight as I had first imagined it to be. She pulled it down further. Self-consciously.

Anna gathered up her things and threw her purse over her shoulder. Then she said, "I don't give out my number, but if you want to see me again, I'll be at *Champions* Friday night. For happy hour."

Champions was a popular sports bar. I knew it well. I often went there after my workouts to catch the Cubs in the spring and summer and the Bears in the fall and winter.

"I don't drink," I blurted out after I hesitated.

If I could slap myself across the side of my head, I would. Another stupid thing to say.

She let out a chuckle but ignored my dumb comment. "It was nice meeting you. Maybe I'll see you again sometime."

Then she was gone.

I was left standing with my mouth probably hanging open.

What just happened?

My body was filled with mixed emotions. On the one hand, I enjoyed it. It felt good to talk to a person of the opposite sex for longer than a minute. On the other hand, I was filled with regrets. Analyzing the conversation. Wondering why I didn't handle it better. Still feeling guilty for talking to someone who wasn't my wife.

I let out a half sigh and groan and decided to get out of there. The last of my smoothie took only one more big swig. I left the shop and boarded my motorcycle determined to put the girl out of my mind.

Certain I'd never see her again.

* * *

City Morgue

Getting to the morgue took longer than I'd expected.

A text on my phone said that my Lieutenant had called a meeting of the detectives and going to the morgue would have to wait. The meeting took over an hour. Procedural stuff. Afterward, I took the opportunity to go through my files.

A drive-by shooting on the south side. That one was at a dead end. The odds of finding the shooter were slim to none. Eyewitnesses weren't talking. Video surveillance identified the car, but it had been stolen. Our local snitches hadn't heard any chatter.

Another file was a crime of passion. The wife's murderer was behind bars. It didn't get any easier than that one.

By the time I left the office and headed for the morgue, lunch rush hour had set in, and traffic was near a standstill. Fortunately, I was on my bike and could maneuver through it, saving a lot of time.

When I arrived, my pace slowed. I dreaded going in. The morgue was unlike any other place on earth. Cold and antiseptic, yet I imagined it to be what hell was like. Hundreds of lifeless faces. Young and old. In various stages of decay. Void of any future.

I went through security and to the basement where they kept the bodies. There I met the assistant to the coroner. His job was overseeing and processing the bodies. A thin man with a brainy demeanor. All business. He barely had time for introductions.

Since I knew that about him, I got right to the point. "What ya got for me today?" I asked.

"A Jane Doe. Early thirties. Gunshot wound to the chest. We haven't had a chance to check her out. You got here quickly."

That seemed like a strange comment.

He opened the door to the holding room and the cold hit me like I'd just walked into an icebox. In a way I had. The room was nothing more than a large freezer lined with tables filled with bodies with white sheets over them. On both sides of the room were bins where more bodies were held. The ones on the tables were either overflow or unprocessed.

He got in front of me and walked briskly to the last one on the right.

An eerie silence filled the room as neither of us said a word.

I stood against the far wall a safe distance away but close enough to see her face.

He pulled back the sheet.

I couldn't believe my eyes.

I recognized her immediately.

Anna.

2

It seemed like all the oxygen had been sucked out of the room, and my breath became shallow and rapid. Seeing Anna's lifeless body on a table in the city morgue made me feel like I'd been hit by a semi-truck doing eighty on the freeway while riding my motorcycle.

I paced back and forth. To the extent I could in that confined space. Just a couple steps in each direction.

"I take it you know this woman," Patel, the assistant to the coroner asked me.

I didn't know how to answer.

"Yes. I mean... We've met."

"Good. I need a name." He walked to the foot of the table and pulled up a clipboard attached by a thin chain. He grabbed a pen from underneath the clip and stared at me waiting for an answer.

I hesitated.

Was Anna really her name? I had my doubts. She never said her last name.

Then I decided not to answer. The coroner didn't need her name to do his job. He only wrote it down for the investigator's benefit. The investigator was me. Jane Doe would have to do for now.

"I don't know her name," I said.

Not really a lie. I'd keep the information to myself until I knew more.

Patel abruptly dropped the clipboard, and the sound of it banged against the steel table echoing through the room like a church bell sounding off in a belfry. He walked back to the head of the table.

I wished he'd cover Anna's face.

"How do you know her?" he asked.

Another piece of information that was none of his business. All he needed to concern himself with was forensics and the time and cause of death. Then I hesitated again. He did need an answer, or it'd raise alarm bells in his mind, and he might mention it to my Lieutenant who might mention it to me.

"I don't know that I do," I answered truthfully. "I think we met. But I'm not sure who she is."

By this time, I had gotten over the shock and started to think like a detective. Information was gold in an investigation, and I needed it fast. Once I thought about it, the timeline didn't make sense. The clock on the wall said 12:33. Anna left the coffee shop at a quarter to nine. It seemed nearly impossible that she could be shot, the crime scene investigated, the coroner called, and her body transported to his office and placed in the morgue in... a little over five hours.

No. A little over four hours.

"When was she shot?" I asked.

Patel walked back to the clipboard.

"The call came in around nine fifty this morning."

Obviously... it was possible.

"Where did it happen?"

"On Belleview Road."

I quickly did the math. Belleview was thirty minutes from *Hipsters*. Anna would've had time to get there, but barely. She also said she had to be at the high school by nine. Did she even work at the high school? Probably not. But why would she lie? And how did she get in such a precarious situation in broad daylight.

"She was shot going into a coffee shop," Patel added.

What?

A coffee shop?

Now I was really confused. She'd just had coffee. With me. Something I wasn't going to tell Patel.

Wait a minute.

My mind suddenly regained more focus. Yesterday was when the Lieutenant told me to go to the morgue. A good fourteen hours before Anna was shot.

There's another body.

"Is there a second victim?" I asked.

"No. Just her."

He misunderstood the question. "I mean... did you call our office about another homicide yesterday?"

A look of recognition came over his face as his eyes brightened and his eyebrows raised.

"Yes. Alfred Sweeney."

Then it hit me. Anna wasn't my case. Sweeney was. My mind raced as I tried to figure out a way to get assigned to investigate Anna's death. More than likely, I was too late. Cases were assigned to the next detective on the list by the dispatcher as soon as they came in. Somebody would've already been notified to make a trip to the morgue.

A pain shot through my heart like I'd been the one struck by a bullet. It quickly turned to anger as I wanted to be the one to find out who did this to Anna. We'd only had twenty minutes together, but this was personal to me for reasons I didn't even understand. She'd made an impression on me. I didn't realize how much until that moment.

A wave of sadness came over me.

Loss. Again.

My wife had died in a drive-by shooting. Thirteen months before. The case was still unsolved.

Obviously, not the same even though the pain felt similar.

I barely knew Anna. I didn't know if I would've gone to *Champions* on Friday night, but now I wouldn't get the chance. Some scumbag took that from me. That's why I wanted to be the one to investigate this case. Be the one to throw Anna's murderer on the ground and handcuff him. Maybe force a confrontation and take him out of this world.

I hadn't gotten that justice for Gabby. My wife. Her murderer still walked the streets.

Patel stared at me with his mouth twisted to the side and his forehead furrowed in confusion.

I needed to pull myself together and fast.

"Show me Sweeney's body and file," I said, in a feeble attempt to sound nonchalant. He started walking and I followed. As I got to the end of the table, I touched Anna's foot.

"I'm sorry," I said to her under my breath. "I'm so sorry."

***

Sweeney was already in a bin across the room. Patel rolled it out and pulled back the sheet.

"Fifty-seven-year-old male," he said.

"Cause of death?" I asked.

"Single stab wound to the chest."

"How did one stab wound kill a man with this much fat on him?" I asked. Sweeney was huge. He had to weigh at least four hundred pounds.

"Fluke. The knife penetrated just above the stomach region and nicked his heart. He bled out internally. Killed by a pizza delivery man."

"That makes sense."

The quip seemed funny to me, but I bit my lip to maintain my professionalism. In my experience, jokes in the morgue were frowned upon. These men and women took their jobs seriously, and they should. Some of them even had thin skin and considered jokes a slight on their profession and disrespectful of the dead. Homicide detectives joked about the perps and the dead all the time. Probably to relieve the tension from the stress of seeing them day in and day out.

To prove my point, Patel ignored my comment and pulled back the blanket further so I could see the wound. Fortunately, I no longer got queasy seeing a dead body. An uncomfortable and awkward feeling was all I felt now at the morgue. Although, when I saw Anna lying on that table, I felt something I'd never felt there before. More of a shock. Like someone had tasered me.

Patel kept talking, bringing my mind back to the task at hand. He gave me all the technical analysis of the cause of Sweeney's death.

To the right of the stab wound was a huge autopsy incision that went from just below Sweeny's neck to his belly button, closed up with oversized staples. Sweeney had obviously been there for a while. By the looks of the body, my guess was two weeks.

When he finished talking, Patel stood there and stared at me as if he wanted me to say something or ask a question. I should be asking questions, but none came to mind. I couldn't get Anna out of my mind.

My phone rang. We both jumped.

Shay. My sister.

I should've let it go to voicemail, but I needed to hear a familiar voice.

"Hello."

"What ya doing?" she asked.

I turned my back to Patel and Sweeney and walked to the other end of the room for privacy. Patel didn't need to know I was wasting his time with a personal call.

"I'm looking at an extremely large, naked man in the city morgue."

"Cliff! Too much information."

"You asked."

"I'm sorry I did," she said almost angrily.

I didn't know if she was offended by the large man comment or the naked part. Could be the fact that I was talking to her from the city morgue. I remembered the last time that happened, she told me not to answer my phone when I was near a dead person. Shay was also one of those women who was creeped out by my job. My wife and Shay were best friends and allies in their quest to get me to change professions. Something I couldn't do. This job was in my blood.

"I probably should go," I said. "Can I call you later? I don't want to keep the dead man waiting."

"Very funny."

"Later."

Patel had already closed the bin and had a file in his hand. I was thinking more clearly.

"Go ahead and release the body to the next of kin," I said. "I don't need anything else."

"Good. We need the space."

We started to walk out together. As we got to the door, I took another look back. At the table on the far right where Anna lay. For the first time ever in the morgue, and for the first time since my wife died, I had to fight back a tear.

It wasn't my case. I barely knew her. But I had to know.

Who was she? And who killed her.

I was resolved to find out.

3

Detective Lance Carson was assigned to Anna's case. I couldn't stand the man. Why did it have to be him? Carson was arrogant and lazy. Two traits I couldn't tolerate. We'd gotten into several arguments in the past and almost came to blows on one occasion. If some other detectives hadn't been around at the time of the confrontation, I would've wiped the smug look off his face permanently.

Whatever.

I'd do my own investigation under the radar. If I found out something important, I'd let him know. Otherwise, I had to satisfy my own curiosity. Better that he didn't know I might've been the last person to interact with Anna before she died.

In reality, I didn't have much to go on. Especially if Anna had lied to me. There were ways to find out if she had. Carson would eventually get around to running her prints through the database to see if he got a match. That would most likely be a dead end. Anna didn't seem like the type who'd been in trouble with the law.

On the other hand, if Anna really was a high-school guidance counselor, she would've been fingerprinted as part of a background check. Carson would never check that database. He had no reason to. I would. Because I never left any stone unturned.

Probably why I should give him what information I had.

Not going to happen. Not yet anyway.

I'd do the groundwork for him. I couldn't run the database because a log was kept of every person who accessed it. I had no logical explanation for why I was meddling in his case. I had other methods at my disposal. The local high schools would be a good place to start. The lead was easy enough to disprove. The guidance counselor pictures would be on the school websites. In a little over an hour, I could know if Anna had told me the truth. If not, I did Carson a favor. He wouldn't have to chase the lead.

At least that's how I rationalized not telling him.

I replayed the coffee shop conversation in my mind to see if I missed anything. Any subtle clues.

"I have to go. My first students start coming at nine," Anna had said.

She left at quarter till. That meant the high school was within ten to fifteen minutes of the coffee shop. I made a list. Even expanded the radius to twenty minutes. Twelve schools.

Turns out not all schools had the guidance counselor's name or picture on the website. Some did and some didn't. I checked off the ones that had pictures who were clearly not Anna.

The next step was to call the schools.

I knew exactly what to say. "My name is Detective Cliff Ford. Chicago PD. Do you have a guidance counselor named Anna?" Simple and straightforward.

I started calling the schools on my list and repeated the spiel a half dozen times. The answer I got each time was no.

One by one I marked them off my list. I got near the end and lost optimism. If this was a dead end, then I had no other leads. Maybe I could go to *Champions* on Friday night and snoop around. See if anyone recognized her. The problem was that I didn't even have a picture. My only hope was that she used the name *Anna* when she was there.

I dialed another number. Only three left. An unfriendly voice answered at South Skyline High School.

"How may I help you?" she asked almost angrily.

I couldn't blame her. My wife and Shay had suggested I become a high school gym teacher. My college degree was in Physical Education. I actually had the hours for a teaching certificate. I laughed in their faces. Within two weeks I'd be arrested for wringing one of the kid's necks. I don't think I could take the insubordination and back talk.

Instead, I chose a career where I carried a gun. If somebody spouted off at me, I could take them down or threaten them if need be. Most people were hesitant to give me any guff given my physical build and overall tough-guy attitude.

"My name is Detective Cliff Ford. Chicago PD," I said to the rude lady. "What is your guidance counselor's name?" I asked, getting right to the point.

"We're not allowed to give out that information."

I resisted raising my voice.

"This is part of an ongoing investigation."

While that was true, technically, I wasn't part of that investigation and not authorized to make these phone calls. Carson would be upset even though I was trying to help him. The Lieutenant wouldn't like it either but would probably only give me a slap on the wrist for show. At this point, I didn't care. I had to know. What they didn't know wouldn't hurt them.

It probably didn't matter. I was pretty sure there was no high-school guidance counselor named Anna.

The woman on the other end of the phone hesitated.

"Ma'am. I'm just asking for a name. I'm sure it's public information. You'd save me valuable time looking for it."

"Her name is Anna Navarez."

I about fell out of my chair. My heart started to race.

"Is she in? Can I speak to her?"

"She's not in today."

"Can you describe her to me?"

I could hear a phone ring in the background.

"Please hold," the lady said.

I stood to my feet and left my desk and walked around the bullpen now. Unable to stay in one place for longer than a few seconds.

She came back on. "Like I said, Anna's not in today."

"What does Anna look like?"

"Tall. Pretty. Dark black hair."

"Is she of Spanish descent?"

"Cuban. I think."

My heart did a complete somersault in my chest.

"When did she call in sick?" I asked.

"This morning just before nine o'clock. I took the call myself. She actually didn't call in sick."

"Did she say why she needed the day off?"

"She said she needed a personal day."

"How was her demeanor? Did she seem upset?"

"Now that you mention it, she did seem rushed. It's very unusual for Anna not to be in her office by eight thirty. She's very diligent about her schedule. I don't believe she's ever called in sick or taken a personal day before today."

"Do you know of anyone who has threatened Anna? Has she received any unusual phone calls? Do you know if she had made any enemies?" I regretted using the past tense. I wondered if the lady would pick up on it. I also needed to take a breath. The questions came too rapid fire. Before the woman even had a chance to answer the first one.

"What's this about?" she asked.

"Never mind. Thank you. You've been extremely helpful."

Those questions were better asked in person. So, I could see the reaction on their faces.

I hung up my cell phone slowly. Almost numb.

Anna didn't lie. She was a high-school guidance counselor. Her parents were from Cuba. She was late for work that morning. I knew why. It was my fault she was late. I almost felt guilty. She would've been at her desk by eight thirty if I hadn't distracted her.

But what happened to her?

Sometime after Anna left me, she suddenly couldn't go to the school. Why? By my calculations, it had to be right after she left the coffee shop. Something took her to Belleview Road. Thirty minutes away. To another coffee shop. Did she get a call? I'd really like to get my hands on the cellphone records. Talk to witnesses at the coffee shop.

It had to be a call. Who was it? The killer?

More importantly, what should I do with this information? I now knew the name of Carson's Jane Doe. He should really be the one to investigate the matter. Interview everyone at her high school. Search her apartment. Pull her phone records. I already had a list of things I would do.

I had to tell him. Or did I? If I did, the Lieutenant would tell me not to go near the case. Especially if he knew I had a personal interest in it. We weren't allowed to investigate murders of people we knew.

Should I tell Carson about Champions?

Did I have a choice? The Lieutenant would probably fire me on the spot if he knew I was withholding the name of a Jane Doe and investigating it personally.

Maybe I should just go there myself.

Today was Wednesday. What difference did another two days make? Carson probably wouldn't even pick up the file before Friday.

What if someone called in to report a missing person?

It'd still take Carson a couple of days to make the connection.

The decision was made.

I was all in. Past the point of no return. I was going to *Champions*. I'd ask around. Discreetly. Did Anna have a boyfriend? Ex-husband? Jilted lover? A stalker? Was she afraid of anyone? Did she mention anything suspicious? Was she meeting anyone else there? A girl-friend perhaps.

Friday night. Two whole days suddenly seemed like a long time to me, although I wouldn't sit on my hands and wait. I'd do what investigating I could. Under the radar.

I hoped I wasn't making a huge mistake.

4

Friday

When I foolishly decided to ask Carson about Anna, we almost had our first confrontation over his handling of her investigation.

"Any luck identifying the girl in the morgue?" I asked.

He sat at his desk as I stood over him.

"How do you know about her?" he replied, with a slight tone of consternation. Clearly annoyed that I would ask about one of his cases.

I already had a prepared answer.

"I was there when she was brought into the morgue. Lieutenant assigned me to another guy who was there at the same time."

"I actually haven't had a chance to work on it," Carson said dismissively. He roughly pushed some papers around his desk. "I've got a lot on my plate right now," he added.

I didn't think that was true. He didn't have any more cases to work on than the rest of us.

Truthfully, I was happy he hadn't started looking into it. At the same time, it made me mad. In a homicide investigation, the first forty-eight hours were the most critical. After that, eyewitness testimony got sketchier. People's recollections faded. Sometimes, their imaginations kicked in, and they added details they didn't actually see.

The murderer also had a chance to cover his tracks. Dispose of the weapon. Maybe even leave the area. Manufacture an alibi.

Then he said something that almost sent me through the roof.

"She's the prettiest stiff I've seen in a long time," he said, in what could only be described as a creepy voice.

Anna is not a stiff!

It took every bit of restraint not to shout those words at the top of my lungs. Really, I wanted to take my forearm and place it around his throat and choke him out.

Instead, I had the presence of mind to say, "I can take the case off your hands if you're too busy. My load's pretty light right now."

"Nah. I'm good," he retorted. "Besides... maybe she's got a pretty sister I wouldn't mind meeting." He looked up at me and said it with a lustful grin.

I'd have thought that statement inappropriate even if he weren't talking about Anna. Because he was, I had to leave, or I'd do something I'd regret. Carson was a louse and undeserving of working a case of a woman with the grace, beauty, and elegance of Anna. She deserved better than someone like Carson assigned to find her killer.

I wondered if he even would. He was lazy and approached every case without a sense of urgency. Still, I was surprised he'd done nothing. He should've at least looked at the missing person's report and run a fingerprint check. That took almost no time at all. Even I had checked the missing person's report. I found nothing, but still.

Another thing that surprised me.

I figured the school would've called when Anna didn't show up for work on Thursday or Friday. Anna must not be that connected if no one had noticed her missing.

That didn't change my anger toward Carson. Even though he wouldn't have found anything on the missing person's report, I'd at least appreciate it if he'd make the effort to do the basics of police investigation.

Not that I was one to throw stones. I'd done nothing on Sweeney. The dead, humongous guy in the morgue killed by the pizza delivery man. Admittedly, my whole focus had been on Anna.

That didn't let Carson off the hook. Our two cases weren't the same. His had a lot of unknowns. He didn't know the identity of the killer or the victim. In my case, I knew who stabbed Sweeney. The pizza delivery boy admitted as much. My investigation revolved around his claim of self-defense. According to the pizza guy, he got in an argument with Sweeney over the tip. Things escalated quickly after that. Words were exchanged. Sweeney became combatant and made a move for him. Sweeney was a big man so I could see how a hundred and fifty-pound pizza boy could feel threatened.

According to pizza boy, he pulled out a knife and stabbed Sweeney just in time. As the man was going for him. If his story were true, then lucky for him he had a knife. Not so much for Sweeney.

A man walking his dog saw the whole thing. I had the statement he made to the police. He pretty much corroborated the pizza guy's story. I just had to piece it together and decide. I had a problem with why the pizza guy didn't run away. The only hole in his defense. Sweeney couldn't run ten steps if his life depended on it.

I was still undecided. The prosecutor would ultimately decide whether to press charges if I chose to pursue it. My recommendation would hold weight, but he'd have the final say. If I didn't see a crime there, the kid was off the hook. Even if I did, the prosecutor might override my decision.

Since neither Sweeney nor the pizza delivery boy were going anywhere, I didn't feel any sense of urgency to get the file off my desk. I wouldn't be able to focus on it anyway. Until I figured out what had happened to Anna.

So, I attacked her investigation like a hungry dog going after a piece of raw meat.

The first thing I did was look up Anna's driver's license record. Anna Marie Navarez was thirty-two years old. Five foot seven. A hundred twenty-five pounds. Brown eyes. My memory was that her eyes were amber colored. A warm and slightly brownish tint. Friendly and inviting.

Anna's home address was also on the driver's license. Armed with that information I looked for public information. Going through official police channels wasn't an option because that would leave a trail. No one could know that I had looked at this case. Still, I found a lot even with the limited resources I had available to me. It never ceased to amaze me how much information anyone could find about a person by just looking on the internet.

Anna was born in Miami, which I already knew but was able to confirm. I found a birth certificate with the name of her father and mother who fled Cuba before Anna was born and came to America as refugees. They became US citizens several years later.

One loose end: I couldn't find why Anna moved to Chicago from Florida. I had some ideas. Maybe school. Maybe work. Maybe she followed a boyfriend to Illinois. A minor detail, but one that left me curious. I might not ever know the reason. Regardless, she did move. A tragic mistake as it turned out.

Anna had no social media presence to speak of. Probably because of her job in the teaching profession. My experience was that a lot of educators stayed off of social media for obvious reasons. She was probably worried that she'd say the wrong thing or like the wrong post that could get her into trouble. Maybe she didn't want her students to know too much about her personal life. I understood the need for privacy. As homicide detectives, we were forbidden to have social media accounts.

As I dug deeper, my investigation turned up more questions than answers.

From the DMV, I learned that Anna drove a late model, Kia. A four-door SUV. Silver color. The problem was that I couldn't locate the vehicle. I went down to the scene of the crime. Pieces of yellow police tape still littered the ground. I searched all the adjacent parking areas but couldn't find Anna's vehicle.

My assumption was that she drove there after she left me at the coffee shop. She could've taken a car service or taxi, but the ride would've been expensive. So, where was her car? If she drove there, the car would be parked near the coffee shop.

Did the killers steal her car? That seemed unlikely to me.

Then I thought of the impound lot. Perhaps, her car was towed. The meter might've expired and, after issuing several tickets, the local cops might've impounded the car. I checked. No silver Kia had been brought in recently.

More confusion.

I went back to the crime scene a second time with a copy of the police report and tried to piece together what had happened. Several people saw the murder. According to eyewitnesses, Anna walked south on the sidewalk toward the coffee shop. I tried to retrace her steps. As she neared it, a man came up from behind and grabbed her purse. Anna spun around to confront him and held onto her purse, unwilling to give it up. A struggle ensued.

I remember thinking that Anna looked like she was in good shape and maybe had martial arts training. She didn't seem like someone who could be overpowered easily. I remembered the purse being oversized and that she carried it over her shoulder.

When Anna resisted, the attacker pulled a gun and shot her in the chest. As she fell to the ground, he ripped the purse off her shoulder and fled. The assailant ran back to the north, away from the shop, and got into a black Lexus driven by another man. No one got a license plate number.

The descriptions of the man varied. The consensus was that he was about six feet tall. Medium build. Crew cut.

Military?

No one saw the face of the man who drove the car.

More confusion.

The area bustled with people and was in the center of a number of retail shops. Why try to pull off a robbery, then a murder, with that many witnesses around?

My anger at Carson returned with a vengeance. Any number of the surrounding shops would have video cameras. Another reason why the first forty-eight hours were important. Many systems taped over footage after a couple days. At the very least, Carson should've confiscated the tapes and looked through them by now.

If it were me, I'd already have the security tapes and be on the trail of the killer and a black Lexus. I desperately wanted to ask around and find the tapes but couldn't. The last thing I needed was for someone to mention to Carson that another detective was there asking the same questions. Carson would no doubt be curious and ask for video footage to determine what detective was asking questions about his case. He'd see me on the tapes, and all hell would break loose.

Another place I wanted to go was the school. I was dying to talk to someone there who knew Anna. From my experience, most people were killed by someone they knew. Work was always a good place to start. But a high school wasn't a hotbed for murderers.

The school was still a logical place to start doing interviews. That wasn't possible for the same reason. Eventually, Carson would make it there. Someone would mention me, and I'd be toast.

Something else still bothered me. A nagging feeling that ate away on my insides. Why hadn't the school reported Anna missing? All I could assume was that they figured she'd taken a couple extra personal days. Eventually, they'd call the station and that's how Carson would solve his Jane Doe problem. That's probably the only way he could solve the case given his level of gross incompetence.

I went back to the crime scene again filled with nagging questions. I ordered an iced coffee from the shop. Not my usual smoothie. I'd feel like I was cheating on *Hipsters*.

Back to my questions.

Who steals a woman's purse in broad daylight? For that matter, who steals a woman's purse when they can afford to drive a Lexus? The sidewalk had a steady stream of people even though it wasn't the morning or lunch rush.

That led me in a different direction.

An organized hit?

That made more sense. Most people who stole purses weren't murderers. The profile of a purse snatcher was a petty thief needing money to score drugs. Or kids in a gang fulfilling a requirement to join. Most serious thefts of purses with weapons happened at night. At bus stops. Or while unsuspecting victims were walking home. From drunk patrons leaving a bar. Vulnerable women whose cars had broken down. Not at nine fifty in the morning in broad daylight in front of a crowded coffee shop.

If an organized hit, then clearly Anna was the target. It couldn't be random. But why? A better question. Who? Anna didn't seem like the type to get caught up in organized crime.

Drug dealers?

Even more improbable. I knew what drug dealers and junkies looked like. Anna was clean. I could tell by her eyes and complexion. The dress she was wearing didn't have long sleeves. Druggies wore loose fitting clothing and covered their arms. They also didn't work out four to five times a week like Anna clearly did to maintain her level of fitness.

I made a mental note to check fitness centers in the area.

The more I thought about it, the more I believed this was an execution. Someone sending a message. The purse was stolen to make it look like a robbery and to make it harder to identify Anna.

My experience was that most younger women like Anna didn't carry cash anyway. She would've had debit and credit cards. Another reason to work the case in the first forty-eight hours. Once Carson knew her identity, he could put out a trace to see if those cards had been used. If they had, the killer was probably on video using them. At an ATM or in a store. Using a stolen credit card outside the view of a security camera was almost impossible.

After I left the crime scene, I turned my attention to Anna's house. I drove by. Twice. Sat outside of it for more than forty-five minutes one of the times. Every fiber of my being wanted to pick the lock on the back door and search the premises.

The house was unremarkable. Anna lived in an older, remodeled two-story home. Small but quaint with a swing on the front porch. The lawn and the house were well maintained. I pulled the real estate records. The house was owned by the next-door neighbor, so I surmised Anna probably rented it. A one car unattached garage was in the back of the house. I wanted to look inside to see if a silver Kia was parked there.

The curiosity was almost unbearable.

I couldn't, though.

If a neighbor saw me and called the police, I had no explanation for being there. Even if I had one, the Lieutenant would be all in my business. Even if it were my case, I couldn't look inside the garage without a warrant unless I thought someone was in imminent danger. In this case, Anna was in no danger at all. She was dead.

That thought sent sharp pains through my heart like a dagger. I couldn't explain the hold Anna had on me. We shared a coffee. Had a twenty-minute conversation. I had learned more about her in the last two days investigating her death than I had in the conversation.

Even with all my efforts, I was no closer to finding her killer than Carson was.

One thing was for certain, though. Now it had become an obsession.

5

Friday night

*C*hampions Sports Bar and Grille was a typical Chicago hangout
for rabid Chicago sports fans. Anna's house was about ten minutes away from the bar which was mostly empty when I arrived. It'd
be packed later when the work crowd started to file in.

I got there early to secure a seat with my back against the wall.
From my vantage point, I could see everyone who came in and out
of the bar and most of the areas where the patrons congregated.

I printed out a picture of Anna from her driver's license and intended to discreetly show it around.

The waitress who waited on me recognized Anna immediately.

"Yeah. I've seen her in here a couple times," she said.

"Was she alone or with someone?"

The waitress twisted her lips to the side.

"I don't think I should answer. Who are you? An ex-boyfriend?"

I flashed my badge. I figured there was no chance Carson ended
up there. The bar wouldn't be on his radar. It was totally unrelated
to the murder.

"What happened to her?" the girl asked, as her eyes suddenly
widened in concern.

"Routine investigation," I said. "Can you think of anyone who
might know her?"

"I don't think so. Like I said, she only came in a few times. I work
most nights. That's why I remember her. Nice girl. I took her order a
few times."

"Do you remember anything unusual? Any guys hanging around her?"

The waitress laughed. "There are guys hanging around her all the time. She's a pretty girl. Some guys come for the sports. Most come to find a hook up. Anyway, like I said, I never really talked to her except to take her order."

"Did you ever see her leave with anyone?"

I felt a twinge of jealousy, although I didn't know why. Maybe I did know.

"No. I don't think so. She was pretty good at putting off the advances. She didn't seem like the type to leave with a random stranger."

I felt a breath of relief suddenly leave my body. I realized I'd been holding it in.

"Thanks. You've been helpful. If you think of something, let me know."

"I will. Can I get you something to eat or drink?"

I ordered a soda and sat back and waited. When the bar began to fill up, I gave up my table and started to circulate. No one recognized Anna from the picture. I didn't flash my badge, though, not wanting to draw attention to myself any more than I already had.

After a couple hours of striking out, I began to think this might be a waste of time. Even if someone did recognize her, it was in a casual bar setting. They weren't likely to know anything. Especially, if the murder was an organized hit.

I'd also overstayed my welcome. So I grabbed a table when one came available and ordered another soda.

Shortly before nine, the manager approached me. Obviously concerned that I was approaching the patrons.

"Can I help you with something?" he asked roughly.

"Have you seen this girl?" I asked, as I shoved Anna's picture in his face.

"What's this about?" The flash of recognition in his eyes told me he did know Anna. Or at least recognized her.

I took out my badge and showed it to him, so he'd lose the attitude.

"I'm not at liberty to say," I said sternly. "Can you answer my question?"

Being the manager, if anyone knew anything, it'd be him. If he was doing his job, he knew everything that was going on in his bar.

"Is she in some kind of trouble?" he asked.

I ignored the question. "I understand she comes here often. When was the last time?"

"I wouldn't say often. Just occasionally. Maybe once every couple of months."

That wasn't often.

"She was supposed to be here tonight. Any idea who she might be meeting? Have you seen anyone hanging around her who seemed suspicious to you?"

I had softened my tone by this point. If he didn't know anything, it was time for me to give up and leave.

"You can ask her yourself?"

"Huh?"

He pointed behind me.

"There she is."

I turned around.

My heart started doing laps around my chest.

Anna had just entered the bar and had stopped to look around. Our eyes met. She saw me and smiled.

I thought I'd seen a ghost. The blood drained from my face.

Anna walked straight toward me. When she got close, she reached in and kissed me on the cheek. Her lips brushed mine and sent waves of desire through me.

"I'm surprised to see you here," she said.

"Not as surprised as I am," I said, reaching for the table so I could hold myself up.

Anna sat down on the stool next to me.

Before I could say anything, my cell phone rang.

The Lieutenant.

Even though I was off the clock, technically, we were on call twenty-four seven. I didn't want to take it but didn't have a choice.

"I need to take this," I said to Anna.

I had a thousand questions. Did she have a twin? If so, did she know her sister was dead? I'd have to tell her. Should I do it in the bar? Based on procedure, Carson was the one who should notify the next of kin.

Definitely not a good way to start a first date.

Was this a date?

Anna certainly seemed happy to see me.

I reluctantly answered the phone and excused myself from the table.

Anna raised her hand to call the waitress over.

"Ford," I answered. We always answered official police business by stating our last name.

"Autopsy came back on the Figaro body. Asphyxiation."

Why was he calling to tell me this? I'd already figured that out from the marks on the victim's neck. Twenty-eight-year-old woman. Found dead in the bed. In her apartment. By a boyfriend who became concerned when he couldn't reach her.

"Ligature or manual?" I asked, even though I already knew. The victim had red marks on her neck consistent with a constricting band. Something soft like a piece of thread or ribbon. Not a rope or wire which would leave significant red marks and bruises. Also, not throttling. Or manual. Throttling was choking someone with your hands. Those left distinguishing marks as well. Fingers and palms left bruising over a large area. Sometimes even noticeable fingerprints.

"According to the autopsy, the face and neck appear congested," the Lieutenant said. "Present is confluent scleral hemorrhage and petechiae of the conjunctivae."

I knew from experience that petechiae was present 85-90 percent of the time in ligature strangulation. The Lieutenant was only telling me this because he liked to hear himself speak big words. I'd read it all in the autopsy. Which I could do later. Nothing was going to happen on the investigation that night. My boss was a micromanager. A workaholic. The first one in and last one to leave.

In a way, it made our jobs easier, because he was so hands-on, he solved a lot of cases for us. On the other side of the spectrum, it annoyed me like nobody's business. Especially at that moment. When my mind was totally focused on Anna.

I looked over at her and was reminded by why I was so mesmerized by her. She looked stunning. Even more so than that morning at the coffeeshop if that was even possible. Anna flashed me a smile. The waitress brought her what looked like water with lemon. I wondered if that meant she didn't drink. Or maybe she was with a cop and wanted to make a good first impression. Don't drink and drive.

"The victim was likely incapacitated when the strangulation occurred," the Lieutenant continued, much to my consternation. "That's why the ligature didn't leave much in the way of markings around the victim's neck."

He said some other things, but I didn't really process them. After another good two minutes of prattle, the phone went silent. That meant it was my turn to speak.

"We looked in her apartment for anything that might've been used by the killer," I said. The first thing that came to my mind. "I'm assuming he took the murder weapon with him."

I was fidgeting now. Rocking back and forth on my feet. Trying to figure out a way to get off the phone.

Anna suddenly bolted from her seat.

It startled me as well. I couldn't remember if I was in mid sentence or what I was even saying.

She made a beeline to the restrooms which were in the back of the bar. I walked back over to our table. Totally confused as to why she left so suddenly.

The Lieutenant blathered on about all the things I needed to do.

"Look again for other objects in the apartment. Based on the autopsy, the murder weapon could've been a towel, a T-shirt, even a pair of underwear. Something soft but strong enough to cut off the windpipe if enough pressure is applied."

The chances of the murderer leaving the item he strangled the victim with was slim to none. Especially since it would be so easy to get rid of. Not like a bloody knife or gun. A towel or T-shirt could be tossed in any trash can, and nobody would even notice. Or thrown in the wash, and all evidence would go down the drain in the rinse cycle.

What was wrong with Anna? She disappeared into the ladies' room and hadn't come out.

What spooked her?

I looked around the bar. In the same direction Anna was looking when she was startled.

Then I saw it.

A woman was walking around the bar area holding a picture in her hand. The lady was tall and fit. Blonde hair. Strikingly beautiful. She went from table to table showing people the picture.

My curiosity went through the roof. The mystery surrounding Anna was already testing every ounce of detective skill I possessed. Meeting her in the coffee bar then seeing what I thought was her dead body in the morgue. Then seeing her walk into the bar that night. Throw in another mystery woman, and my head was going to explode.

It would anyway if the Lieutenant didn't shut up. I wasn't paying attention to a word he was saying. How do I end the call? Ending the conversation without a good excuse was never a good idea, so I had to let him continue until he quit talking. Especially when the reason was related to Anna. He'd given me specific instructions to stay away from her and the case.

At least the case. We all thought she was dead.

How would the Lieutenant react if I told him she was very much alive? Well... the woman in the morgue was obviously dead. So, who was Anna and what was the relation? This was clearly the best lead to determining the woman in the morgue's identity. He'd tell me to call Carson and leave immediately. Something I wasn't prepared to do. I had to know. Carson would keep me out of the loop.

"Interview the boyfriend again," the Lieutenant said. "Canvas the apartment building. Look for security cameras in the area. Did they capture any suspicious cars or pedestrian traffic? Check her phone records. Talk to her employer."

Shut up! These were all things I already knew to do.

Where was Anna?

Anna still hadn't come out of the ladies' room. It seemed like it'd been long enough. Although, I couldn't be sure. I had lost track of time with the Lieutenant's continual droning on and on about the Figaro case.

The blonde-haired lady was nearing my table. I had to know who was in the picture and what it might have to do with Anna. By that point, I was beginning to doubt myself. Maybe Anna going to the restroom when the woman walked in the bar was a coincidence.

I didn't think so. I saw the look on Anna's face. Her eyes widened when she saw the woman. Her mouth flew open. She quickly gathered her purse off the back of the chair. Didn't even look my way. Just took off walking. Wouldn't she have said something to me about needing to use the restroom?

Anna practically ran to the restroom. It seemed like she was walking as fast as she could. Like she was trying to get away from something. Did she leave? I wondered if there were any exits around back. Of course, there were. The fire laws would mandate them. Did they have alarms on them? Only to be used in case of emergency. No alarms had sounded. Anna had to still be in the building.

Time to get off the phone. Past time.

"Lieutenant, I've got to go. I have another call coming in on another case."

I hated lying to his boss, but I was about to lose an opportunity. The blonde lady might leave before I got a chance to find out what she was doing in the bar. She was doing the same thing I'd done earlier that evening. Circulating a picture. Clearly asking people if they'd seen that person.

I hung up the phone and walked right up to her.

"My name is Cliff Ford. I'm a detective with Chicago P.D. Is there something I can help you with?"

The lady flashed a smile, although the concern on her face was overriding her fake friendliness.

"I'm looking for this girl. Have you seen her?"

She showed me the picture. A younger girl. Probably seventeen or eighteen. Korean. Jet black hair. Cute features. You could walk down any street in Chinatown and see a dozen girls who looked like her.

"Is she missing?" I asked.

"She ran away from home. I'm trying to find her."

"Is she in danger?"

"Would you want your seventeen-year-old daughter on the streets of Chicago, alone on a Friday night?" the blonde lady said.

"Point taken. I'll keep an eye out for her. "What's her name?"

"Bae."

Before I could say anything else, two suspicious men walked into the bar. The blond woman saw them as well and reacted. Strangely. She walked to a corner of the bar out of sight of the men while keeping her eyes firmly affixed on them.

What's going on?

6

T he scene unfolding before my eyes was unsettling. The blond woman was acting suspiciously. As were the two hoodlums who were clearly up to something. Looking for someone.

To add to my angst, Anna had been gone too long. I started to worry about her. My anxiety jumped another notch to the point I was almost beside myself.

I touched the gun on my hip for reassurance. Even though I couldn't use it except under extreme circumstances. Even watching the two men in a leather jacket and determining that they were up to no good, was against my training and protocol.

In Chicago, we weren't allowed to profile. Stupid. These men had trouble written all over them. From their dress to the manner in which they carried themselves, to their rough scowls and hardened demeanors, they looked to be up to no good. In the old days, a cop could approach and even search them for weapons with nothing more than suspicion. I was beyond suspicious. The bulky clothes were a dead giveaway. The men were packing heat.

The question was why.

My hands were tied. I couldn't do anything unless provoked. They immediately walked over to a third man sitting in the far corner of the bar. I hadn't noticed him. He pointed to the restrooms.

My heart did a somersault. Then started to race. Anna was in the restroom.

The two men walked toward the area at the back of the bar where the restrooms were located. The third man followed close behind.

Could they have something to do with Anna? They were clearly looking for someone. What interest would these three hoodlums have with a high school guidance counselor? I tried to force myself to relax. They might just be going to use the head and the third man pointed them in the right direction.

Out of the corner of my eye, I saw a flash. The blonde woman was moving. With a purpose. Toward the restroom. Like she was following the men. Something about the manner of the woman seemed familiar. She didn't act like a civilian. Her gait was that of someone with a military background or law enforcement. FBI or CIA. Her actions were clearly intentional. She probably had noticed the threat as well.

But who were the men targeting? Blond woman seemed like she knew something I didn't.

All I could do was observe. Following them wasn't an option. I had to follow procedures. Of course, I wasn't even supposed to be anywhere near Anna. The Jane Doe was Carson's case. I could always say being in the bar at the same time was a coincidence. The Lieutenant wouldn't buy it. Not for a second.

When the three men and blonde lady disappeared behind the wall, I could barely control myself. I remembered a hallway led to the restrooms and pictured it in my mind.

I had to sit and wait.

No one came out for a good five minutes. Anna had been gone for almost ten minutes. Something wasn't right.

I could no longer contain myself.

My gun was in its holster. I touched it again. Contemplating under what scenarios I was allowed to use it.

I need to use the restroom.

The argument sounded hollow in my mind. What could the Lieutenant say or do? Tell me I'm not allowed to use the restroom? He couldn't prove I didn't need to go. That thought almost made me laugh. I would have, if not for the seriousness of the moment. A woman's life could be in danger. A woman I had feelings for.

Did I? That seemed strange to me. I wasn't sure I even knew her name or who she was, and yet I had feelings for her. The first woman I'd thought about in that way since my wife was murdered.

Maybe the blond woman was in danger. Certainly, I had an obligation to help her if she were in trouble.

The political correctness angered me and almost caused me to not be able to see straight. I hesitated. Even if I walked in the back and was able to prevent a murder, every one of my actions would be scrutinized like an old woman at a garage sale looking over a five-dollar piece of junk.

I could almost hear the defense attorney now.

What were you doing in the bar?

Having a drink. I go there often.

So you were drinking? Your judgment was impaired?

I was drinking soda.

Why did you follow the men?

I didn't follow them. I needed to use the bathroom.

Did you know Anna was there? Did you see her? Did you talk to her?

As soon as the question got around to Anna, I was screwed. Screwed if I did act; screwed it I didn't. The bar probably had security cameras. Anna might even be called to testify. I had no way to explain my behavior. Lying wasn't an option. I busted people for lying and impeding an investigation.

Yes. I saw Anna. I talked to her. She invited me there on a date. Yes. I noticed the resemblance between her and the Jane Doe in the morgue. How could I not notice? She went to the restroom before we had a chance to talk. When she didn't return, I became concerned. No. I noticed the three men but wasn't following them.

A white lie, but one I could justify. I wasn't following the men. My date had been gone for ten minutes. I was concerned.

The arguments were solidifying in my head. I could hear me making them to the Lieutenant.

What were you doing, Cliff? he would say.

Going to the bathroom. Do I need your permission to use the bathroom?

41

Am I not allowed to check on my date and make sure she's okay? I prevented a murder. Doesn't that account for something?

Murder?

Why did my mind go there? My imagination was running wild. I needed to rein it in. What I really needed to do was find out what in the world was going on. I was a detective. This was what I did for a living. I investigated crimes. That was the problem with my job. I never prevented crimes. I'm not allowed to. I had to wait until someone did something bad to someone else, and then I could act.

So what? I'm breaking protocol. My judgment shouldn't be second guessed. My gut told me something was wrong, and I had an obligation to look into it further. If I was wrong, so be it.

The arguments didn't matter. Whether I was right or wrong, I had to know.

Where was Anna? Was she in danger? Where was the blonde woman? Why was Anna hiding from her? Were the three thugs after Anna? Were they after the blonde woman? Who was she? Who was Bae?

When I turned the corner to the hallway that led to the restroom, no one was there. To my surprise, the three thugs and the blonde woman had disappeared. I stopped at the door of the ladies' restroom and listened. I didn't hear anything. Then I heard a toilet flush. Water running. The sound of the paper towel being dispensed.

"Anna," I said. "Are you okay?"

The door opened.

It wasn't Anna. Another woman stood in the doorway looking at me with skepticism.

"Is anyone else in there?" I asked.

The girl looked back at the door. "No," she said. "I didn't see anyone."

Strange.

The men's restroom was further down the hall. I opened the door to it and entered cautiously. No one was there either.

There had to be a rear exit. Now I grew more concerned. I considered drawing my gun but thought better of it. I did have my hand on it, ready to draw it at the slightest provocation.

At the end of the hallway was a red exit sign with an arrow pointing to the right. I walked carefully toward it. When I got to the end of the hallway, I peered around the corner. Another hallway led to a door. A sign with bright red letters glared at me. *Do Not Open. Alarm Will Sound.*

Apparently, that wasn't true. The alarm hadn't gone off. This was the only way out. Anna had to leave that way. So did the three men. And blondie.

This time I drew my gun.

Opened the exit door slowly.

Thankfully, the alarm didn't sound. The last thing I needed was to draw attention to myself and set off a panic in the bar. I was banking on the fact that the outside didn't have security cameras and wouldn't catch me coming out of the bar with my gun drawn. Our guns were to remain holstered unless we saw an imminent threat. Another stupid politically correct rule.

The door led to an alley. One lone light illuminated it and cast eerie shadows in each direction.

Even though the area was dark, I could make out three figures on the ground at the end of the alley. I kept my gun drawn and hurried over to them.

The three thugs.

On the ground.

Unconscious.

I checked for pulses.

They were all alive. I didn't notice any obvious injuries. No gunshot wounds. No knife wounds. No blood anywhere.

What happened to them?

Did Anna do it?

The blonde woman?

Whoever it was, they were good.

I kept my weapon drawn and walked cautiously to the end of the alley. The parking lot for the bar was in the back and to the side. When I rounded the corner, I saw a late model Sports Kia silver SUV driving away.

The driver looked at me.

Our eyes met.

Anna.

She hesitated, then sped off.

The blonde-haired woman was running after her. Anna had a head start and cleared the parking lot and sped away, leaving the woman standing in the parking lot watching her. The lady put her hands in the air and dropped them in exasperation.

I shouted at her.

She turned and looked at me.

I didn't know whether to raise my weapon or holster it, so I kept it in my hand but to my side.

The woman took off running in the other direction.

By the time I got to the exit of the parking lot, she'd disappeared.

I pulled out my phone and called for an ambulance.

The police would arrive shortly after that.

I only had approximately five minutes to get my story straight.

7

Police Headquarters
The next morning

I wasn't under oath, so the truth, the whole truth, and nothing but the truth wasn't the plan. As expected, the Lieutenant grilled me like a wife who'd found lipstick on her husband's collar.

"Why were you at *Champions* last night, Cliff?" he asked gruffly.

He wasn't sitting at his desk. The Lieutenant was standing. With his back to me. I didn't know why.

"I had a date."

"Who was she?"

Not that it was any of his business. I was on my personal time, but I answered anyway.

"A girl I met at a coffee shop. It wasn't really a date. She told me she was going to be at *Champions* on Friday night and invited me to show up and we'd hang out."

I hoped he didn't ask me her name.

"What was her name?"

"Actually, we didn't really talk. She showed up. Then left right away."

Deflection. I'd seen suspects do it a thousand times. We'd see if it worked on the boss.

The Lieutenant got a nasty grin on his face and gnarled his stained teeth and said, "So she took one look at you and turned around and left?" Then he bellowed with a deep belly laugh that had to be heard by the people in the bullpen outside his office.

Fortunately, his mind was elsewhere. He saw an opportunity for a dig and took it. I shrugged my shoulders.

Over the years, I'd had to testify in court many times. The prosecutors always instructed me to limit my answers to yes and no when possible and not to say anything unless asked a specific question. I was employing that tactic now.

The office smelled like an ashtray. We weren't allowed to smoke in a government office building, but the Lieutenant smoked so much that his clothes, hair, fingernails, and every other part of his being smelled like a chimney. I didn't smoke. I was allergic. Even secondhand smoke affected my breathing. I'd only been in his office for less than ten minutes, and my eyes were already watering. I'd start sneezing soon if I didn't get out of there.

To make matters worse, several times a day, the Lieutenant dipped his finger in aftershave and dabbed it on both sides of his neck. The air was filled with the smell of scented alcohol and stale cigarettes. I had all I could do to keep from gagging.

For whatever reason, the Lieutenant had lost his train of thought and hadn't asked the next question.

Torture. My stay was being involuntarily extended. I'd just as soon get on with it.

Going to his office for longer than one minute was considered cruel and unusual punishment according to the running joke in the office. Waterboarding would be better.

"When did you see the three men?" he finally asked, getting to the real reason for the interrogation. Three men were severely injured outside the bar. An investigation would be commenced shortly if it hadn't already. The Lieutenant wanted answers. What he didn't know was that I wanted them more badly than he ever would.

"Two of them came in together," I said. "One was already there sitting in a booth at the back of the bar."

"How much had you had to drink, Ford?"

"Two sodas."

I didn't drink. Except maybe for the occasional glass of wine on a special occasion and only when at a fancy restaurant. The Lieutenant already knew that fact but was covering his bases.

"Okay. Continue."

I shifted my body in the chair and leaned forward, dipping my head down slightly. Trying not to breathe through my nose. The Lieutenant was still standing and facing sideways, staring off into the far wall. Some kind of intimidation tactic, I presumed.

"The men were acting suspicious," I said.

"How so?"

"They just had that look. Like they were up to no good. Baggy clothes. Bulges in their shirts. Steely eyes."

"All the kids wear baggy clothes these days."

"These weren't kids. They were men. I'd say in their late twenties. Rough looking. Their noses looked like they'd been in more than one fight over the years."

"Did you see a weapon?"

"Like I said, I saw bulges in their shirts that looked like a gun. I didn't actually see one, but I suspected they were all carrying one. Turns out I was right. They were taken off of them in the alley."

"What happened next?"

"The three men went to the men's room. Or at least in the back area where the restrooms were."

"And then you followed them in?"

"No. I didn't follow them. I stayed at my table and waited for them to come out."

"What were you doing at the table?"

"Finishing my soda."

I wasn't about to tell him I was sitting there worrying about Anna. The whole thing still puzzled me. Why did Anna leave so abruptly? Why did the blonde lady follow them? Who were the men? Maybe the Lieutenant could answer some of my questions.

"Who were the bad guys?" I asked. "Do we have an ID?"

"Local thugs. Into the usual. Drugs. Sex trafficking. They are Strikers."

The Chicago Strikers were a local gang. Powerful. Operated mostly on the south side of town. More mafia than gang. Or at least they liked to think so. Small fish in the bigger and more sophisticated pond of organized crime. Mafia without the money. Violent and ruthless, though. They lacked any restraint. They'd rather shoot you than talk about the weather.

How in the world did Anna get in their crosshairs?

"Strange that they would be downtown at *Champions*," I stated.

The Lieutenant grunted with what I interpreted as him agreeing with me.

The Strikers generally stuck to the seedier areas in town. Something brought them to *Champions* that night. To me, it seemed like they came there looking for Anna. Even more puzzling was how the blonde girl took down all three of the vicious killers without them firing a single shot.

I assumed blondie did it. Anna was a high school guidance counselor. A job that took some fortitude for sure, but nothing like dealing with local gang members.

"I want you to find out what the three men were up to," the Lieutenant said. "They're in Chicago Memorial Hospital."

I couldn't have been more surprised. "You want me to question them?"

"I don't want you to play tiddlywinks with them!"

I'd heard that joke a hundred times.

"Of course, I want you to question them," he added. "I'm assigning their case to you."

The Lieutenant held his hand in the air in a gesture like he wanted me not to respond. "I know it's not a homicide case. Look into it anyway. Since you were there. It might lead to something more sinister, and I want one of my best men on the job."

The Lieutenant had no idea that I was ecstatic. He'd given me a license to investigate Anna and the girl in the morgue without realizing it. The two cases were tied together. I was sure of it. I could easily argue that I was simply following the thread where it led. To Anna.

"I assume these men had priors," I said, trying not to sound too excited.

"A whole notebook full of them."

Before the ambulance arrived, I had searched the men for weapons. Each of them was carrying a gun. Possession of a firearm by a convicted felon was illegal and violated their probation which I assumed they were on. Even if they had a right to own a gun, a concealed carry permit was required to carry one. I was sure they didn't have one and couldn't get it. Even if they had a permit to carry a gun, having one in places where alcohol was sold was illegal. The men were violating the law no matter which way they turned. I had a reason to hold them and interrogate them.

I'd hoped the Lieutenant's interrogation was over. I was ready to get started.

No such luck.

"Why did you follow the men into the restroom?" he asked.

My answer was already prepared, and I rattled it off without hesitation.

"I didn't. The sodas went right through me. I needed to use the head. When I got to the restroom, it dawned on me that I hadn't seen the three men come back out. But they were nowhere around. So, I decided to investigate."

Investigate was the wrong word to use. The Lieutenant didn't pick up on it.

"I went into the alley and saw the men laying on the ground," I added before he could say something.

"Did you draw your weapon?" the Lieutenant asked.

"Yes. As soon as I exited the building and saw the men on the ground, I drew my weapon."

Not exactly the truth, but close enough. Before the ambulance arrived, I checked for security cameras in the alley. There weren't any.

"Go down to the hospital right away and see what you can find out."

I couldn't believe my luck. This was my inroads into the case. In a way, I could link the Jane Doe in the morgue to the men at the bar. They were related somehow. I just had to find out how.

8

Chicago Memorial Hospital

The level of violent crime was such in Chicago that most of the hospitals had their own wing to treat prisoners who were under arrest and required twenty-four-hour armed guards to watch them. Guests going in and out had to go through metal detectors and were scanned with a wand. Generally, guests were limited to attorneys and next of kin for security reasons.

Security cameras were on every hallway and at every exit. When possible, the patient/inmate's legs were shackled, and one wrist handcuffed to the bed which was fastened to the floor. The doctors and nurses had some level of self-defense training and were paid more than other medical professionals in the area for obvious reasons. No one would voluntarily submit themselves to the horrors of working a prison medical ward without some additional incentive.

I hated going to the ward, but this time I was excited. Maybe I'd finally get some answers.

The first prisoner on my list to question was Mick Ball. I chose him because the nurse said his injuries were the least severe. Mick was also lower in the pecking order than the other two. I recognized him as the one in the bar waiting for the other two men. The one who pointed at the restrooms.

I mainly had two questions. Were they targeting Anna? If so, why? Well... three questions. Also, what happened in the alley?

As a detective, the mystery was intriguing. Three armed men were brutally assaulted by either Anna or the blonde-haired woman.

Unless someone else was hiding in the alley which seemed unlikely. I didn't see anyone. A lot of damage was done to those three men apparently without them having an opportunity to fight back. That took considerable skills. A remarkable feat. Even for a man.

When I walked into Mick Ball's room, I realized I had underestimated the extent of the damage that person had inflicted on the three men. If Mick's injuries were the least severe, I'd hate to be either of the other two men. The side of his head was swollen and bruised like he'd been hit by a bowling ball. His mouth was wired shut and his left arm was in a cast. His left eye was completely swollen shut, and his right eye was nothing more than a slit. I wondered if he'd even be able to see the picture of Anna I brought with me. Even if he could, would he be able to communicate with his mouth wired shut?

I'd soon find out.

"Mick, I'm detective Cliff Ford. Chicago PD. I'd like to ask you a few questions about what happened last night."

He turned his head sideways away from me in defiance.

That didn't deter me. "I understand you've been read your rights and know that you don't have to speak to me. You also have the right to an attorney. I understand that you have not exercised that right as of yet."

He didn't answer. The Strikers would provide the attorney. Word had likely not gotten back to the leadership yet, which was why one hadn't shown up. We had a small window to extract information. Once the attorney did show, the men would be instructed to clam up. They probably already knew to do so anyway, but often men like this thought they were smarter than law enforcement and would occasionally let something slip.

"I'm going to show you a picture. Tell me if you recognize this woman."

I showed him a picture of Anna. He kept his head turned to the side. I reached over and pulled his chin toward me. He let out a huge yelp. Technically, what I did would be considered police brutality in today's day and age, but no one was in the room. There were no cameras. His word against mine. I didn't mind getting a little rough to get answers.

It did the trick. He didn't turn his head away again. His jaw was probably tender even with the pain medication which was being fed to him through a drip. I noticed a button in his hand, which he pushed a couple of times after I had manhandled his chin.

"Do you recognize this woman?" I said more strongly. This time shoving the picture in his face in front of his good eye.

He didn't answer. I was trained to detect recognition in someone's eyes. In this instance, I couldn't tell if he recognized her. The eyes were too badly swollen.

I decided to try a different tactic.

"You don't have to answer," I said. "One of your pals already did. He said you were after this woman. I want to know why. I saw you point to the restroom. You saw her go in there. You told your buddies where she was. Why were the Strikers after her?"

Lying was an acceptable police interrogation tactic. Within reason. A gray line somewhere between a white lie and a whopper. I tended to play more good cop and keep the lies to a minimum. Some detectives would say anything no matter how outlandish to trick a suspect into a confession.

When it came to Anna, I was willing to push the line further than normal, although in this instance, I didn't think it'd help. The man's mouth was wired shut. He couldn't tell me anything anyway.

I had one more card to play.

"How come you let a little girl beat you up?" I said mockingly.

I heard what I thought was an expletive escape out of his mouth. Then he winced, like it hurt to even allow any sound to come out of his mouth. Confirmation that a woman was the one who beat them up. Either Anna or the blond-haired lady.

"Wait until word gets out on the street. Back to your Striker buddies. You got messed up by a girl. You'll be the laughing-stock of your gang."

I could see his right-hand ball into a fist. I'd struck a nerve. Image was everything to these men. To even be in the gang they had to prove their toughness. In some cases, they had to fight several gang members at once to pass initiation. If they showed the least little bit of cowardice, they were out. Sometimes even killed and thrown in a garbage dumpster somewhere.

"Was it the blonde or the black-haired girl?" I showed him the picture of Anna again. Pointed at it.

"Is she the one who did this to you?" I said, raising my voice several decibels.

He shook his head no.

"Did the blonde do it?"

He nodded.

At least that was something. I didn't know who blonde lady was, but I was thankful she had taken them out. She might've saved Anna's life. These men were clearly targeting Anna. I needed to know why.

Time to pay Anna a visit. At her school.

I liked Anna, but I was a detective above all else. I was investigating a case and deserved answers.

Feelings or not. She owed me that much.

Satisfied that I'd gotten all I was going to get out of Mick Ball, I went to the next room. Eddie Ryan was older and had done more time than Mick. His rap sheet was littered with assaults. Armed robberies. He beat a prostitute nearly to death because she held back some of the money she'd earned one night. He'd be in jail right now, but the woman didn't show up at trial to testify against him.

Eddie was so heavily sedated that he was unable to answer the most basic questions. He had a shattered kneecap and a concussion. Apparently, one blow caused both injuries. Probably a kick to the side of the knee with considerable force shattered every bone, cartilage, and tendon in his knee. He'd walk with a limp the rest of his life. The head injury likely occurred when it smacked against the concrete when he fell to the ground.

My last hope for information was Chill Malone's room. The worst low life of the three. Although, debatable. What's worse, cancer or a heart attack? Being bit by a pit bull or by a Doberman? Was a tornado worse than a hurricane? Didn't matter if your house was destroyed. Any of these three men would shoot you and cut out your heart at the slightest provocation. Malone was higher up in the Strikers. So he'd simply had more opportunities to inflict terror on the streets of Chicago.

I had no idea why the courts let men like this breathe.

To my surprise, another man was in the room. Wearing a suit. Clearly his sleazy looking lawyer.

"Detective Cliff Ford," I said, knowing just how to play this.

"Clayton Mills," he said, extending his hand. "Aren't you in homicide?" Mills asked.

I didn't recognize him but wasn't surprised that he knew the names of the homicide detectives in our precinct.

"Normally. Yes. I'm here to investigate the assault on your clients. Have they given you a description as to who did this to them?"

He didn't trust me, but this was the quickest way to get his men to talk.

"Chill is still in a coma. According to Eddie Ryan, it was a blonde haired woman. She ambushed them. Beat them with a baseball bat."

I had the confirmation I needed. My intuition was correct. The lady did it. Not Anna. She also didn't do it with a baseball bat. She didn't have one in the bar. I didn't recover one in the alley. She wasn't carrying one when she ran after Anna.

I couldn't help but smile. She'd beaten these men to within an inch of their lives with her bare hands. To me, she was a hero.

I needed to find her and thank her.

First, I had to find out who she was.

9

According to the Striker's attorney, the blonde woman caused the injuries to the three men. Did she commit a crime? Was it self-defense? Did she use an illegal weapon?

Did I care?

If her motive was to protect Anna, I was grateful. That's certainly how it looked from my vantage point. My imagination had pieced together a theory. Spliced it together into a movie in my mind which I played over and over again.

Anna saw the blonde woman and made a beeline for the restroom. Clearly spooked. Why was she afraid of the woman? Perhaps the lady was bad news after all and not the hero I had made her out to be. While I wouldn't lose any sleep over the fact that she put the three men in the hospital, it could be that she needed to be put behind bars as well. I needed more proof before I could make that leap.

I presumed that Anna saw the men coming and bolted out the back door to get away from the danger. Maybe to get away from the blonde woman. Hopefully, Anna would clear that up for me. For whatever reason, the alarm at the bar wasn't working. I needed to go by the bar and tell them. They needed to get that fixed. Had it gone off, the men would've been spooked. The bar management would've been alerted, and a confrontation probably avoided.

To continue with my movie, I saw the men in the alley. Chasing Anna. The blonde woman right behind them. She recognized the threat the three men posed. Perhaps she had law enforcement training. Because of the imminent threat, she had sprung into action.

Unafraid. Blonde woman attacked the three men from behind with the element of surprise. Beat the heck out of them. In my line of work, I had to use the least amount of force necessary to subdue the subject. Apparently, those rules didn't apply to her. Or if they did, she ignored them.

Anna took off running to her car. For whatever reason, the blonde woman had an interest in Anna because she chased her out of the parking lot.

As detectives, we're trained to look for motives. That was what had me stumped. Why did Anna run? What was she afraid of? How did she get involved with the Strikers? Why would men like that be after her? Who was the blonde woman and why was Anna afraid of her? My imagination could not piece together a plausible explanation.

That's what I intended to find out. The mystery had gone on long enough. The only person who could answer my questions was Anna. So, I drove by her house. The silver KIA was in the driveway. Today was Saturday, so she didn't have school.

I was tempted to knock on the door but decided to observe for a while. Truthfully, I needed the time to drum up the courage. For whatever reason, I didn't want the fantasy to end. Like somehow, we had made a connection. I'd convinced myself that I had feelings for her. For the first time since my wife died. It felt strange. Still, I was afraid that if I confronted Anna, I wouldn't like what I heard. The dream would die.

I had to prepare myself for that possibility.

Above all else, I was a detective and had a job to do. Something happened in that alley. Anna also owed me a personal explanation. Why did she run out on me? Then I realized that from a personal standpoint, she didn't owe me anything. We barely knew each other. Fortunately, I had the investigation angle that I could use to understand the situation.

If she didn't provide answers right away, I'd be left with no choice but to take Anna down to the station for questioning. As much as she intrigued me, and I was interested in a relationship, it wasn't at the expense of my job. My hope was that I could help her. Maybe she got caught up in something that she wasn't able to extract herself from. It could be anything. Wrong place at the wrong time. Trying to help a friend. A student at her school. Something as simple as cutting off one of the Strikers on the freeway and they were pursuing her.

I hoped there was a simple explanation. I refused to believe that Anna wasn't who she said she was. A good judge of character, I thought Anna was a good person. I hoped I wasn't wrong.

But I had a dead woman in the morgue, three men in the hospital, a blonde woman on the loose who assaulted them, and Anna, who ran away from the scene of the crime. Or whatever it was. A bit of anger rose up inside of me. I deserved an explanation and would demand one.

Rather than jumping right into an interrogation by knocking on her door, I decided to turn it into a stakeout. Less than a half an hour later, lights came on in the house and I could see activity through the windows. Apparently, she was a later sleeper. I didn't actually get a glimpse of Anna, but I saw her shadow and silhouette a couple of times through the curtains.

A little after ten, the front door opened, and Anna appeared. Dressed in workout gear. Black form fitting shorts and a tank top over a sports bra. Her hair was in a ponytail. She was carrying what looked to be a gym bag and was wearing sneakers.

I followed her to a fitness center a couple of miles away in a strip shopping mall next to a major grocery store chain. The club had windows all along the front so I could see in. To my knowledge, Anna didn't know my car which made it easy for me to get close without being detected.

The day we met at the coffee shop I was on my motorcycle. Today, I was driving a four door Ford sedan. All detectives had the same make and model car. Something I always thought was stupid. It made undercover work difficult. All the bad guys knew what kind of car we drove. Presumably, Anna wouldn't know.

That's why I rode my motorcycle most of the time, except when on official police business. In this instance, the tinted windows worked to my advantage in that I was able to pull the binoculars out of the glove box and watch Anna through the windows without people in the parking lot thinking I was some kind of pervert.

Anna greeted the person at the front desk and went immediately to the step machine. I watched her for thirty minutes attack the machine with the intensity of a tenth-grade boy playing a video game. She certainly was fit enough to make a quick get-away, which she somehow managed to accomplish the night before. I wondered how she could be so calm considering the close call. She didn't seem the least bit concerned about being seen in public.

When she was finished with the cardio workout, Anna wiped off the machine with a towel and then wiped the sweat off her face, neck, and arms. Then she moved to the weight machines and did two circuits. Lighter weights and higher number of reps. That's how she maintained her perfectly toned arms and legs which was one of the first things I had noticed about her.

After that, Anna did several sets of sit-ups on the medicine ball and then several stretches. She got off the mat and took a few large drinks of water from the cooler. Sat down on a chair and took a couple of minutes to cool down. Then left the fitness center waving goodbye to the person at the front desk on the way out.

From my vantage point, I never saw her interact with anyone else. The gym was a local establishment and not one of the fitness chains. Everyone there seemed focused on their workouts. Even the men seemed oblivious to the beautiful woman in their midst, and she had no gawkers.

Except me. I was the only one fixated on her. Why did she have that effect on me?

Anna left the gym and put her bag in the back seat of her SUV. I expected her to get in and drive off and was prepared to follow her. Instead, she walked next door into the grocery store.

That gave me an idea.

Inside, I could orchestrate a chance meeting. Make it look like I just happened to run into her. She wouldn't know I was following her. A much better plan than walking up to her unexpectedly and giving her the third degree at her house. Maybe she'd even go with me to get coffee or something and I could get my explanation.

I waited for Anna to disappear into the store, and then I got out of the car and walked in. Nonchalantly. Like I was doing some Saturday morning shopping. Not a cop following a suspect. A normal single guy doing a little grocery shopping.

I grabbed one of the hand baskets and put the first three things I saw in it. So, it wouldn't be empty when I bumped into her.

Anna was in the produce section.

I hung back and slowly made my way to her vicinity. She seemed intent on shopping, oblivious to everyone around her, including me, even though I was within ten feet of her. Since she wasn't going to notice me, I decided to make the first move.

Anna was by the avocados. Squeezing one after the other. Clearly trying to find the right one.

"Anna?" I said, in the most surprised sounding voice I could muster.

She turned and looked at me. Smiled and then said, "Hi."

Her lips twisted to the side and her forehead furrowed like she was straining to recognize me.

What?

"I'm sorry. Do I know you?" she said. "I mean... obviously, I do. You know my name. Remind me where we met?"

Does this woman ever tell the truth?

10

My mind was totally blown.

I was standing in the grocery store next to Anna and she was pretending not to know me. Although, I had to admit it seemed genuine. Like she really didn't recognize me. Was she hit over the head last night? Did she have amnesia? My imagination was running wild like an out of control, roller coaster.

When I followed her into the grocery store, this was the last thing I expected to happen.

"I'm sorry," Anna said apologetically. "I'm so bad with names."

"Cliff Ford," I said, not knowing what else to do. Why was I introducing myself? I felt like a fool.

Should I play along? Or confront her?

Was she afraid of something? I looked around the produce area and didn't see any threats. No one else was in our vicinity. She had no reason to carry on the ruse.

Anna held an avocado in her hand and was squeezing it.

"I can never pick out the right one," she said. "It's always either too soft or too hard. Do you ever have that problem?"

"I stick with the easy vegetables like carrots," I said, immediately wanting to kick myself. What was I doing? I wanted to shout at the top of my lungs, *Anna it's me!*

"Technically, avocados are a fruit, not a vegetable," Anna said, in a teacher kind of voice, although she flashed me a smile, so I knew she was kidding.

"I didn't know that."

"Where did you say we met?" she asked, with her eyes squinted slightly in confusion.

"I didn't say. Although you asked me. Sorry. I forgot to answer."

I was stumbling for words. They didn't seem to come out right. My mind felt like a skillet full of scrambled eggs. I had no idea what to say or do. So, I told her the truth even though she already knew it. "We met at a coffee shop. *Hipsters*."

"Oh okay," Anna said hesitantly, like she was pretending to remember but didn't.

"We also met at *Champions* bar," I added.

Remember. Last night. When you ran out on me. Some men chased you. Do you really think you're fooling anybody?

"It must've been a while ago," Anna said. "I haven't been to *Champions* in ages."

Last night. Are you an idiot or an incredibly good liar?

Maybe a great actress. She certainly seemed believable.

"I'm sorry I don't remember you," Anna said, seemingly with sincerity.

"You work at South Skyline High School," I said. "As a guidance counselor. If I remember correctly."

Her eyes widened.

"You have a good memory," she said.

This clearly was Anna. And she didn't remember me. I studied her closely. She was definitely the woman I met at *Hipsters*. The one who told me her name was Anna and that she was a high school guidance counselor. She didn't actually tell me it was at South Skyline High School. I figured that out on my own.

"Have you had breakfast?" I asked. "I'd love to catch up. Or we could grab a cup of coffee and get reacquainted."

"That's so sweet of you to ask," Anna said. "But I can't. I'm meeting my fiancé."

My jaw almost fell off my neck for the second time.

Anna flashed a large diamond ring at me. On her ring finger. Clearly an engagement ring. She wasn't wearing that the night before. That would explain why she was pretending not to know me. She was going to secretly pursue an affair and didn't want her boyfriend to find out. Anna was concerned that I'd tell him about us.

There was no us. Nothing happened.

"We're going to pick out the food for our wedding reception," Anna said, putting down one avocado and picking up another. "There are so many details to work on."

"When are you getting married?" I asked.

"In six months. It's like, ages from now. Seems like it."

A pain shot through my heart. Whatever I thought was going to happen between us was dashed like an avocado dropped from the top of a skyscraper. Splattered on the concrete below.

"It'll be here before you know it," I said, sorrowfully. I felt like I'd lost my best friend.

"I know, right."

My ears perked up. I could tell a subtle difference in personality. This wasn't the Anna I met at the coffee shop or the one at *Champions* bar. This one talked more like kids these days. Like. And right. This Anna probably picked it up from hanging around teenagers all day long at the high school. My Anna didn't talk like that.

"I'm going to pick out a wedding dress tomorrow. With my sister. The wedding is starting to get real. I can't believe I'm getting married!"

"Well... congratulations."

"Thank you."

I was convinced this wasn't my Anna.

"I'd better be going," she said, "I hate to be rude. It's nice seeing you again."

She touched my arm, sending a chill down my spine. She might not be my Anna but was the spitting image of her.

In the time it took me to blink my eyes twice, Anna was gone around the corner of the aisle. I put the items in my basket back on the shelf and walked out to my car.

Stunned.

Speechless.

Totally incapable of wrapping my arms around what just happened.

Was Anna engaged and that's why she pretended not to know me? Was she afraid of something because of what happened the night before? Was I right and it wasn't her after all?

I got in my car and fixed my eyes on the front of the store. A few minutes later, Anna came out, got in her car, and I followed her. All the way back to her house. She took her groceries and gym bag out of the car and went inside.

If this wasn't Anna, why was she driving Anna's car? I clearly saw Anna leave the bar the night before in a silver KIA SUV. That car was parked in the driveway in front of that house. Was I losing my mind? Was she playing me for a fool? Pretending not to know me because of what happened the night before?

Anna knew I was a homicide detective. Was she in some kind of trouble? If so, why would she even come to the bar last night? Nothing made sense. I had to erase the movie in my mind and start all over. That often happened in an investigation. I'd pour all my energies into making a case against a suspect, and then be thrown a curve ball and find that I was so off base, I wasn't even in the ballpark.

How could I have been so wrong about Anna?

I remembered something.

At the coffee shop. Something about our conversation.

Several times I got the distinct impression that Anna was lying to me. Now I had proof. But why?

I sat across the street from Anna's house for a good hour. That gave me plenty of time to think. I came to several conclusions. The woman in the grocery store was the real Anna. The address was the same as what was on her driver's license. So was the vehicle. A silver Kia SUV. She worked at the high school as a guidance counselor.

She also didn't know me. That was clear as well. No one was that good an actress.

That's when everything got murky. I rubbed my eyes hard. The situation was so confusing that my head started to hurt.

The woman in the coffee shop pretended to be Anna. Sped away last night in a silver Kia. SUV. I saw her. Only a glimpse, but it was clearly her.

I was tempted to go knock on the door and flash my badge. Demand answers. I had every right to interrogate the woman.

Before I could, Anna came out of the house, got in her car, and drove to a restaurant. A man was out front and greeted her. Kissed her on the lips. Her fiancé I presumed. They were inside for more than two hours.

When they came out, they drove to a hotel. Parked their cars and went inside. Probably there to talk to catering about their wedding reception.

I used that opportunity to look inside Anna's car. I tried to be inconspicuous, but I was prepared to flash my badge if necessary. If she happened to come out and saw me there. I almost wished she would. I didn't see anything remarkable, so I got back in my car and waited.

An hour later, the couple came out of the hotel and drove back to Anna's house. The man parked his car behind her in the driveway. I snapped a few pictures of him to run through my database to determine his identity. I'd also check the paper for wedding announcements.

I observed them go into the house. At that point, I felt like a voyeur. I had to get out of there, so I left and drove to my house.

Totally confused.

When I got there, I popped a soda can and plopped down on the couch. As deflated as a popped balloon.

Fifteen minutes later, something Anna said caused me to sit up.

A sister.

Anna was going to pick out a wedding dress tomorrow. With her sister.

Twins?

I'd considered that possibility when I thought about the woman in the morgue. It was the most logical explanation. The only thing that made sense before was that Anna had a twin sister who was killed in front of a coffee shop.

Was that who I met in the coffee shop?

Her twin?

For whatever reason, the woman told me her name was Anna and that she was a high school guidance counselor. Why would she say her name was Anna?

The headache was so strong now, my temples were throbbing.

If Anna had a twin sister, then who was the dead woman in the morgue?

The twin obviously.

I'd know tomorrow. I intended to follow Anna to the wedding shop. When her twin sister didn't show, then I'd know my theory was correct. I wouldn't know everything. Like why Anna's sister lied to me? But I'd know enough to put more pieces of the puzzle together.

What would I do if her sister showed up at the dress shop?

My head started hurting again at the thought.

11

The next morning, I was up early and at Anna's house at the crack of dawn. Determined to see if my hunch was right. The girl I met at the coffee shop and at *Champions* bar was Anna's twin sister. Or so I was thinking.

I probably got there *too* early, but I didn't care. I couldn't take the chance that I'd miss her. Anna said in the grocery store that she was meeting her sister today to try on wedding dresses. The stores probably didn't open until later, but they could be meeting for breakfast or had errands to run beforehand. A risk I wasn't willing to take.

I intended to follow Anna to the bridal shop and confirm my suspicions.

What would I do then?

I hadn't a clue.

This much was clear. Someone was lying to me. Either the girl in the coffee shop or the girl in the grocery store. Coffee shop girl said her name was Anna, and she was a guidance counselor. I knew a lot about that Anna. She did indeed work at a high school. She lived in the house I was staking out at that very moment. The silver KIA was sitting in the driveway. I had confirmed that Guidance Counselor Anna drove a silver KIA with the license plate I was staring at through my binoculars.

That's where things got murkier. My detective skills were being tested.

The girl in the grocery store acted like she'd never met me before in her entire life. I considered myself a good judge of character. I didn't always know when someone was lying to me, but I could usually tell. Grocery Store Anna should win an academy award if she was the girl I met in the coffee shop.

Other scenarios crept into the far recesses of my mind. What if Grocery Store Anna and Coffee Shop Anna were the same person? Why would she lie? That was obvious. Anna was engaged. I saw the ring on her finger at the grocery store. I also confirmed she had a fiancé. He followed her home. They kissed in front of the house.

Coffee Shop Anna didn't have a ring on. If they were the same person, why not? Again, the reason was obvious to me. That Anna was flirting and invited me to meet her at a bar. Perhaps one last fling before she got married. A motive to lie and pretend not to know me.

But our meeting was by chance. How could she have possibly known I'd come up and talk to her?

She was a pretty girl and said three guys had already approached her. Of course, she'd get hit on. Perhaps I was the only one she considered having the fling with.

The thought made me feel something as my chest bowed out. I quickly tamped it down. My imagination was out of control. I needed to rein it in. It had been flattering that a woman as pretty as Anna had been interested in me. When she ran out on me at *Champions*, my ego took a hit.

Now that I'm thinking it wasn't the same girl, the feelings were stuck in neutral, like a car that had blown its transmission and would idle but not run. I didn't know what to think.

I raised the binoculars back to my eyes.

It has to be the same girl!

Champions bar Anna was driving a silver KIA.

But she didn't recognize me at the grocery store!

The debate raged in my mind.

It can't be the same girl. It's her sister. She told me her name was Anna as a joke. Maybe some silly game the two of them played.

But what were the odds that they both drove silver KIAs?

And who was the girl in the morgue?

The spitting image of both of them.

The problem with getting to Anna's house so early was that I had a lot of time to ruminate. After three hours, I was more confused than I was when I got there. Also, more determined to crack the case than ever. I looked at my watch for the umpteenth time in the last half hour.

My curiosity was driving me crazy.

Hopefully, the sister would meet Anna at her house, they'd drive together, and I'd get my answer sooner rather than later. That'd tell me a lot. It'd confirm if they were twins who drove the same color car.

Twins. That's what I was hoping for.

Two silver KIAs.

Impossible.

Not impossible, but improbable.

I rubbed my eyes roughly.

This didn't make sense.

When it seemed like there was no logical explanation, I had to remember that there was. I had a case once where a woman was murdered. The body was discovered by a relative on her own kitchen floor. The beat cops were the first on the scene. After they confirmed the woman was dead, they secured the area and left the house so as not to contaminate the scene.

I was called in. I checked the body as well and determined the woman was dead. Then went outside to wait for forensics. I preferred to get right to the investigation, but the Lieutenant at the time had set up those procedures, so I followed them.

Forensics was backed up, and it took them a good two hours to get there. When they did, I led them to the body. Except there wasn't a body. The woman was gone. Vanished into thin air like a puff of smoke in the wind.

No evidence she'd ever been there. The woman I saw on the floor appeared to have been strangled. So, there wasn't any blood. No sign of a struggle. A clean crime scene as we call it.

Where was the woman? My first thought was that she somehow came back to life. Maybe she'd had a faint pulse and I missed it. I searched the house. No sign of her.

Her car was still in the garage, so she didn't drive away. We'd been out front the entire time, so she didn't walk out of the house. A cop was at the back door. He didn't see her come or go. No one else entered the premises until forensics got there.

A mystery.

No logical explanation.

I drilled the beat cops.

"Did you search the house for the killer?" I demanded.

"Yes. We didn't find anything."

"Did you check everywhere?"

"Of course."

We searched again and didn't find anything. After several hours, we gave up and left the scene. Even sent forensics home when they arrived.

The next day, I went back to the house. The woman's body was lying on the floor. Right where she'd been the day before. It seemed like she was in the exact same position.

My mind was playing tricks on me. How was that even possible?

When there's no logical explanation, remember that there is.

A rule for every detective to live by. Turned out, the house had a safe room. The murderer had been hiding in the house the whole time. Hidden cameras were throughout, and we hadn't seen them. The murderer, an ex-boyfriend, watched our every move from the monitors in the safe room. When we went outside, he moved the woman's body into the room hidden behind a bookshelf. Later that night, he moved it back.

He admitted that he did it to mess with us. What he should've done was taken the body and disposed of it. He might've gotten away with it had he done so.

It took me nearly a month to find the safe room and six months to solve the crime. We found the man's DNA in the room, but it wasn't in the database, meaning he had no prior convictions, so

I didn't have a match. But I did have a list of ex-boyfriends to work through. His name wasn't on it. He wasn't on anyone's radar because they had only dated for a short time.

Someone remembered something. A name. Richard somebody. I looked around and found him. Something about his manner seemed off when I questioned him. He agreed to a DNA test. Turned out he was a match. Case closed.

Something I was determined to do with Anna. Crack the case. Technically, it wasn't even a case. This was personal. I had no way of justifying following Anna other than that we lived in a free country, and I was sitting on a public street. My Lieutenant would have a cow if he knew. Especially, considering I was in my undercover police car and using work-issued binoculars. And the binoculars might be considered inappropriate at best, creepy at worst under normal circumstances. I didn't care. I had to get a good look at the sister if and when she arrived.

When Anna came out of the house alone, I almost dropped the drink in my hand as I scrambled for the binoculars. She got in her car and pulled out of the driveway giving me time to regroup.

I followed behind at a distance.

Anna stopped at a coffee shop and came out with a to-go cup in her hand.

I looked at my watch. *11:33.*

Anna got on the 290. An interstate leading out of Chicago proper. She took 290 until it changed to 88. Past Midwestern College. There she got on 355 South. Another interstate. That made it easy to follow her. Tailing a mark was harder on city streets when there were starts and stops. Green lights and red lights to consider along with traffic and pedestrians.

We weren't on 88 for long. She got off on Highway 34. Which turned into East Ogden Avenue which changed to West Ogden and eventually led into Naperville. An affluent suburb of Chicago. I followed Anna into a residential neighborhood. She parked in front of a house. A sign out front read *Missy's Bridal.*

Anna got out of her KIA and walked around back. From my vantage point, I could see a shop. Probably where the lady worked out of. I sat in my car and waited. Excitement was building. The time was approaching noon. That's probably when she told her sister to meet her at the bridal shop.

I made sure I was out of sight but could still see the front of the house clearly.

My phone rang, startling me.

My Lieutenant.

What did he want?

I had to answer it.

"Ford, I need you in Chatham. ASAP."

My heart sank. Of all the inopportune times he'd called me, this had to be the worst.

"I'm kind of busy," I said hesitantly.

"What do you want me to tell the three dead bodies?" he asked roughly. Then he mocked me. Acted like he was talking to the corpses. "Detective Cliff Ford says he's too busy to come and help find your killers. He's getting a pedicure at the moment."

His voice dripped with a mix of sarcasm and vitriol.

"My mistake," the Lieutenant said to me. "Sorry to interrupt you."

"Can you give me an hour?"

"410 Dexter Street," he responded roughly. "Be there in ten minutes or don't bother showing up at work in the morning."

"I'm in the suburbs. At least thirty minutes out."

I made up a town about the same distance as Naperville.

"Blue light it. You'll get here in twenty," he insisted.

Meaning turn on my police lights and rush over. The undercover cars had lights in the grill and on the back windows.

"Who are the dead guys?" I asked, stalling for time. Mystery girl should be there any minute now.

"Three more Strikers."

"What happened to them?"

"Gunshots. Efficient. A pro did this."

"Is this case related to the three gang members who were assaulted at *Champions*?" Those three men were Strikers as well.

"That's your job to find out. Any more questions? You only have nineteen minutes now to get here."

I hung up the phone swearing under my breath. The clock was about to strike noon. I was certain Anna's sister was going to drive up any minute.

Didn't matter. I couldn't wait any longer.

12

The crime scene on Dexter Street looked eerily familiar.

Similar to the scene at *Champions* bar on Friday night. Unusually so.

Three gang members. Strikers. Wearing black leather jackets. Lying on the ground.

One main difference though. These three thugs were dead. Gunshot wounds to the head. The three at *Champions* were fortunate, so to speak. They were only permanently maimed and disfigured.

The thought brought a smile to my face.

The scene was bustling with activity.

The good thing about getting there late was that I didn't have to coordinate forensics and the coroner. Timing could sometimes be tricky. Call the coroner too early, and they had to stand around and wait. Too late, and you could have dead bodies lying around longer than anyone wanted. Nobody wanted to deal with dead bodies that had been out in the sun for an extended period of time.

Both teams were already there, which I was sure had the Lieutenant riled up. The coroner was off to the side, leaning against his service vehicle, smoking a cigarette. Clearly annoyed. Someone had called him too soon.

The forensics team was working on the bodies. The Lieutenant was still at the scene barking orders to the dozen or so support people who were scurrying around trying to appear busy.

I noticed a couple of cops going door to door. Canvassing the neighborhood to see if anyone had seen anything.

It ticked me off that the Lieutenant was still there. He had no doubt waited to see how long it took me to arrive. I made good time getting there, but it's not as if I could just blink my eyes and magically arrive. I got there with a minute to spare, but he still found a way to razz me.

"Glad you could make it, Ford," the Lieutenant quipped. "I'm sure the killer's glad you gave him a head start."

"How do you know it's a he?" I asked, ignoring his snide remarks.

"Do you know any women capable of taking down three gang members in broad daylight without them getting off a shot?"

I shrugged my shoulders.

"Good point though," the Lieutenant admitted in a rare concession. "Never assume."

I figured he didn't have any information. If he did, he would've shared it with me, so I walked over to the bodies and squatted down. I wasn't wearing gloves but didn't see the need since forensics was already examining the three men. They could tell me more than I could observe. So, my approach method at the scene was look but don't touch.

I noticed immediately how pristine the crime scene was. I'd seen my share of gang shootings, and this was unlike any I'd ever seen before. Most were a mess. Bullet holes everywhere. Shell casings littering the ground. Bodies generally had several bullet wounds in the oddest places. Legs. Shoulders. Arms. Midsections.

Most of the time, when bullets started flying, all sense of order went out the window. Thugs with guns shoot wildly. Randomly. They lose all sense of balance and equilibrium. Most bullets missed which was a pain to track them all down. We'd find them in the weirdest places. A time-consuming and annoying waste of manpower when we could be spending that time solving crimes.

That wasn't the case here. The three victims were killed with three bullets. Red dots formed little circles just above the bridges of their noses. The bullet entries on all three were almost uniform in fashion.

Strange.

Even impressive in a dark sort of way. Definitely a professional, dedicated to the craft of sharpshooting. It took training to get that proficient. Judging by the bullet entries there had been no hesitation on the shooter's part.

I stood and looked around the area. We were in a back alley. More of a road behind a row of modest houses that accessed the garages and driveways. We were in a known gang area. Shootings and trouble in general were commonplace there. Yellow tape surrounded the entrance to one particular house where I assumed the Strikers were operating out of. The Lieutenant was probably waiting for a warrant before entering the premises.

Whoever had been there was likely long gone. Hopefully, they fled in a hurry with lots of clues left behind.

"What do you think?" the Lieutenant asked me.

Not in a way that he wanted to know. More like a teacher springing a pop quiz on a student. He stood there looking cocky.

I paused, calculating my answer, while the details of the scene spun around in my head.

"Obviously a professional shooter," I said, still looking around to try and play the part of the detective.

"Duh, Junior," he said in a condescending tone.

For some reason, the Lieutenant had started calling me Junior. I didn't know why. I was sure it was meant as some kind of slight. Like I was a Junior Detective, even though I'd been promoted to Senior Detective a couple years before. A lot of people had more seniority than me, but not many solved more cases in a year, so I thought I'd earned his respect. If I had, he had a funny way of showing it.

What did he want me to say? I looked around again. There was nothing to see. The crime scene was shy of clues. If there weren't three dead bodies lying on the ground, no one would think anything had even happened there.

"What kind of professional?" he asked.

"I don't know."

Wrong answer.

"You don't know?" the Lieutenant boomed. "That's not what I want to hear! You're paid to know!" He continued on his tirade. "It's your job to know."

I could argue that I just got there, but defensiveness wouldn't get me anywhere. I wanted to say as little as possible without getting underneath his skin. That would only make solving the case that much harder. Working well together was necessary whether I liked the Lieutenant or not.

"What I mean is that it doesn't make any sense," I said. "Why would a professional be in this part of town? The Strikers don't cross paths with organized crime very often. What kind of beef would Mafia types have with the Strikers?"

"I wouldn't rule anything out," the Lieutenant replied crassly.

"I haven't. Just spit-balling here."

My tone changed so I'd sound as sophisticated as possible.

"And... Mafia hits are more execution-style," I added, even though he already knew that fact. "Usually, some violence is associated with it."

"Being dead isn't violent enough for you?"

He knew what I meant but was just being a jerk. The Mafia liked to beat up their victims. Send a statement. They preferred to club a man to death with a baseball bat rather than shoot him. They also wouldn't leave the bodies in the middle of the road. They'd dump them in the river. Or in someone's front yard. To send a message.

"I don't think it could be a professional hitman," I continued to muse. "These lowlifes aren't worth the trouble. Who'd pay to off them?"

"Another gang?" the Lieutenant replied.

"They don't hire out this kind of thing," I answered. "They prefer to do it themselves. To show how tough they are. If a gang hired a ringer, they'd be the laughingstock of the neighborhood. It would take years to live that down. They won't do it."

A beat cop approached. One of the ones I'd seen canvassing the neighborhood. A job I'd do if I had to but preferred someone else do it. Nobody liked a cop showing up at their door. Most people were hesitant to get involved. Especially in these rougher neighborhoods. Retaliation was always a worry.

The man approached the Lieutenant even though, technically, he should've given the information to me first. I was the lead detective. I cut him a break since I hadn't been introduced as such.

"What you got?" the Lieutenant asked.

"A blue hair down the street saw somethin'," the beat cop replied.

I jumped in and introduced myself, so he'd know I was in charge. After the brief formalities were over, I asked. "What did she see?"

He looked down at his black notebook which I could also see and that looked shy of details.

"It's sketchy. She doesn't see things real good without her glasses. But she heard gunshots. Er... rather, she said she heard three bangs. At first, she thought they sounded like firecrackers. But then she recognized them as gunshots. She's heard 'em lots of times in this neighborhood. The woman's lived here all her life. She said the neighborhood's overrun with thugs and gangs. Which, of course, we know. She's sick of 'em, but she ain't leavin'. Says it's her house. End of story."

"Just tell us what she saw," the Lieutenant barked.

"Like I said, she heard gunshots."

"We know what she heard. I want to know what she saw!"

For the moment, the Lieutenant's rudeness was directed toward someone else which was a welcomed reprieve.

"So... she walks over to the kitchen window and looks out."

"Did she see the shooter?" I asked, feeling my frustration starting to boil as well as the Lieutenant's.

"I'm gettin' to that. She didn't actually see who pulled the trigger."

That wasn't surprising considering the shooter likely took less than two seconds to fire the three shots. The men on the ground didn't even have a chance to draw their weapons.

I glared at him. He looked back down at the notebook.

"She saw a woman. With blonde hair. The shooter jumped that fence right over there. That's not a small fence, I might add."

He pointed in the direction of a fence on the other side of the road. It was about five or six feet high. Typical neighborhood fence.

"The ol' woman said the shooter jumped over it like a rabbit," he continued.

"How do you know it's the shooter?" I asked. "You said the woman didn't actually see the gunshots. She just heard them."

He fumbled with his notebook again. "I'm just assuming the person she saw was the shooter. Why else would she be running away?"

I let it go. He wasn't a detective for a reason.

"Did she say anything else?" I asked.

"She could hardly believe her eyes and even told me so. But then she told me she just had 'em checked by an eye doctor. Even without her glasses, she knows what she saw. She said it ain't every day you see a blonde, white girl jump a fence around here."

He hadn't mentioned before that the woman was white, but I figured as much since she had blonde hair.

"Did she say which way the woman went?"

"Nah. Got nothin' on that."

The beat cop closed his notebook like he was saying he had nothing left to add.

I asked him to write up a report and let me know if anything new was discovered. He agreed, and went to his squad car, and left us to our business at the crime scene.

Then I looked around again. Mostly for show. To make it look like I was thinking.

When I finally made eye contact with the Lieutenant, he was staring straight at me. We both had to be thinking the same thing.

The woman who beat up the three Strikers at *Champions* bar was a blonde-haired woman.

What were the odds?

He might be the Lieutenant, but he'd also been wrong. Apparently, a woman could take out three armed men without them getting off a shot.

13

Missy's Bridal Shop

Anna was starting to worry.

At first, she was only annoyed. Her sister, Rita, her Maid of Honor, was supposed to meet her at the bridal shop in Naperville to pick out a dress and help her with the fitting. It wasn't like Rita to be late. That wasn't her style. She was punctual and she could generally count on her.

Anna kept checking her phone. It felt like she must've looked at it a thousand times. Where was Rita? Why wasn't she there? How could she let her down like this? Rita knew how important picking out a dress was to her. Thinking about her sister distracted her from the task at hand.

Then she began to think the worst.

A car wreck?

No! She tamped down that thought. Rita must be stuck in traffic.

Anna just came that way and the traffic was fine.

Her mind began imagining all kinds of horrendous things. Rita had better have a good explanation for why she was late for something this important.

This wasn't the first time something like this had happened. While generally Rita was as dependable as a toaster, it *was* like her to disappear for long stretches of time. Mysteriously. Sometimes they went weeks without hearing from her. But she always let them know in advance when that was going to happen. They'd solved that problem a couple years before when they didn't hear from her for nearly two weeks, and Anna had become fraught with worry.

Anna and Rita had always had a bizarre ability to almost know what the other was thinking. They could sense when something was wrong with the other. Not all the time, but more often than not. When Anna couldn't find Rita that summer, she started to panic.

So worried she called the police and filed a missing-person's report, although the cops were slow to react. They said that Rita was a grown woman, and they found no evidence of foul play, so they wouldn't do anything until she'd been missing for forty-eight hours. Even after forty-eight hours, they opened a case but didn't do anything as far as Anna could tell.

Anna was beside herself. She called the cell phone company to have them track Rita's last-known location. Because she wasn't on her sister's account, they couldn't give her any information for privacy reasons. Understandable, but irritating nonetheless and only added to the worry.

Rather than sit back and do nothing, Anna took matters into her own hands. She printed flyers and put them up throughout Chicago. A waste of time though. The odds of anyone calling were slim to none. Especially in a city as big as Chicago. People were always scurrying to and from work, home, and wherever with little interest in flyers tacked to poles.

But she couldn't sit around and do nothing.

Anna had a key to Rita's apartment and went there looking for clues. She found her sister's computer and logged in by guessing the password. On the first try. It hadn't been that hard to do. Bongo was the name of their dog when they were kids. Another example of how they were connected. They thought alike.

Turns out Rita wasn't in trouble at all. She was on a business trip. Out of the country. Anna had been furious. She insisted that in the future, Rita tell them when she was going out of town for an extended period of time. She said she would and had kept that promise.

Until now.

Perhaps that's where she was. On a trip. Away for work. That had to be it. Rita forgot to tell her. Didn't remember the appointment at the bridal shop.

The anger returned and overrode the worry.

How could Rita be that inconsiderate?

Then the ominous feeling returned.

Why won't these feelings go away?

She tamped them down again. There had to be a good explanation. Rita was predictably unpredictable. When it came to normal, everyday things, she was as strait-laced and boring as one could be. Anna couldn't imagine a scenario where Rita would forget an appointment. The only explanation must be that Rita had been called away on business with short notice and had forgotten to call.

When it came to Rita's job, everything was a mystery. No one knew exactly what she did for a living. Some kind of international sales. That's why she said she had to be out of touch for long periods of time. Her work took her overseas. To places with sketchy cell phone service. When grilled about it, Rita finally blurted out that she was a fabrics buyer for a major fashion house.

"Why the secrecy?" Anna had asked in an almost harsh tone.

Rita insisted that she had a nondisclosure agreement which prevented her from saying anything more.

"Even to your own sister?" Anna argued.

It didn't matter. Rita still maintained the veil of secrecy and Anna knew that once Rita dug her heels in, she wouldn't budge. She was a strong-willed woman. So was Anna, but that shouldn't take the place of common courtesy. The least Rita could've done was called and said she couldn't make it.

They had lunch last week and it seemed like everything was normal. One of their favorite lunchtime rendezvous was an Italian beef sandwich joint on the South Side. The beef with peppers was legendary, and people drove from numerous neighborhoods to indulge in one of Chicago's finest eating establishments. They almost always had a line, and neither cared. The food was worth the wait.

They'd confirmed the bridal shop appointment at lunch that day. Rita didn't give Anna any indication that she'd be out of town. Even confirmed the address.

Anna sat at a conference table in the bridal shop with catalogs spread out in front of her. Pictures of various dresses. Some of the most spectacular wedding dresses she'd ever seen. So many that she suddenly felt overwhelmed.

That's why she needed Rita to be there. For her fashion sense. Anna valued her sister's opinion. More importantly, she was excited and wanted Rita to be there to share in the excitement.

And Rita would know which dress to pick. She often helped Anna pick out clothes. Rita was always trying to get Anna to take more fashion risks.

"I work at a high school!" Anna had argued. "We have a dress code. I have to dress conservatively."

"Conservative, yes," Rita said. "Frumpy, no."

The dressmaker pointed to a dress in the catalog, interrupting Anna's thoughts.

"Anna let out a gasp." The dress was beautiful. She couldn't help thinking that Rita would love it. It was definitely not conservative and certainly not frumpy.

"Thank you again for doing this," Anna said to Missy, the owner of the bridal shop.

"You're welcome," she said. "I'm glad to do it. I want to show you something." Missy stood and left the room.

Anna thumbed through the catalogs again, looking at her options. The woman was gone for nearly ten minutes.

Anna looked at her phone again. She still hadn't heard from Rita. Booking another appointment for another day wasn't possible. The bridal shop had been booked weeks in advance. Anna had only gotten into this dressmaker as a referral from a teacher friend at her high school.

A few months before in the teacher's lounge, the conversation came up about wedding dresses. "I'm going dress shopping this weekend," Anna had said. "With my sister."

Clearly, she was excited, and the other teachers seemed to enjoy the positive energy. One of the older teachers, Mrs. Hatcher said, "My daughter's a dressmaker. I could get her to make you a dress."

"I don't think I could afford a custom dress. Not on my salary," Anna replied. And then while thinking out loud she said, "We'll be lucky to afford a wedding." She felt her cheeks turn pink when she realized she'd said the last part aloud.

Mrs. Hatcher waved her hand dismissively. "I'll talk to her. She'll make you a good deal. Consider it a wedding present from me."

Anna did some research. Turns out the woman's daughter wasn't an ordinary dressmaker. She was world famous. Designed dresses for celebrities from LA to London and parts in between. Her services were in great demand. Fittings were scheduled months in advance. Anna felt fortunate to have such an opportunity. She couldn't believe her good fortune. When she accepted the invitation, she left the teacher's lounge glowing and feeling like the luckiest person alive.

Now that she was looking at the dresses, she wasn't disappointed. The selections were spectacular. And the woman's daughter was only going to charge her for the cost of the materials.

Missy came back into the room with something in her hand. She handed it to Anna. The catalog wasn't an ordinary catalog. Printed on a type of high-end paper she'd never seen before. When she held it, she felt like she was holding a precious piece of artwork.

Missy pointed to a particular dress.

Anna could feel her mouth gape open.

She described it for her. An alluring crepe fit-and-flare wedding dress with a plunging, off-the-shoulder neckline. The long sleeves were stunning, adorned by carefully hand-placed lace sewn into the dress. Beaded lace appliques, as Missy called them, covered the bodice, and extended down onto the skirt where it attached and created a breathtaking shaped cutout train.

Anna was beyond ecstatic. She'd never imagined being married in something so gorgeous. She hesitated to ask how much it cost; but she had to. Certain it was more than she could afford.

The price was more than she wanted to spend, even at cost, but she was forced into a decision and made it. Her fiancé, Hayden, was just getting started in finance, and her salary was modest.

"You only get married once," Missy said. Then she knocked on wood and added, "Hopefully."

Anna signed the contract, paid a deposit, and left the shop with mixed emotions. Feeling like a princess but steamed that her sister hadn't been there to share in the experience. She couldn't believe Rita didn't call. Didn't show. Didn't text. Nothing. She should've been there to help her make the decision.

A sadness came over her.

She would only get married once, and Rita was ruining it. She loved her sister to the depths of the earth, but surely Rita knew how important this was to her. And she didn't show up.

Not even a phone call!

Before she drove away from the bridal shop, Anna dialed her sister's number.

No answer.

"Rita, where are you?" she exclaimed to her sister's voicemail. "I had the dress fitting. The appointment was at noon. You didn't show up. I needed you there. I can't believe you stood me up! What... the ...You'd better be dead or in the hospital!"

She immediately regretted the last comment as the ominous feeling came over her again.

What if something bad has happened to her?

Anna called right back. "I'm sorry. I didn't mean that. Where are you? Call me. I'm starting to get worried about you. Love you. I got the most amazing dress. I can't wait for you to see it. Call me!"

The rest of the afternoon, Anna looked at her phone more times than she could count. Her mind ran wild with all kinds of scenarios. She went back and forth from being afraid to wanting to yell at her sister for missing the bridal gown appointment. One of the most important days of her life.

She had to recharge her phone because she kept checking it every few minutes.

Six hours later, she still hadn't heard from Rita.

14

Dexter Street

The warrant to search the gang's house arrived shortly after the Lieutenant left. He stayed longer than usual, probably because he was as intrigued by the crime scene and the mysterious blonde woman as I was.

Who was she? Why did she take down Strikers in the back alley? What was her motivation?

To say it was unusual to have a blonde, white woman as a suspect in a crime in that neighborhood would be a gross understatement. Add the fact that she potentially took down numerous armed thugs was both baffling and impressive. Being a victim would've made much more sense. The Lieutenant commented that he'd never seen anything like it. He'd been on the job for almost thirty years.

Now there were two crimes for me to investigate. Three Strikers who were shot and killed in the back alley and the other three thugs who were lying in hospital beds perhaps permanently incapacitated. A blonde-haired woman was seen fleeing both scenes. Since I didn't believe in coincidences, I could assume I was looking for the same person. Although, assumptions were also dangerous in my line of work. I didn't have any proof, but my gut instinct told me it was her. When I followed my gut, I was rarely wrong.

I wanted to meet the lady for several reasons. One to find answers. The other was to shake her hand. Her combat skills and sharpshooting accuracy were mind-boggling.

The coroner hauled off the bodies, and the cops did more canvassing but turned up nothing of significance. The little bit of information they were able to get out of neighbors was limited.

The crime scene held virtually no clues. All I had to go on was the information the little old blue-haired lady gave to the canvassing cop. I interviewed her myself to see if I could extract any more information. By the time we were finished, the old lady wasn't even sure it was a blonde-haired girl.

"I might've been mistaken," she said.

That put me back to square one. Some might say, including my Lieutenant, not to put too much effort into it. Investigating the deaths of gang members was a mixed bag. As a law enforcement person of any kind, you wanted to make the world a safer place and fulfill your oath.

However, gang-related problems were ongoing, and we all knew they weren't going away. That made it hard for any of us to put much energy into it when the crime was against them. On the one hand, I wanted to do my job and solve the crime. On the other hand, I had a stack of innocent victim files laying on my desk.

In this instance, I wasn't sure a crime had actually been committed. It might've been self-defense. Although, leaving the scene was definitely a crime even if the shooting were justified.

The Lieutenant would expect me to make minimal effort, then wrap up the case in a nice little bow and move on. No one would lose any sleep over three dead Strikers. The joke around the office said it all.

What do you call three dead gang members at the bottom of Lake Michigan?

A good start.

Another office favorite was: *The killer was just doing our job for us. We should send him a thank you note.*

That wasn't going to happen in this instance. Because of the connection to Anna, this case interested me more than it normally would. The blonde woman might hold the answers to my mystery.

I had met her once.

Sort of. At *Champions*. She came in and circulated a picture. Asked around. Went from table to table. She approached me, but I was distracted by my thoughts of Anna. I'd been blind-sided when Anna walked into the bar that night when I thought she was dead.

I strained to remember the conversation which lasted no more than ten seconds. All I could piece together was that she wanted to know if I had seen the young, Asian girl in the photograph.

She mentioned a name. I couldn't remember it for the life-of-me. I replayed the scene in my mind.

The rest of the movie was a blur. One Striker was already in the bar. I remembered he sat in the corner. Clearly suspicious. Anna came in. We spoke briefly. She ordered a drink and then left for the restroom.

Actually, I was on the phone with the Lieutenant. That's why I didn't get a chance to talk to Anna for any length of time. She left and went to the restroom after she saw the blonde-haired woman. Unexpectedly. Like something was wrong.

Then two more Strikers entered the bar. The one sitting in the corner pointed to the back, and all three Strikers took off to the area where the restrooms were. They appeared to be focused on Anna. When the blonde woman saw them, she followed. Her walk was de-liberate, strong, and rapid without drawing attention to herself.

The next thing I knew, the three Strikers were on the ground in the back alley, Anna was driving out of the parking lot, and the blonde woman was chasing her. It happened so fast, had I waited even a few more seconds, I wouldn't have seen anything but the scumbags on the ground. Not even that, if I hadn't gone into the back alley.

Then I reminded myself. Not Anna. Her sister was the woman in the bar that night. I couldn't make myself quit calling her Anna. I would associate that face with Anna until I discovered another name to put with it. Hopefully, I would put all the pieces together soon.

The most important thing was that the blonde woman connected the two cases. Six Strikers had been assaulted. Three killed. It couldn't be a coincidence.

The woman in the morgue was also connected. I just didn't know how. That made it three cases I was working on.

The Lieutenant didn't know what I was doing, which was why I was glad he left the scene at the house when he did. He left me there to search the house myself. Coordinate the forensics team. Something I was happy to do. I might find answers in there.

When the warrant arrived, the first thing I did was clear the house, even though the beat cops had done so before they sealed it off and filed for the warrant. I wasn't taking any chances. I went room to room to make sure no one was hiding in the premises. The investigation would have to wait until I was satisfied the area was safe.

What I found was not what I expected to see. Not your typical gang house. The location was definitely used for trafficking women. This was clearly where the Strikers were keeping girls. One way I could tell was how neat and clean the rooms were. Generally, gang members were slobs. The sink was usually filled with dirty dishes. Pizza boxes and beer cans were often piled up on the floor on the counter or in an overflowing trash can.

I didn't see any of that.

The beds were even made. In the upstairs anyway. That's where the gang members clearly slept. Three upstairs bedrooms had no noticeable clues which was a clue in and of itself. My first thought was that the girls were kept up there. Then I dismissed it because it wasn't secure enough.

These girls were likely held against their will. Not all, but most. Those who were voluntarily pushing tricks for the gangs didn't need to be kept at a house. They lived in their own residences. They came and went as they pleased, and everything was great as long as they paid the gang their share of the money from the tricks.

Looking around, I was certain I'd find a more secure area. A makeshift prison. I found a door off the kitchen that led to the basement. The door had huge locks laying on the floor next to it. The cops had obviously cut the locks and searched the basement. Then secured the area until forensics arrived.

My heartbeat inched up a few more notches as I opened the door to go down and look around. My instincts told me to approach that area carefully. With my gun drawn. Going down the steps not knowing what was at the bottom was always one of my biggest fears. I was a sitting duck if someone was waiting to ambush me. Even though the cops had searched the area, I wasn't confident that they were thorough enough.

I opened the door cautiously. Identified myself and crept down the steps like a cougar sneaking up on a prey. Although I'd already made enough noise to give away my intentions.

A beat cop followed behind me.

My breathing became shallow as my heart started to beat even faster.

The beat cop was right behind me. Another stood at the top to guard our backs.

The room was empty. No bodies. No hidden compartments. I breathed a sigh of relief.

It definitely had signs that girls were being held there against their will, though. Mattresses lined the floor. I counted six of them. Women's clothing was strewn on the floors and stuffed into a dresser up against the wall, confirming what I'd already suspected. The area had one bathroom, and it was filled with feminine products, makeup, and such. Girls were being held there. Against their wills. As sex slaves.

The sight of things sickened me. The worst part of my job was dealing with women and children who were victims of sexual or domestic abuse. Rape and other violent crimes against the most vulnerable.

I walked through each area of the room. Didn't touch anything. Just observed. Clearly, whoever was there had fled in a hurry and left a lot of things behind. Forensics would be there several hours just working on that room.

Satisfied the house was clear, I holstered my weapon and went back upstairs to notify the forensics team that they could begin their work.

Then I walked them from room to room again giving them instructions on what to look for. The forensics team would, no doubt, find a treasure trove of clues in every room. Fingerprints. DNA. Maybe some ID's or weapons were left behind in their haste to abandon the premises and keep their valuable merchandise—the girls.

We didn't see any drug paraphernalia. Not surprisingly. The Strikers sold drugs, not used them. The leadership didn't want the grunts blowing the gang's profits up their noses. They probably gave some to the girls though. One of the ways they controlled them. Forensics would be able to tell me if they found any drug residue down in the basement.

That's where I told them to start. That area held the most interest for me. Although the other areas were important, clearly the makeshift prison would most likely hold the most information.

Twenty minutes later, one of the members of the team came upstairs to find me.

"Detective Ford," she said, "I have something I want to show you."

I followed her down the stairs. A set of lights had been set up to illuminate the basement.

"Over there," the lady cop said, pointing toward the dresser which had been pulled away from the wall.

"What am I looking at?" I asked.

"There's writing on the wall," she said. "Looks like a list of names."

I walked over to get a closer look.

The words were clear.

They were names of girls. First names. That didn't necessarily do me a lot of good. A clue, nonetheless. The girls, for some reason, wanted to document that they were there. It was their way to let someone know what had happened to them.

I read through the list. Searing their names into my memories.

My mouth flew open when I saw the last name on the list.

Bae.

Then I remembered.

The blonde-haired woman at *Champions*. The picture of the North Korean girl. The conversation came flooding back into my mind like a tsunami. It replayed in my head like it had just happened.

I could hear her ask me, *Have you seen this girl? Her name is Bae.*

I thought she meant B. A. Y. The spelling on the wall was B. A. E. Then the words, WAS HERE.

Was it the same person? It had to be. An excitement welled up inside that only happened when I had a big break in a case. Now I was certain the two crime scenes were connected. There wasn't a single shred of doubt. The blonde-haired woman was looking for a girl named Bae. I now had evidence the girl was being held in this house by the Strikers.

That's why three scum bags were dead and three more were in the hospital. That's why the blonde-haired girl was leaving a trail of dead bodies. She was after the girl. The Strikers had her, and she was willing to kill any of them who got in her way.

For some reason I felt proud of her even though the questions were swirling around in my head.

Who is the blonde girl?

Who is Bae?

A relative? Friend? Law enforcement?

Was Blondie a good guy?

Apparently.

Whoever she was, the lady was on a mission. And she had unbelievable skills.

I suspected there would be more dead Strikers if I didn't find her soon.

15

The forensics team finished their work, and the only people left at the scene were the two policemen who were standing watch over the front and back doors.

Seconds before, a suspicious, nondescript, four-door car drove by the house. It slowed down deliberately. As soon as I came out the front door, the car sped up and then was gone in a flash. I wasn't able to get a plate number, and if it was a gang member, the car most likely had stolen plates. Clearly, one or more of the Striker thugs were checking out the scene.

That gave me an idea.

As soon as it popped into my head, I knew it was a bad idea. Good plan, but bad idea.

Without hesitation, I walked over to the front door and ripped down the yellow police tape, wadded it in a ball, and stuffed it into my pocket. Another deviation from standard police procedures. Unconventional at a fresh crime scene. If the Lieutenant knew what I was doing, he'd have my head on a platter, maybe even my badge.

I couldn't worry about that right now. I had to put this plan into motion before dark.

"What are you doing?" the rookie beat cop at the front door asked.

"You're free to go," I answered. "We're done here."

I didn't elaborate. The less said the better in case things went south.

Then I walked through the house, exited the back door, and did the same thing to the yellow police tape blocking the entrance to the back door.

The woman cop guarding that door didn't say anything. More experienced, she knew I was in charge of the scene, and beat cops rarely challenged the detective's authority. Her eyes widened in obvious surprise, though. Like a deer in the headlights. Although a seasoned cop, she was briefly speechless, confused, and seemed to be frozen in place.

I ignored her reaction.

Another cordoned-off area set apart by yellow police tape was in the yard by the road in the back alley. That's where the three Strikers had met their demise. I walked over there and tore down the yellow police tape tied to the stakes in the ground.

Then walked to my vehicle with a purpose. The two cops followed. I opened the trunk and threw the wadded tape inside it then slammed the lid down.

They stood there staring at me.

"You're both free to go," I said for a second time. "Good work. And thanks."

They didn't leave right away. Instead, they looked at each other, then back at me like they deserved an explanation. When one wasn't offered, the rookie cop said, "Why did you take down the tape?"

His name plate said, Kiffin. He wasn't going to drop it. Not that I blamed him. He had to answer to the Lieutenant as well. He'd be required to write up a report. Kiffin didn't want him, or his partner blamed for the removal of the crime scene tape. The whole thing clearly made him uneasy. The senior cop seemed bothered by it as well, but she probably would've let it drop. Not her concern. The rookie cop would learn that eventually.

"I'll put it back up later," I answered.

Kiffin shook his head from side to side, "I'm sorry, Sir, but procedures are to secure the crime scene until we release the house back to its owners. The tape lets everyone know not to enter the premises until we are done with the scene."

Kiffin was making perfect sense. Rookie cops often felt a compunction to follow the rules. Understandable, but annoying at that moment.

I stepped in closer to him. Off to the side, so I wasn't right in his face. Technically, I was in charge of the scene and could do whatever I wanted to do. Throw my weight around if need be. Chew him out if I wanted. Tell him to never question my actions again. But I cut him slack because he was right. I was breaking procedures. The two cops needed an answer for CYA reasons.

"Did you see the car drive by earlier?" I asked.

"I did, Sir. The car looked suspicious to me."

Not all cops called detectives *sir*. This one was trying hard not to make a mistake. I appreciated that. I'd never walked a beat but was thankful for those who did. They had a harder job than me, in some ways.

"You're right. It was suspicious," I said. "More than likely gang members checking out the house so they can come back after we're gone. Or it could be gawkers. But that's unlikely because they took off like their hair was on fire as soon as I walked out the door."

"They'll likely be back," Kiffin said. "That's why the tape should stay up. It'll keep them out."

I did my best not to roll my eyes at the rookie's naive concept that our crime scene tape would stop thugs from entering the house. Wishful thinking but highly unlikely. Bolted doors and windows wouldn't stop them if they wanted in that house. Thugs didn't follow rules.

"I'm counting on there being more," I explained.

"I'm not following you, Sir."

I didn't feel like explaining and was losing patience. "I need you to get your patrol cars out of here. I'm going to move mine down the street. When more Strikers show up, and I think they will, I'm going to be here to question them."

"That could be dangerous, Sir," Kiffin retorted.

I shrugged my shoulders. "Yeah. Well, it comes with the territory, right?"

The woman cop spoke up. "Where's your partner?"

She had a good point.

My partner, Greg Doyle, blew out his knee at a police league bas-ketball game a few days before and had a torn ACL. He'd be out of commission for at least six months. The Lieutenant hadn't gotten around to assigning anyone to me yet. Something he'd likely do to-morrow at our Monday morning briefing. You were always sup-posed to have the support of a partner in the field at all times. Tech-nically, the Lieutenant was breaking procedures. Doyle would think my plan was brilliant. I learned to think outside the box from him. Unfortunately, he wasn't there to back me up.

"He's on medical," I answered.

"I think we should stay here with you," Kiffin said.

"I'll be fine. I don't want any cruisers in the neighborhood. I want them to think we've cleared out. I'm going to park my car the next block over."

Kiffin started to object, but I raised my hand in the air to stop him. I appreciated the thought and knew there was some merit to it, but I wanted the house to look like we were gone. It was the only way to catch the Strikers off guard, should any of them return to the scene of the crime.

"I'm only going to stay until dark," I said reassuringly. "If I run into trouble, I'll call for backup. When I'm done, I'll put the tape back up. I've got several rolls in my trunk. Not that the tape's going to keep them out. I'm sure they'll be back in the house before we know it."

That seemed to convince them because neither voiced any further objection. They got in their cruiser and left. I moved my unmarked car to the next street over and locked it up. Not before getting my pump action shotgun out of the trunk and carrying it with me as I walked briskly back to the crime scene. I didn't want one of the nosy neighbors noticing me brandishing a weapon and calling the cops back to the scene.

When I got back to the house my stomach started to growl. I was hungry. I looked around the kitchen to see if they had anything edi-ble. I found a cold soda in the fridge and some packaged food which I heated in the microwave. Then I went into the living room, moved a chair so that it faced the front door, plopped down in it, and waited.

Not an ideal situation. I couldn't see the back door from my vantage point. I hoped that I'd hear them drive up if they came in from the back alley.

When darkness fell, I began to wonder if this was such a good idea. Too late. I couldn't leave. I was already committed. Certain the Strikers would come by again.

Who would come by?

Gang members who had heard about the murder? I hoped not. My thinking was that word hadn't spread through the entire organization, and some Strikers might show up who were unaware of the events that happened earlier that day. I'd have the element of surprise. I should be so lucky.

Gang members who had heard of the murders would be more cautious. Also fired up. Angry that three of their own had been killed. They wouldn't like the fact that a detective was in their house setting a trap for them. They'd enter with more caution. Maybe drive by a few times. Get a lay of the land. Maybe even approach the house with guns drawn.

My mind began to play games with my imagination. What if a carload of gang members came? With semi-automatic weapons? One against two or maybe even three was what I had counted on. Start upping the numbers, and the odds of it ending well for me plummeted. What would they think if they arrived at the house and found it completely dark? With no cars in front of it? With no police tape and no lights on. They might think it was a setup.

So, I went upstairs and turned on several lights. Then came back down and turned on the kitchen light to make it look like there was activity in the house. Fellow thugs at home holding down the fort, so to speak. Hopefully, whoever would come hadn't heard the news and would think everything was business as usual.

Satisfied, I sat back down and tried to make myself relax. Calm my racing heartbeat. Remind myself why I was there.

This wasn't about three dead Strikers. The average lifespan of a gang member in Chicago was twenty years and six months. Those three idiots lying naked in a morgue had outlived their life expectancy. They seemed older than that to me. But ninety miles of bad road aged people quickly. Nevertheless, they got what was coming to them. If it hadn't happened today, it would've happened eventually.

I was there for the girls.

The fourteen names scribbled on the wall in the basement. Their names were permanently etched in my mind.

Without question, those girls were being held against their will. Scared out of their wits. Wondering how they'd gotten themselves into such a horrible predicament and if they'd ever get out of it or see their families again.

Was I breaking procedure? No question about it. Drastic problems called for drastic measures.

Would the Lieutenant throw a fit if he knew? Without a doubt.

But my idea was creative. I was thinking outside the box. If some gang members showed up, I was certain I could find a reason to arrest them. They'd have illegal weapons or drugs on them. Maybe even a girl or two who was being held against her will. With any luck, it would only be a few thugs, not four or five. I was in a numbers game, and right now I knew I was rolling the dice.

If I could get the jump on a couple of Strikers, that'd give me a bargaining chip. If they told me where they took the girls, I might even let them go. If they resisted, my 9mm striker-fired semi-automatic pistol Luger, pressed strategically against someone's nose could be very persuasive. Most people caved when it came down to life and death.

It made me laugh out loud to think that my gun was a striker, and it might be pointed at a Striker in a matter of minutes. The funny thought released some tension.

I let out a deep breath, feeling my shoulders relax even more.

The tension returned with a vengeance, when a car pulled into the driveway, and two Strikers stepped out of the vehicle.

16

Two car doors shut.

Two Strikers got out and walked toward the front door.

I moved away from the window to the inside of the hallway that led to the kitchen. I was in a position where I was confident that they couldn't spot me until it was too late for them to ambush me even if they were planning to set a trap for me.

I took a quick deep breath—my lame attempt to calm my heart which was beating out of my chest. I raised my gun, clutching it with both hands, ready. Pointed at the door. It would be a matter of moments before they came into the house. Any second now. No time to think or do anything but be ready for the moment of action.

Focus.

Intense focus.

As if my life depended on it.

Which it did.

Kill or be killed.

They had the advantage. I had procedures to follow. The Strikers had no rules. Before I fired my gun, I had to take that one millisecond to ask myself if I was doing the right thing. It was a thin, grey line and could be a life-changing choice.

For me and for them.

Cops had gone to jail for life for making the wrong one.

I was already on shaky ground. I'd promised the beat cop I'd call for backup. I should've. But I didn't want the scrutiny on my actions. I'd say there hadn't been time. I was going through the crime scene again. Thinking. It's how I solved cases. Alone with my thoughts. The two Strikers drove up. Startled me. No time to call it in.

Satisfied I had the story set in my mind, I moved to the shadows of the hallway. I took another deep breath as if that would help.

The element of surprise was on my side but was also working to my disadvantage. I wasn't sure what to expect.

They'd certainly be armed. Would the men barge in with their guns blazing or still in their pants?

Would they knock?

Enter totally clueless?

I could only hope.

They didn't knock. The door swung open by someone who clearly wasn't in a hurry. No drama, just a few people coming home after work or to hang out and have a beer. They weren't being cautious. The two men stepped into the room. I waited until both had cleared the door then I stepped out of the shadows.

"Chicago PD! Hands on your heads!" My commands were sharp and authoritative. Meant to surprise them.

They didn't immediately obey. Nor did they look shocked. Why not?

"I said to put your hands on your heads where I can see them!"

Their hands were out in front of them where I could see them, but they weren't following my instructions. Why weren't they afraid? What did they know that I didn't know?

"On your knees! Now!" I barked my commands with the fierceness of a Doberman.

If they didn't comply, I wasn't sure exactly what I'd do. I couldn't use deadly force unless there was an imminent threat. They hadn't given me any reason to believe they were going to harm me, even though I knew they would if they could.

While I considered two armed thugs who weren't complying with the orders of a detective an imminent threat, the powers that be would scrutinize my every decision and come to their own conclusion. Easy for them. They didn't have to worry about getting shot, maimed, or killed. The biggest threat they faced were paper cuts from shuffling the mountains of paperwork that would be the aftermath of a brutal situation.

I took two steps forward and waved the gun menacingly. Hoping they'd get the message. They both had smirks on their faces.

Then I heard a sound.

Behind me.

If I looked that way, I'd give the men in front of me the advantage. Was that what they wanted me to do? If I didn't, I'd have no idea what was behind me.

I suddenly had the eerie feeling they were expecting the noise, which sent a dread shooting through my body like a dart.

A trap!

There were three of them.

I thought I was setting a trap for them.

A panic came over me, not knowing the nature of the threat behind me but imagining the worst. I halfway expected to hear a gunshot fired at my back at any moment.

Was this how I was going to die?

A split second later, I heard a yelp.

Then a thud.

I changed my angle so I could keep my eyes on the two men in front of me and get a glimpse of what was happening behind me.

The hallway was dark.

A figure suddenly emerged.

A blonde-haired woman. Dressed in all black. Holding a gun. Pointed at the two men by the door.

"You heard the man," the woman barked with authority. "Get on your knees! Spread eagle! Now! I'm not going to tell you twice!"

The men had stunned looks on their faces.

Confusion.

Their eyes flitted back and forth. Between the woman and me.

The blonde woman didn't wait for them to comply. She took several quick steps toward them and threw the man on the right side to the ground. Then pointed her gun at the other man's head.

"Three of your lowlife friends are dead. Do you want to join them?" she said to the second man. Her foot was firmly planted in the back of the Striker on the ground.

He quickly got on his knees and went spread eagle. The woman took their guns out of the back of their pants and tossed them across the floor in my direction. I kicked them so they were behind me.

A couple steps back to my right, and I could see a body lying on the floor in the hallway to the kitchen. Unconscious.

"Do you have two pairs of handcuffs?" she asked me.

I nodded yes.

"Toss them to me."

I reached into my back pocket, pulled them out, and slowly moved toward her until I was close enough to hand them to her. She skillfully secured the handcuffs on the two men, then patted them down. She pulled out a knife from one of their pockets and a pair of brass knuckles from the other guy's side pocket.

"Do you have another set of handcuffs for the other guy?" she asked.

"No. I only have two."

My voice was cracking as I said it. I felt almost as stunned as the Strikers laying on the ground in cuffs.

"No problem," she said nonchalantly.

The woman stood and went into the hallway and dragged the body of the unconscious man into the living room.

"He's out cold," she said. "But you can never be too careful."

She took out a pair of zip ties from her pocket and secured the man's arms behind his back. Then holstered her weapon, stood to her feet, and wiped the sweat off her brow. She took a deep breath and relaxed her shoulders a bit.

"You can put your gun away," she said to me.

"Who are you?" I asked. I lowered it so it wasn't pointed at her, but I didn't put it away.

"Let's go in there, where we can talk."

She pointed toward the kitchen.

I put away my weapon, even though I was hesitant to. Only because of basic protocol. She wasn't on my team. I had no idea who she was. But on the other hand, her timing had been brilliant as had her skills in taking the men down. They were all in cuffs or zip ties. From my vantage point, she had clearly saved my life. If she was a threat to me, she'd have already acted on it.

Once out of earshot of the bad guys she said, "What's your name?"

"Cliff Ford. Chicago PD. Homicide."

The woman grinned.

"May I call you Clifford?"

I nodded. A slight smile formed on my lips. Both from relief that everything was under control here for the moment, and that I was talking to the blonde. The mysterious, gorgeous, hyper ninja-like skilled woman who could take down men like they were feathers.

Actually, I preferred she didn't call me Clifford. A running joke in elementary school. At least, until I settled it with the school bully and beat the daylights out of him one afternoon after school. He didn't call me 'Clifford' any more after that. None of the other kids did either.

Blondie could call me anything she wanted. This was suddenly her show. I wondered if she would mind if I called her 'Blondie.'

In the light, I could see her clearly. The same woman I'd seen in the bar. She was stunningly beautiful. Also, extremely fit. Her handshake was firm and easily matched my strength. The woman had an air about her which immediately impressed me. Confidence I didn't remember seeing in another person before. Male or female. Not to this extent.

The Lieutenant was cocky and pretentious. But that didn't translate to confidence or being capable. This woman was the best of the best on steroids.

She also didn't appear to have any guile. More of a confidence in her ability. Fearless. I had no doubt that she could disarm me and put me out any time she wanted. I had to assume she was on my side. Something she confirmed, with her next words.

"Your plan was a good one," she said, as she leaned against the counter.

"Take down the police tape and wait for them to show up." She paused as if in thought. "If you hadn't done that, I intended to."

It amazed me that she knew my plan. Was it that obvious? Had she been watching me the entire day?

"How did you know the Strikers would show up?" I asked.

"The same way you did. Intuition. It seemed logical. Three of their men are dead. They'd be curious. They'd also be livid. They'd want to know who took their guys. Several of them already drove by during the day. They slowed down when they saw the cruisers and the coroner hauling off the bodies."

"Did you kill the three men?" I asked.

She answered me with a question. Classic deflection.

"Like I said, your plan was a good one, but it had a fatal flaw. Do you want to know what it was?"

"What's that?" I asked.

"Your shadow. They could see it through the window."

I hadn't thought of that. The light from the lamp and kitchen must've reflected off the mirror on the wall. Or off the curtains. I wanted to kick myself. I thought I'd considered all the angles. Apparently not. Luckily, I was still standing to talk about it.

She continued, "I saw them drop off one man down the street. Then they drove slowly back to the house, so he had time to sneak in through the backdoor. I had intended on seeing how it all played out, but I figured you needed help. He was coming from your blind side."

"You probably saved my life. I owe you big time. Thank you."

"You're welcome."

"Who are you? FBI? CIA? DEA?"

To say I was intrigued, baffled, and curious would have been a gross understatement. I'd worked in the trenches of underworld lowlifes for numerous years and had never come across someone like her.

She was like a Wonder Woman or a Catwoman. Was she on the side of good or evil? Catwoman wore black. Blonde woman wore black. Was she more like a Bond girl? A spy? The thought occurred to me that she might be CIA, but I knew they weren't allowed to operate on US soil.

My imagination was out of control, but somehow, I managed to keep my mouth shut and from saying something stupid. I was completely blown away by the events of the last few minutes. Or was it seconds? I didn't know. My head was spinning. At least the Strikers were incapacitated. I was feeling a bit incapacitated myself.

We stared at each other. Neither of us said anything for what seemed like an eternity.

"Seriously," I finally said. "Who are you? I need to know if you're a good guy or bad guy."

"I'm someone who can help you," she said. "I've been following these three thugs for a while. These are the guys who killed the girl in front of the coffee shop."

I could feel my eyes widen. My mouth was probably agape.

She said it in a relaxed manner. No drama. Just the facts. I could hardly believe what I was hearing.

Was she talking about Anna?

She had to be!

17

"What do you know about the girl at the coffee shop?" I asked the blonde-haired girl who was standing in the kitchen with me. The three Strikers were in the other room. Lying on the floor, restrained. Their three weapons were on the kitchen counter.

My heart was doing somersaults about the possibility that the lady might give me information that would clear up the Anna mystery. I was desperate to know.

She still leaned against the kitchen counter with her arms crossed. She still hadn't told me her name. I doubted she would. Any name she gave me would probably be fake.

"The woman was murdered," the blonde-woman answered. "Shot in cold blood. The three guys in the living room were the ones who did it. Like I said, the one I took down was the shooter. The other two were in the car. I don't know which one was driving."

"How do you know it was them?"

"The car out front is the getaway vehicle. Black Lexus. I confirmed the license plate. I've been tracking them. I saw the whole thing. The girl was walking in front of the coffee shop. One of the thugs got out of the car, walked up to her, grabbed her purse, and then shot her point blank in the chest. On the sidewalk. She didn't have a chance. I didn't have a chance to save her either. The shooter ran back to the car, and they were gone in a flash. I tracked them back to this location."

The woman had all the facts. That's exactly how it happened.

"Can you describe the woman who was killed?" I had to be sure.

"Beautiful girl. Jet black hair. Probably Cuban. Maybe Dominican. Thirty-four or thirty-five, I'd say. Medium height. Thin. Fit."

It sure sounded like the girl in the morgue. She could've been describing Anna. Or the girl I met in the coffee shop.

I thought I'd get answers. It seemed like more questions were coming up.

"What else can you tell me about her?" I asked.

"Not much. I never met her. It's a shame though. A total waste. You've got her killer. He's in the other room. Is it your case?"

"No. Another detective has it. I'm investigating the three murders here at the house from earlier in the day."

I saw her roll her eyes when I mentioned murders. I'd done it on purpose to see if I could get a reaction. That'd be evidence that she was the shooter. The look was telling but not definitive.

The woman was good.

"Where were you last Friday night?" I asked.

I wanted to see what she knew about the three thugs who were beat up at *Champions* bar. There was no doubt in my mind that she was the one who did it, but I wanted to hear it from her. She definitely was the woman asking about the Korean girl and the one running after the car in the parking lot.

She ignored the question and asked her own.

"Do you know where they took the girls who were in this house?" she asked.

I ignored her question. Two could play that game.

"I saw you at *Champions* bar. Friday night. You beat up three gang members in the alley."

Dead silence. She simply stared at me. Her face and demeanor neither confirmed nor denied my accusation.

"I need to take you in for questioning," I said.

The woman uncrossed her arms and was no longer leaning on the counter.

"Good luck with that," she said.

That sounded like a threat.

"You're obstructing an investigation," I exclaimed, in as strong a voice as I could muster.

"From my vantage point, I just solved your investigation. Run ballistics on the gun. You'll see. That's the murder weapon. You wouldn't know that if it wasn't for me. You'd also be dead right now if I hadn't come along. So, drop the obstruction nonsense."

She had a point.

"Look," she continued. "We need to work together on this. I'm looking for a girl. The gang kidnapped her and were holding her in this house."

"I can confirm that," I said, breaking any number of protocols. Sharing details of an investigation with a third party was against every rule in the book. It seemed like the right thing to do.

"Your girl wrote her name on the wall downstairs. Bae."

Her eyes lit up.

I continued. "That's right. We found a list of names written on the wall. Behind the dresser. Presumably the names of girls held in this house. Bae was one of them."

Her forehead burrowed in deep concern.

"Do you know where they took them?"

"No."

"Well... those scumbags in the other room know. Let's go question them."

She started to walk that way, but I held out my hand to stop her. Fortunately, I only brushed her arm. I didn't want her to think I was trying to restrain her. I didn't think I could, even if I wanted to.

"I need to read them their rights," I said.

"Let me do it," the woman replied. "Follow my lead. You play good cop."

Before I could say anything, she left the room. I scurried to catch up to her.

She grabbed one of the men by the scruff of his neck. He was face down on the floor. She flipped him over. Roughly. Her gun was in her hand. I felt the urge to stop her but thought better of it. I'd seen her handiwork and knew how dangerous she was.

"Where did they take the girls who were being kept in this house?" the woman said to the man sharply.

The man glared at her and then turned his head to the side. From my experience, Strikers didn't talk. They had a code. Ratting on one of their own would get them killed.

We weren't allowed to use force to make them talk, so the only thing we could do was read them their rights and hope we could make a case from the evidence. Most of the time, their slick lawyer had them back on the streets in no time.

While the other man on the ground, the one trying to sneak up on me, may have been the one who killed the girl in front of the coffee shop, I had no proof, other than the word of the blonde woman. Getting her to come down to the station and give a statement didn't seem like it was going to happen. And I didn't see how I could make her.

She ratcheted up the intensity. The gun was suddenly against the man's forehead.

"Stop!" I shouted. "You can't kill him."

"I'm going to read him his rights first."

He tried to squirm away, but she had him pinned down. The other man looked on. His face was racked with fear. The third man started to stir.

"You have the right to remain silent," the blonde woman said. "If you choose to remain silent, I have the right to put a bullet in the back of your brain!"

"You can't do this," I said, realizing what she meant by me being the good cop. She wanted me to pretend to talk her out of killing the man. If the man on the floor thought she really would pull the trigger, maybe he'd talk. I couldn't get away with such tactics, but it might just work with her doing it.

She was breaking any number of laws, but it didn't seem like she cared. Her tone became even more menacing. Even I was scared.

"You have a right to a coroner," she said. "If you can't afford a coroner, one will be provided for you at no charge. Do you understand your rights?"

He didn't answer. Simply looked up at her with widened eyes, clearly petrified.

"Do you understand your rights?"

"Yes," he said meekly.

"I'm going to ask one more time. Where did they take the girls?"

His eyes flitted back and forth. Like he was considering his options. From my standpoint, I couldn't tell if she was bluffing or not. He was probably wondering the same thing.

"I'm done with you," she said. "After I blow your brains out, I bet your friends will talk."

She made an exaggerated gesture like she was ready to pull the trigger.

"No!" I shouted. "Don't kill him."

"I'm going to count to three," she said, ignoring me. "You'd better answer me, or you're as dead as your three friends who were hauled away by the coroner earlier today."

I wasn't sure if she had just confessed to killing the three men.

"One!" she shouted.

What should I do? I wasn't sure I could stop her even if I wanted to. At that point, I didn't want to.

"Two!" she said in an even louder voice.

Should I let her kill him in cold blood right in front of my eyes? I'd have no choice but to turn her in.

The woman had saved my life. I decided to let it play out.

Before she could say three, the man caved. "I'll talk! Don't shoot me. I know where the girls are!"

"Where?" she said.

"Shiv has them."

I was familiar with the name. Shiv was the leader of the Strikers. Had been for several years. He was known as being a ruthless and cutthroat head of the gang. We had no idea where he was.

"Address?"

She pressed the gun back down on his forehead.

"He's in a warehouse on the south side. Down by the docks. That's where he's at. I don't know where they took the girls, but he'll know."

It seemed like he was telling the truth.

"Which warehouse?"

He spewed out an address.

The woman stood to her feet.

"Alright. Detective, you need to put police tape on the front and back doors. Seal off the house. Then call for backup. Take these three in on suspicion of murder."

For whatever reason, it felt like she was in charge. I went to my vehicle, got the police tape, and put it up while she stayed inside and watched the three men. I secured the three guns in evidence bags and searched the suspects more thoroughly. One of the guns had the serial number filed off. That gave me a reason to arrest them. I could also charge them with attempted assault of a police officer.

I wasn't sure yet if I was going to mention the woman in my report or to the Lieutenant. The Strikers wouldn't say anything. As soon as they were in custody, they'd clam up. They'd mention the blonde-haired woman to their attorney, but he wouldn't say anything. If he did, he'd be admitting that his clients were trying to ambush me.

Blonde-haired lady had gone back into the kitchen.

When I was finished, I went to look for her.

She was gone.

18

I took the Strikers into custody and booked them into a holding cell but hadn't charged them yet.

Technically, I could detain them for a reasonable period of time while I investigated. *Reasonable* being a relative term. Seventy-two hours at most. Less than that once the Lieutenant got wind of it.

That was my biggest concern. I had a short window of opportunity before he stuck his nose into the situation and with questions I wasn't prepared to answer. I could already hear him peppering me. He'd want to know why I was still at the house. Alone. When everyone else had already left. What were the circumstances of the confrontation with the Strikers? What proof did I have to detain them for murder? Who was the woman they allegedly shot? How was it related to the three Strikers who were killed earlier that day? Is it related to the three Strikers in the hospital?

Have I lost my mind?

Fortunately, the Monday morning meeting of the detectives would occupy the Lieutenant's time. Hopefully, long enough for me to call in a favor. A complicating factor was that the Lieutenant might assign me a partner at the meeting. If he did, that'd significantly hamper my efforts. I'd have to spend the better part of the day getting acquainted with my new partner. Going over cases. We'd have to discuss the events of the night before. Having another set of eyes scrutinizing my actions was the last thing I wanted.

Thankfully, the Lieutenant ended the meeting with no mention of a partner. In fact, he didn't give me a second glance. I was grateful. This would give me a chance to implement my plan. Several people wanted some of the Lieutenant's time, so I sneaked out undetected. I wasn't actually sneaking. It just felt like it.

I bolted downstairs to ballistics to see my friend Mans Bergmann. Everyone called him "Magnum" which fit the job, if not the man. Mans was the antithesis of Tom Selleck—the original Magnum PI—making the nickname kind of humorous. Mans was five-foot five, a hundred fifty pounds, if wearing a winter coat that was soaking wet. Magnum PI was six four. Mans was scrawny and best suited for a lab. He'd be broken in half like a toothpick if he were to ever brandish a gun and walk a beat.

Everyone had their place. I'd be lost as a goose running a ballistics lab. Mans had tried to show me on more than one occasion how he matched bullets in the microscope, but it all ran together to me. I nodded my head and pretended to know what he was talking about.

A German transplant, Magnum had a Master's in Physics from the University of Chicago. He was an expert on all things metallurgy. A ballistics genius. Some say one of the best in the business. With no point of reference, I had no reason to disagree with them.

Especially since his help was exactly what I needed at that moment.

Right now.

ASAP.

The ultimate rush job. Even if we were best of friends, Magnum wouldn't be happy about the intrusion.

Magnum was always busy. There were no shortage of deaths or murder weapons in Chicago. His job was to analyze the guns and the bullets. Eighty-to eighty-five percent of all Chicago homicides involved a gun. Magnum had the ultimate job security. A matter of supply and demand. Chicago provided him plenty of both.

I was praying he wasn't too busy to run a quick test. On the way to the ballistics lab, I checked out of the evidence locker for the gun I'd taken off the Striker from the night before and the bullet the coroner had taken out of Jane Doe's chest. The blonde woman said the Striker's gun was the one used to kill the Anna lookalike in front of the coffee shop. She'd been adamant. You could see from the steely look in her eyes that she had no doubt about her information.

I was skeptical. The shooting happened so fast I couldn't believe she could be that certain. The Lieutenant would be even more skeptical than me. That's why I needed the report. Definitive proof. My word for it would mean nothing. The Strikers would be back on the street before lunchtime.

The report would also give me cover. I was determined to not tell the Lieutenant the whole story. If I gave him the slightest hint of what had happened, he'd demand to know why I hadn't arrested the blonde-haired woman on the spot. At least brought her in for questioning.

Having replayed the scene in my mind a dozen times, I don't think that was even possible. After seeing her skills, the woman could break me in two like a toothpick if she wanted. Something I didn't want to admit to the Lieutenant. She'd also saved my life. Another fact I hoped my boss never learned.

Magnum needed to come through for me. He could confirm beyond a shadow of a doubt if the woman were telling the truth. No reason to doubt her, but also no reason to believe her. Even if the man in custody was the shooter, that didn't mean he was still carrying the same gun. He could've ditched it. Maybe he had more than one gun. Perhaps she had identified the wrong person. Numerous scenarios were running through my head, and they all pointed to her being wrong. It just didn't seem feasible.

From eyewitness reports, the whole shooting happened in a flash. A matter of mere seconds. No one else had been able to give a detailed description of the shooter or any valuable information. Somehow the blonde woman knew exactly who he was. The ballistics report on the gun would confirm it either way.

That's why I was in the lab as soon as possible. I had to know. If it were a match, I'd march right into the Lieutenant's office with proof I'd solved the murder. Although not my case, I'd get serious credit. At least that's the way it should work. The Lieutenant wouldn't be happy that I'd overstepped my bounds, but the important thing would be that the case would be solved. A Striker would be put away for a very long time. Cold-blooded murder came with a hefty sentence. A judge would be thrilled to have such a clean-cut case against a Striker. The Lieutenant often overlooked our indiscretions if he got credit for an arrest.

In all likelihood, I wasn't stepping on Carson's toes anyway. The Jane Doe file was probably still sitting on his desk. Unopened. I doubted Carson had made any progress at all. Might not have even started a murder book. With a bullet match, the Lieutenant might even take the case away from Carson and give it to me, giving me free rein to pursue the Anna thread and get to the bottom of the mystery once and for all.

I bolted through the door to the lab, evidence in hand, and found Magnum exactly where I expected him to be. Standing at a table, with his eyes planted in the lenses of a large microscope. No doubt analyzing bullet markings on another case.

He looked up, smiled, then put his eyes back on the microscope lenses.

"I need a favor," I said, after the necessary greetings.

Magnum chuckled slightly.

"Join the crowd. Take a number. There's a long line."

He pointed to a table with a dozen weapons on it.

"I'm supposed to get through that pile of evidence this morning," he added. "You need a favor? Not going to happen."

Magnum spoke with a strong German accent but with perfect English diction. He'd been in America for most of his life. His mother spoke with a heavy German accent which still influenced him since he saw her every day after work. His father was killed in a construction accident when Magnum was a teenager, and being an only child, he felt a responsibility to look after her.

I only met her once when he invited me to dinner after my wife died. Probably felt sorry for me. I enjoyed the home-cooked meal. The mother was kind and interesting. She was an excellent cook, and from my perspective, had the constitution of a mule and could take care of herself. That night I learned her son never neglected the daily visit. His mother told me as much. My opinion of him ratcheted up a few notches. His actions were noble, caring, and impressive in my opinion.

"This is important," I said. "I need to check a gun."

I held the evidence bag out in front of me and tried to hand it to him. If Magnum were holding it, he'd feel more of an obligation to run the test. He didn't take the bait. He turned his focus back to what he was working on and ignored me, leaving me still holding the bag.

I stood there waiting patiently, so he'd know I wasn't taking no for an answer.

"What do you need to check?" he finally asked, disengaging from the microscope.

I knew I had a very small window of opportunity that I needed to take advantage of. No fluff. Just the facts.

"Fingerprint," I said.

Every gun left a ballistic fingerprint on a bullet. When fired, the markings on the bullet would be the same every time. Like a person's fingerprint. An identifying mark that was foolproof evidence in court. Defense attorneys had long since given up serious attempts to discredit the evidence.

Under normal circumstances, I'd leave the evidence with him, fill out the proper forms, and wait two to four weeks for the results. I rarely asked Magnum to rush a job. Only once before, in fact. This was only the second time I had a personal motivation.

The first time was when my wife was shot and killed by a drive-by shooter. I blamed myself for months. I kept thinking the shooting wasn't random. Somehow, I'd gotten her killed because of one of the cases I had worked on. I wanted Magnum to check the bullet that killed Gabby with all the bullets from my cases.

A major undertaking, but one he did because of the personal nature of the crime and as a personal favor to me. He didn't find anything, and I was devastated. I desperately wanted answers to who killed my wife.

The crime was still unsolved. Something I still had trouble living with.

I almost felt a similar desperation in this case. I needed expedited results. For some reason, this case provoked the same emotions. I hadn't had time to analyze why. No way I could wait two weeks or more. And the Lieutenant would get wind of it, and pandemonium would break loose. Things wouldn't end well for me, and on top of that, we wouldn't have the answer.

It couldn't simply be expedited. It had to be immediate. I wanted him to drop everything he was doing, fire the gun into his machine, and compare the markings on the test bullet with the markings on the bullet taken out of Jane Doe's chest. Right then. It'd take him half an hour.

A big ask, but I had to know.

"When do you need it?" he asked.

"Now."

"Must be important."

Fortunately, he didn't ask why. Magnum knew me and under-stood by my tone that this was of extreme importance. I was making it sound like a matter of life and death.

"It is. I wouldn't ask if it wasn't."

Magnum let out a sigh.

Truthfully, it didn't matter to him, and I knew it. So what if all the cases in the works had to wait an additional thirty min-utes to get their results? Magnum got to the cases when he got to them. A few got moved to the front of the line for various rea-sons, but no one got a bullet looked at on the spot. I was pushing the envelope, but he was the only one who could help identify the bullet.

"I'll call you when it's ready," he said.

"I'll wait."

No way was I leaving until I had definitive information. I also didn't want to run into the Lieutenant on the off chance he was wandering the hallways.

Magnum peered at me over his wiry glasses with a look of acceptance in his eyes. He knew me well enough to know I wasn't going anywhere. I would wait until I had what I needed.

I walked over to a chair and sat down and let out a deep sigh. I was one step closer to getting answers. Hopefully the blonde woman was right, and the two bullets were a match.

A little while later, Magnum walked over to me with a piece of paper in his hands.

My already-racing heart ratcheted up its pace even more.

I stared at the results.

I could hardly believe my eyes.

The blonde was right!

The bullets were a match.

I had exactly what I needed. I had the gun that killed the woman who looked exactly like Anna.

"Thank you, my friend," I said, as I bolted out of the lab with the results in my hand.

I had to go see the Lieutenant.

19

"I have a suspect in custody on the Jane Doe murder case," I said to the Lieutenant.

He was sitting behind his desk. I was standing in front of it. We were only allowed to sit when invited. Ridiculous in my opinion.

But... his office, his rules.

We had to follow several strange and conflicting protocol rules. His door was always open, and we could walk in anytime. However, when we did, whatever we had to say had better be important or we'd get chewed out for everyone in the bullpen to hear.

In this case, the news would bring a smile to his face. A homicide arrest was always the best news we could bring him.

As anticipated, his eyebrows raised in excitement. Temporarily. His next words caused my mouth to fly open in disbelief.

"It's no longer our case," the Lieutenant said abruptly, with the force of an earthquake inside of me. I hadn't slept the night before, but the adrenaline flowing through my veins would make sleep difficult even tonight.

"What? When did that happen?"

"The FBI took it over. Said they had jurisdiction."

My knees suddenly weakened, and I reached for the back of the chair. What I really wanted to do was sit down before I fell over. Couldn't since it wasn't allowed.

Once I regained my bearings I blurted out, "But I've got the shooter! And we have him in lockup. And two of his minions. Accessories to the crime."

I was speculating at that point. I had no evidence, other than the word of the blonde-haired lady, that the other two were involved. That case still needed to be made. We had the shooter dead-to-rights. Sort of. His attorney would probably argue that he got the gun from someone else. After the coffee shop shooting. Or that it wasn't even his client's gun. I wasn't concerned about those details at the moment.

I sat the ballistics report on the Lieutenant's desk. Something I wasn't supposed to do unless he asked for it. At this point, all caution had been thrown to the wind. He picked up the paper and peered at it with his cold, emotionless eyes.

I knew what was coming next. An interrogation. With an elevated voice.

How did I come upon this information? What probable cause did I have to run the ballistics report? How did I get the test back so quickly?

To my shock, he didn't ask me any of that. He appeared bored. Like he was looking at a random article of no particular interest. It took every bit of restraint to bite my lip and not come unglued.

Especially after he shrugged his shoulders and handed the report back to me. Without another word. No questions. Nothing. I couldn't believe it. I stood there almost frozen in disbelief.

I'd never seen him act this way before. I was giving him a murderer on a silver platter. The ballistic data proved it. The FBI didn't need to swoop in and take over this case. I had this. I already solved the crime. It was mine. I wanted it to be mine. I wanted to finish it. I needed it.

For my own sanity.

For personal reasons unknown to anyone involved. I had to find out how the dead woman was related to Anna. Who was the woman I met in the coffee shop? Why did she want to meet me at *Champions* then bolt out the door as soon as she saw the Strikers?

This was my ticket into that investigation.

"Scully is the name of the FBI agent," the Lieutenant offered, effectively tearing up my ticket and throwing it in the wind.

He wrote down a number on a piece of paper and handed it to me. Presumably Scully's number. Confirmed when he said, "Give Scully a call and tell him what you know. Also tell him to come and get his suspects."

He looked back down at paperwork on his desk, basically dismissing me.

I wasn't going to drop it that easily. I couldn't.

"Why would the FBI take our case?" I asked. "The murder happened in Chicago. It's in our jurisdiction."

The Lieutenant had clearly lost interest. Sometimes I wondered how he had gotten to be a Lieutenant.

"I don't know," he replied, barely bothering to look up. Not even enough to catch my eye. If he had, he'd have seen them on fire like burning embers.

"Maybe the gal was an informant," he said matter-of-factly. "Or a witness. She might even be an agent. Undercover, maybe. I'm just speculating. Could be any number of reasons. Above my pay grade. Not our problem anymore."

Jurisdictional issues were tricky. The Feds certainly had the power to overrule us when it came to cases. From the Lieutenant's perspective, it was one less murder on his plate. From my perspective, it felt like I'd fallen off an emotional cliff.

How could he just let it go?

I couldn't.

"What do you want me to do about the three Strikers who were killed over at the house?" I asked roughly.

I'd already solved that case as well. The blonde woman did it. With the new developments, I certainly wasn't going to tell him how I came across that information. From my perspective, it was a righteous kill. She had done the city of Chicago a favor. I didn't need to know any more than that. Neither did he. Nobody would question me closing the case unsolved.

"Put it on the backburner," the Lieutenant said, confirming what I already knew. "You have other more pressing cases. Seems to me like the Feds have taken an interest in the Strikers. Or at least that's the word from my bosses. Try not to get in their way."

His way of telling me that he didn't care one way or the other. That or his boss had told him the same thing. *Don't get in the Feds' way. Play nice. No running with scissors. Let them handle everything. Don't give the case another thought.*

Not possible. When you work as a detective, you can't just shut your mind off at the end of the day. It's part of why so many people in law enforcement burn out. You wake up in the middle of the night wondering if you'd missed something. Every detail was analyzed ad nauseum. There wasn't an on/off switch.

The Lieutenant could let it go because he wasn't personally invested. I wasn't supposed to be either, but I'd already crossed that bridge to the dark side of detective work. Made it personal. Forget it? No chance. Easier said than done. And I wasn't done.

Even though the conversation was done.

I left his office feeling like a deflated balloon. With Carson on the case, I'd been barely hanging on by a thread. I'd already overstepped my boundaries, but I was able to justify it in my mind, and with a sufficient argument if I were challenged on it.

With the Feds in charge, any action I took beyond calling Scully and handing off the prisoners, would be considered impeding their investigation. Something no detective ever wanted to do. That didn't mean our office didn't sometimes buck the system and claim our jurisdictional rights—even challenging the FBI. But only when the Lieutenant had our backs and was willing to go to bat for us with his bosses.

It seemed like one of those times when we *should* fight it. We had the men in custody. We could make it difficult for the Feds. Claim we had first shot at the men. I wanted this case. I already had hard evidence to identify the shooter. If we just handed it over to the Feds, I'd never know the outcome. No one would keep me in the loop.

But the Lieutenant didn't have my back. He wasn't interested in pursuing it and would cut off my nose if he knew I was still sniffing around the case.

I stared at the number in my hand. FBI agent Scully was my last hope to get information.

Back at my desk, I didn't call him right away. I needed to take a deep breath. Calm myself. I tried to anticipate the conversation and choose my words carefully while mulling it over in my mind. I'd never get more information out of him than at the onset of the handoff.

After that, it was none of my business. It would be on a need-to-know basis. And if my prior experience with Feds was any indication, I was certain Scully didn't think I needed to know anything.

Not who the girl was or what had happened to her. Certainly not any information about the next of kin.

I took another deep breath and dialed Scully trying to organize my last-minute thoughts. I didn't even get far enough to ask any of my questions.

"Scully," he answered, on the first ring.

"My name is Cliff Ford. I'm a homicide detective with the Chicago PD."

"How can I help you, Detective?"

No warmth at all. Totally matter of fact in his tone. It sounded like I was talking to the Lieutenant.

"You recently took over a Jane Doe from our department. A woman who was killed in front of a coffee shop."

Total silence.

"I've identified the shooter," I said then waited for a response.

The case had probably just crossed his desk. My words would be a bombshell he wasn't expecting. Almost expectedly, I heard a loud sound in the background. A bang. Like he had suddenly changed positions and his chair hit his desk. He was probably trying to process this new information. So, I offered more.

"I have him in custody," I said. "And two of his accomplices."

"How do you know it's the shooter?"

"We ran ballistics on his gun. The ballistic fingerprints are a match. He also fits the description of the shooter. So does his car."

"I'll be right down."

Before I could speak, he hung up the phone.

Shell shocked didn't even begin to describe my feelings. Thirty minutes ago, I had a solid to put the scum away, and it would have been my collar. Now that the FBI was involved... poof... the case was gone. It wasn't that I wanted the notoriety. It had never been my motivation for doing my job. I wanted to follow the whole scenario through. More than one case was tied together. I knew it, and the evidence was there.

I sat at my desk, shaking my head. Anyone watching me from the other side of the glass would wonder if they should call an ambulance. They might have thought I was having a seizure. I did feel like my head was going to explode.

A half an hour later, I saw a suit walk in and go directly to the Lieutenant's office. Had to be Scully. Two other FBI-looking suits tagged along behind him. Papers in hand.

I shouldn't have, but I followed them into the Lieutenant's office. It completely went against all protocol, but I felt a magnetic pull. I couldn't help myself.

It was Scully. They were talking about a transfer. The papers in Scully's hands were the authorization to take custody of the three men along with all the evidence I had collected. I stood there while they talked. I was without words. I knew I needed to keep my mouth shut or I was likely to say something I'd regret.

The Lieutenant looked over the paperwork and then looked up at me.

"This is Detective Ford," the Lieutenant said to the three men.

They all nodded in my direction.

"He broke the case," the Lieutenant added.

Each of the men reached out their hands and I shook them. It felt nice to get a positive acknowledgment from each of the Feds and from the Lieutenant, but it didn't calm my angst.

"Good to meet you," I said.

"Good work, Detective Ford," Scully said. "You've done a great service to the FBI."

I had no idea what that meant other than the dead girl had some tie to them.

After more formalities, the Lieutenant said, "Ford, take these men down to the holding cell, and see that the Strikers are transferred into Agent Scully's custody. We're happy to let you get them off our books."

No, we're not! I wanted to shout at the top of my lungs but resisted the urge.

Downtrodden, I led them out of the office and down to holding. Almost like I was leading a funeral procession. That's what it felt like.

Then I felt a burst of energy as I felt the impulse to ask Scully my questions. We had a short window. I finally summoned up the courage, "Have you identified the woman yet?"

"We have," Scully said.

"Who is she?" I asked, knowing full well what the answer was most likely to be.

"I'm not at liberty to say."

"Have you notified the next of kin?" I asked.

"We'll handle that."

As I expected, I was back to first base. In reality, I wasn't even up to bat. It felt like I had struck out and had been taken out of the game. Every baseball analogy I could think of came to mind with a flood of anger.

Thirty minutes later, they drove off in a van with the three Strikers.

And the gun.

And the bullets.

And the ballistics report.

They'd pick up the black Lexus later from the impound lot.

All my hopes of finding my girl left with them.

20

Three days later

My mind was on my work, even if my heart wasn't in it. I couldn't help but think that I'd lost the opportunity to find the mystery girl at the coffee shop forever. There were so many questions still rattling around in my mind and keeping me up at night. The prudent thing to do would be to let them go. My job was too important to me to lose over a girl I barely knew. I'd already taken risks I normally wouldn't have taken.

So far, I'd come out of it unscathed. Even ahead of the game. While the FBI had taken over the case of the Jane Doe, I still got credit with the Lieutenant for solving the case for them. He'd been nicer to me over the last couple of days because of it.

As for Anna, my options were limited. Every idea I came up with was dismissed out of hand. It wasn't a good idea and not in my best interest to pursue an investigation. I had information that I could follow up on, but it could potentially cost me my badge if I went down that road. I had to weigh the risk/benefit of the whole situation.

Was I going off the rails? Unhealthily obsessed? I wasn't even sure anymore. As much as I wanted answers, I was hesitant to go too far off the deep end again.

One thought tempted me. I could stake out Anna's house again. But how would I explain it if someone complained? Most people weren't that observant, but it only took one nosy neighbor looking out a window, seeing my car, and then calling 911. Someone who had nothing else to do but gossip and cause trouble. Many a stakeout had been ruined by a neighbor phoning in a suspicious vehicle in the neighborhood. Cover blown when the blue lights appeared on the scene.

That's why I nixed the stakeout idea. My best option was to run into her at *Hipsters*, the coffeeshop where we first met. I went there every morning and hung out longer than usual. Looked twice every time a jet-black-haired woman walked into or by the coffeeshop. The Anna lookalike never showed. Honestly, I didn't expect to see her, and I didn't. I never asked Katy, my regular bistro server about her either.

The FBI also took over the case of the three Strikers in the hospital. So, I also had no reason to investigate that assault or the mystery of the blonde woman who beat them up. They didn't even ask for the notes from my investigation.

Did I want to keep looking into it? Absolutely. But if I kept diving deeper, and it flew onto someone's radar, I could find myself in hot water I couldn't get out of. Especially if that radar belonged to the FBI and they complained to the Lieutenant.

Probably best to leave things alone. That happened in cases as well. After looking at every angle, sometimes the best thing to do was close the murder book, put it on the shelf, and wait for a break. If it never came, the file became a cold case. It seemed like the mystery of Anna was getting colder by the minute.

Even if it still consumed my mind. The mystery woke me up at night. Usually around two in the morning, my brain would decide to wake me up with a newfound piece of information. Always nothing. Sometimes a new theory. Most of the time, a thread I'd already run through my head a thousand times. Thread was what we called a line of questioning or a theory in a case.

By three in the morning, I found myself having the same conversation.

So, what do you think we should do? I'd ask myself.

I'm not sure. But I really need to find the blonde girl. She seems to be the key to this whole thing.

You won't find her unless she wants to be found.

Apparently, the girl pretending to be Anna doesn't want to be found either.

Which made me angry. Didn't she think she owed me an explanation?

Those middle-of-the-night conversations in my head were not helping. If anything, they made it harder for me to do my job during the day. By mid-afternoon, I was running on fumes. In need of a caffeine fix. The caffeine kept me awake at night. A vicious cycle that I needed to get out of. My late-afternoon workout was suffering as well. I couldn't seem to find the effort to go all out.

Maybe I was a little depressed. The whole Anna thing had brought back too many old memories that I had buried. My wife's murder and the coffeeshop woman's murder were both competing for my attention.

So, I focused on work. I had no shortage of cases to occupy my time.

A new case hit my desk. A drive-by shooting on the south side. Why did they always have to be a drive-by? As if someone wanted to keep reminding me of Gabby. That unsolved case. I'd give anything to go through that murder book and see if I could find something the lead detective had missed. The Lieutenant had strictly forbidden it. I understood why.

This murder would likely go unsolved as well. The odds of finding the shooter were slim to none. Eyewitnesses weren't talking. Video surveillance identified the car, but it had been stolen. Big surprise. Our local snitches hadn't heard any chatter.

I'd soon file the case away. Probably already should've. But I knew I was the last hope for the victim. Although, he wasn't really a victim in my opinion. The dead kid was bad news. A member of a local gang into drugs and other nefarious things. Not the worst of the worst but on track for more trouble. He didn't deserve the death penalty though. As soon as I gave up on the case, the chances of ever finding his killer went to zero.

It'd go into the abyss of other cold-case files to never be looked at again. Part of me was okay with that. You couldn't solve all the murder cases in Chicago. And when the victim was a known hooligan, I found it hard to muster up much sympathy. When their rap sheet was longer than six printed-out sheets, acting upset would be kidding myself. I was never happy when anyone died, but an innocent getting shot was more tragic in my mind.

Also on my pile was a twenty-nine-year-old man who was shot early Tuesday on the far south side. He was attacked around two in the morning while walking with two other people. An older woman who was a schoolteacher once told me nothing good ever happens after midnight. She was right. I was never out that late unless I was investigating a crime.

A man told police he was inside his home and heard the gunshot. He ran outside and found the victim with a gunshot wound to his head. He called 911, and when the medics and police arrived, he told them what he heard and saw, which wasn't much. The victim was taken to the University of Chicago Medical Center, where he was pronounced dead.

One more person who died too young, senselessly lying in the cold morgue. It made me wonder if coffee-shop girl was still there.

The Chicago Tribune called me for a statement.

"Hi, Detective Ford, do you have any suspects?" the reporter asked. She was certainly polite enough and trying to do her job, but even if I had the information, I wouldn't be sharing it with her.

"No. We've got nothing," I replied, in an equally friendly manner. Someday, she might have information that I needed.

She already knew the answer but was hoping for a break. Someday, I might feed her a bone just to shock her. The thought occurred to me that I should give her a tip on the coffee-shop girl. I'd already broken a dozen laws. What was one more? I quickly tamped down that thought, even though a leak might draw a relative out of the woodwork. It might bring coffee-shop-Cuban-girl-not-namedAnna-and-not-a-guidance-counselor down to the police station.

"Come on, Detective, you must know something you can tell me," she pleaded. "I have a boss too. I have to make him happy."

As if we could have a suspect. We had no witnesses. No murder weapon. One of a dozen people killed already that week. Chicago averaged close to twenty murders a week. People had no idea what it was like to be in the trenches when you're a detective or a beat cop. The odds of finding the shooter were slim to none in many cases. We did the best we could, but we weren't magicians. We didn't have magic wands to wave.

Forty-two percent of homicides the year before were cleared. Cleared meant solved. That was a fudged number. The real number was closer to eighteen percent that were actually solved. The cleared category included a category the department called 'exceptional.' Meaning we identified a suspect, but the suspect was dead or there wasn't enough evidence to prove the charges. Or the DA decided not to prosecute for whatever reason.

No one wanted to hear the real numbers. It was depressing. Real and raw. And made people paranoid for good reason.

"Sorry. I wish I could help you," I said to the reporter sincerely. "No suspects at this time."

I hung up the phone and listened to the chatter that was slightly above a slight roar in the room. The belly of the homicide department was nothing more than a large bullpen with cubicles. Each cubicle had a desk and computer.

The cubicle next to me was empty. Where my partner had been working until he blew out his knee. Word was I was getting a new partner soon. Marty Wade. Not who I thought. A newbie who was walking a beat. Supposedly, a fast tracker. Cocky but capable. Which was what I preferred as opposed to cocky and a moron.

Truthfully, I looked forward to it. For one thing, Wade would take some of my workload. Not half, but at least a quarter. Also, it gave me someone to distract me from Anna.

Necessary, since I thought about her constantly.

* * *

Everyone's cell phone alert went off at the same time, sending a crescendo through the bullpen and causing a flurry of activity.

Before I had a chance to even pull my phone out of my suit pocket and look at it, the Lieutenant was out of his office, barking orders.

There'd been an explosion.

At the docks. In a warehouse.

All hands on deck.

The address followed. Along with the words *Gunfight. Casualties.*

I recognized the address immediately.

Same address the lowlife had given the blonde woman in the gang house.

Shiv.

The leader of the gang. The warehouse was at Striker's headquarters.

Was the blonde-haired woman behind the explosion? That brought a smile to my face as I hoped she was.

Then I got a nervous pulse of energy. A dreaded thought.

Was she one of the casualties?

Could it be tied back to me?

21

We were some of the first to arrive at the scene of the explosion at the Striker's warehouse down at the shipping docks.

Surprisingly, Scully was already there. What was the FBI doing at an explosion at a gang house?

The Lieutenant questioned the same thing. When I asked him what he thought, he didn't even try to venture a guess. Everyone was still a distance away from ground zero while the first responders were doing their jobs, and the Chicago PD blues were securing a perimeter. The warehouse was blown to bits.

As detectives, we'd be the last to interject our expertise into the situation. Probably not until forensics finished their work. Or at least when they were wrapping it up. We couldn't even approach the crime scene yet. Certainly not until the area was considered safe. Something that'd take a while, and I wasn't good at just standing around waiting.

It looked like a war zone. Half a city block was leveled, although it didn't appear like any structures other than the Striker's warehouse were damaged. If there were any casualties, they'd be in the main warehouse structure or outside where the shootout had taken place. The odds of any innocent bystander casualties were slim to none from the looks of the overall crime scene.

The Lieutenant motioned for us to follow him into the area of the shootout which was a few meters from the main blast site. A half dozen Strikers lay on the ground dead from gunshot wounds to the head. The scene looked eerily similar to the one behind the gang house not that far from there. The shooter was precise. The entry wounds were in the middle of their foreheads or in the chest area. It had to have happened in a matter of seconds. Several Strikers had drawn their weapons, and they lay on the ground right next to their dead bodies, but apparently, none of them had a chance to use them.

I was certain who was behind it.

This had to be the handiwork of the blonde-haired girl. In not so many words, she had all but told me that she intended to pay Shiv a visit. For whatever reason, the woman had declared all-out war on the Strikers. From my vantage point, the powerful gang was losing.

Big time.

Actually, I knew the reason. They'd kidnapped her girl. Bae. I'd tried to find information on her but had run into dead ends. Finding the identity of the blonde woman or the Korean girl would be like looking for a lost pen in downtown Chicago. Impossible.

The lady appeared to be doing what all of the Chicago Police force could not do. Bring the Strikers to their knees. I was in awe of what she had accomplished in such a short time. Impressive—in a dark sort of way. I'd be lying if I didn't say I was a bit grateful for her doing some of the heavy lifting.

Of course, she played by different rules. Was extremely resourceful. How did she pull off a bombing? Where did she get that many explosives?

I had no proof she was behind it, which was why I felt comfortable not saying anything. This wasn't the place for what would sound like random speculation to others on the force. That would only invite questions I had no intention of answering right now.

Only Strikers were dead. No great loss there.

My phone rang as I was taking in the scene, determined to keep what I knew to myself.

Unknown number.

"Ford," I answered, instinctively stepping away from the others.

"Clifford. How are you?" the familiar voice said.

I moved even further away.

"How did you get my number?" I asked the blonde-haired woman.

Out of all the questions I could've asked her, that was the first one that popped into my head.

"I see you are down at the docks," she said.

I immediately looked around in every direction but didn't see her. How did she know I was there?

"I'm sorry the FBI took your case from you," she said in a sincere tone of voice. "You deserve the credit for solving it," she added.

"How did you know..."

I stopped in mid-sentence. My mind was being blown. Was she with the FBI? How else could she have that inside information? Had she gone rogue? Was I an accomplice? The thought occurred to me that she was even more resourceful than I'd realized.

I had her on the phone. I needed to focus.

I had a more important question.

"Why did they take the case from us?" I asked.

"The woman who was shot at the coffeeshop was an undercover agent with the FBI."

I could feel my heart pounding in my chest. Maybe I could get some answers after all. She seemed well connected. If she could be believed. I ignored all the red flags. I was in too deep to start backpedaling now.

Blondie had to be FBI.

Were we breaking the law by even having the conversation?

Didn't matter. I was past the point of no return. The puzzle pieces were starting to come together.

"You were right," I said to her. "The guy at the house was the shooter. Ballistics were a match."

"I told you they would be. The Strikers killed her. More of an execution, really."

"Why would the Striker's want to take her out? Had she infiltrated their gang?"

I had so many questions, I couldn't ask them fast enough.

"Not exactly. She worked in the sex-trafficking division of the FBI. Her job was to rescue girls. The Strikers were taking girls off the street and holding them as sex slaves. The woman wasn't undercover in the sense that she was part of the gang, but she was working surreptitiously to get girls out. Her work was robbing them of one of their most valuable commodities. Young, beautiful girls. Saving the girls was her passion. My kind of girl. I'm sad we lost her."

"Me too. And the Strikers have one of the girls you're looking for. Bae." A light bulb had gone off as more pieces of the puzzle were coming together.

"Had," the lady said, startling me.

"As in, they don't have her anymore? Was she still alive? Was she in the warehouse?"

The woman hesitated for the first time in the conversation. "I don't know where she is. The FBI undercover agent rescued her. But she was killed before I had a chance to ask her where she was hiding her."

"I take it you still haven't found her."

"No."

"Is that why you blew up the warehouse?"

She hesitated.

"That was an accident. So to speak. The Strikers had a meth lab in that warehouse. A stray bullet set off the explosion. Brought the whole place down. But to answer your question, the Strikers weren't keeping any girls there."

That explained how she could have that many explosives. She didn't. That made sense. Millions of dollars' worth of drugs probably disintegrated in that explosion.

"Why are you telling me all this?" I asked.

"The dead woman has a sister. Her name's Anna."

My heart did a somersault in my chest.

"How do you know Anna?"

She didn't answer the question directly.

"The dead woman's name is Rita Navarez. Her sister filed a missing person's report on her earlier today. The FBI hasn't notified the next of kin yet. My guess is that the family didn't know what she really did for a living. Look up the missing person's report. They need to know what happened to their family member."

It sounded like the phone call was coming to an end. "How can I get in touch with you if I have more questions?"

"I'll text you a number. You can call me at that number. Don't bother trying to trace it, though. It's a burner. Untraceable."

The line went dead.

Her last statement was no surprise. She had her reasons for staying undercover, and I had to respect that. For whatever reason, she was helping me. I was appreciative. More than she would ever know. Maybe I could repay the favor at some point.

A number appeared on my phone. I memorized it. Then deleted it.

I made a beeline for the Lieutenant. I had to get out of there. Hopefully, I wouldn't catch any flack for wanting to leave the crime scene.

"I've got to go back to the office," I said to him. "I may have a break on a case."

He waved his hand for me to go. There were already enough people there. Especially if you included the FBI.

I raced back to the office and went directly to where they received the missing person reports. They wouldn't assign them to anyone for forty-eight hours. The woman said it just came in that morning.

I found it.

How did the blonde lady know it would be there? She might have an inside track in the FBI, but how would she have one in our offices as well?

I couldn't fathom how that was even possible. It almost appeared that she was larger than life. Like a stealth ninja. She was everywhere the action was and had all the information at her fingertips.

Right in my hands was a piece of paper with valuable information I'd been desperately looking for. I scanned through it as fast as I could.

Rita Navarez.

34.

International Fashion Sales.

The blonde lady was right. The family had no idea what Rita did for a living. The person filing the report was Anna Navarez. The guidance counselor. A phone number and address were listed on the report. The same house I sat in front of during my stakeout.

I now had Anna's phone number and a reason to talk to her. I stuck my head in the missing person's supervisor's office. The man responsible for assigning the cases.

"Can I take this one?" I asked. "I think it's related to another case I was working on."

Lying to my associates was coming too easy to me those days.

"What's the name?"

"Rita Navarez."

He flipped through his own files.

"The waiting period isn't over yet."

"I believe she's dead. We have a Jane Doe who matches this description. I don't want to wait forty-eight hours to verify it. If you give it to someone else, they may not know about Jane Doe lying in the morgue."

"Sure. All right then. Go ahead. Take it."

I bolted out of the office before he could change his mind. Practically ran back to my office and plopped down in my chair.

So many pieces of the puzzle were falling into place. I was trying to wrap my head around all of them.

I had to talk to Anna. She obviously didn't know her sister was dead. Since I was given the case, I had every right to tell her.

A debate began to rage in my mind.

Do I go see Anna right away or do I check in with the Lieutenant first?

The grey line was getting fuzzier and fuzzier.

Ask for permission or forgiveness?

Neither.

I was going to see Anna. I didn't need permission or forgiveness.
I wasn't doing anything wrong.   I was just doing my job.
What am I going to say when I see her?

22

The parking lot of the South Skyline High School was packed as expected since it was the middle of the day. A lot of luxury cars. Not like when I was a kid. Nobody got a new BMW for their sixteenth birthday when I was in high school.

I got out of my car and began a less-than-confident walk to the entrance, although I was certain I'd made the right decision not to tell the Lieutenant my plans. My justification was that he was busy with the explosion, the six dead Strikers, and all the fallout from it. I was sure that the crime scene would keep him busy for a while. Not every day that half of a block gets taken down.

Had I gone to him for permission, he'd have said, "Ford, it's not our case. The FBI has it. They wanted it. They can notify the next of kin. Your time's better spent finding a murderer. If you don't have enough cases to occupy your time, I'll find you some more."

I could imagine a scenario where he'd load me down with more files just to make a point.

As it stood right now, this was *my* missing person's case. Assigned to me through the proper channels. I was following official protocol, at least for this part of my investigation. I was well within my rights to walk into the school, flash my badge, and give Anna the news that her sister was dead.

When I opened the door and the smell of the high school hit me, I began to regret my decision.

What was I going to say? Once I told Anna, how would I segue into my questions? They were flashing across my mind like a rapid-fire semi-automatic machine gun.

Who is the woman in the coffee shop who looks just like you?

If she wasn't you, then who was the woman in Champions bar imper-sonating you?

Why did she tell me to meet her there and then bolt out the back door?

Did you know your sister worked for the FBI?

Why were the Strikers after the girl in Champions Bar?

Do you know the blonde-haired woman?

The thought occurred to me that I could make this a preliminary visit. An interrogation of sorts. Not tell Anna her sister was dead. In that instance, it'd be appropriate to ask those questions. I could come back later and tell her the news about her sister and her untimely demise.

How cruel and selfish would that be? When would I stop thinking about myself and start thinking about Anna? She was going to be devastated. All I'd be doing was prolonging the inevitable if I didn't tell her the truth.

Obviously, Anna was racked with worry. Enough so that she would fill out a missing person's report. People didn't do that unless they had serious reasons to question their family member's ab-sence. Probably because her sister, Rita, didn't show up at the wed-ding dress shop. At least that's the conclusion I had come to. In the grocery store, Anna mentioned her sister.

For whatever reason, I thought the mysterious *Champions* girl was going to show up at the wedding dress shop. Of course, Anna was meeting Rita. So, who was the girl I met in the coffeeshop?

Focus.

I tried to put myself in Anna's shoes. Over several days, she prob-ably tried to reach her sister. To no avail. Then she became worried. Called everyone she knew. Family and friends. That's how things went when someone reliable and well-grounded wasn't returning phone calls or texts and seemed to have vanished.

Anna probably kept up her frantic search for several days. No one had heard from her sister. How could they know that she lay in the morgue? A Jane Doe. Stripped of all her identity and future.

My heart began to ache at the thought. In a way it never had before. Actually, it had felt similar to one time before. Thirteen months ago. The day I got the news. Same feelings, but I had been on the other side of the situation.

Blindsided.

When some cops came to tell me that my wife was dead. The victim of a drive-by shooting. The air was sucked out of my lungs. I became dizzy. Nauseous. Then paralyzed with fear. How was I going to live without her? A feeling came over me that I would never forget. Similar to what I was feeling now.

My hand shook as I approached the main desk and flashed my badge. I took a deep breath.

"I'm here to see Anna Navarez," I said, straining to keep my voice from cracking.

The woman picked up the phone and dialed a number.

Thankfully, I was leaning against the counter which was now holding me upright. All the emotions of the day I was notified of my wife's death came flooding back. As did the total numbness. Disbelief. It felt like someone had drugged me. The same fog of war hung over me today.

I barely remembered the details because of my zombie-like state. Mostly I remembered the order of events. I went to the morgue to identify the body. Saw Gabby lying there. Not wanting to believe it was real. Then I met with the investigators while they questioned me about my cases.

The investigator asked me something I hadn't thought of. Could one of my past cases be related to my wife's shooting? Perhaps it was a revenge killing. Did any murderers I'd put behind bars recently get out of jail?

I didn't know of any, but said I'd check. He ended up doing it for me.

The rest became more vivid in my memory. Making the funeral arrangements. The service. Burial. The house full of people. I was in a constant fog, but the events were seared in my brain.

And then everyone was gone. I felt so alone. My world had come crashing down.

Now I was about to impose the same horrible fate on Anna. It was heart-wrenching.

"She'll see you now," the woman behind the counter said as she gave me a lanyard to put around my neck. I knew the drill. Badge or not, everyone had to have a lanyard if they were on school property. Then she gave me directions to Anna's office. Somehow, I managed to put one leg in front of the other because I found myself standing at the door that led to Anna's office. I stood there and stared at it. Trying to get the courage to go in.

Anna Navarez, Guidance Counselor, the gold-plated sign on the door read.

I knocked.

"Come in," a sweet voice said. The same voice I remembered from the grocery store. A similar voice to what was etched in my memory from the coffee shop conversation.

I entered.

No longer wanting to flee. But rather wanting to be there for Anna. Somehow, I was connected to their family. To Rita. To the mysterious girl who looked like both of them. This case was personal. There were so many pieces to this puzzle, and I wouldn't stop until it was solved.

I felt the loss. I understood.

Somehow that gave me a sudden shot of courage. Until I saw Anna's face. I felt her pain as soon as I saw her grimace, then force a smile.

"I'm Detective Cliff Ford," I said soberly.

My badge was still in my hand, but I didn't bother showing it to her. The lady at the front desk had no doubt given her my name.

Anna was as beautiful as the woman I had seen in the coffee shop that day. Except that her eyes were red.

Bloodshot.

She'd been crying.

She was already standing and walked around her desk and extended her hand. Her hand was shaking when ours finally connected. She had the same strong and firm handshake as the girl in the coffee shop.

"I'm afraid I have bad news," I said.

I could feel the tears welling up in my own eyes. I choked them back.

"I know," Anna said. "Someone from the FBI came by earlier today. He told me about Rita. I assume that's why you're here."

I nodded.

"Please have a seat," she said, pointing her hand toward the chair. She sat down in her chair on the other side of the desk. Not before straightening her blouse and skirt. Then her hair. Dabbing at her eyes roughly. She raised her head. Put her shoulders back. In an attempt to exude strength. Professionalism.

She'd no doubt dealt with tragedy with her students. She probably knew how I was feeling. If she'd been a guidance counselor for long, she'd probably given a student similar bad news.

"I didn't know Rita worked for the FBI," Anna said.

I simply nodded again.

"They didn't tell me much. Just that she had been with the bureau for eight years. Eight years she was out there risking her life. Who knew? Working for the FBI. She started right out of college, they told me. I guess what she did was dangerous work. That's why there was so much secrecy. We thought Rita worked in international fashion sales. I know she lied to protect us, but I really wish I had known about her work. I suppose it was for the best."

In my experience, people either clammed up or started overtalking in a way that was out of character. Anna was experiencing the latter. For whatever reason, I couldn't find any words to interrupt her. There wasn't a playbook for that kind of situation. Everyone reacted differently.

Finally, I mustered up, "I'm very sorry for your loss."

"The man at the FBI said they have the shooter in custody."

I nodded.

Then felt the urge to say, "I'm the one who arrested the shooter and his two accomplices."

Anna's eyes widened.

"You're the one who broke the case?"

I nodded.

Anna bit her lip and turned her head away. "I don't know how to thank you," she muttered, barely above a whisper.

"I was only doing my job."

Anna clutched her hands. Clearly trying to hold it together. I figured once I left, the restraint would leave with me, and she'd allow herself to break down.

"Have we met?" Anna asked out of the blue. "You look very familiar."

"Yes. At the grocery store."

Anna got a faraway look and stared off into the wall behind me.

"That's right. In the produce section. I'm sorry. I remember being rude. You said you knew me."

"Yeah. I'm sorry. I didn't. I was investigating your sister's death."

"I thought something was strange. I think I would've remembered you."

"You mentioned you were getting married. Was Rita the one who was supposed to meet you at the wedding shop last Sunday?"

Her eyes widened again. Anna probably didn't remember telling me about the meeting.

She burst into tears. I reached for a handkerchief in my pocket, but she pulled a box of tissues out of her drawer and buried her eyes in one. The reaction gave me the answer.

That left one more unanswered question as an idea popped into my head.

"Do you have another sister who looks like you?" I asked when it felt right to do so.

Anna's eyes widened for a third time, and the tears stopped abruptly. "Julia?"

145

My heart felt like it had completely turned over in my chest. Did I finally have a name?

"I think I met her," I said softly. "Julia."

"Yes," Anna said, matching my soft and somber tone. "There are three of us. Identical triplets. Do you know what the odds are of that happening?"

I shook my head no.

Anna said, "One in a million. Some say one in two hundred million. It's extremely rare. We all look identical. Same black hair. We even wear it the same length. When we were in college, we'd go on each other's dates to see if our boyfriends could tell us apart. They never could. We thought it was funny. We played tricks on our parents when we were younger. They weren't amused."

Anna chuckled. I did as well. Telling me about her sisters had given her newfound strength. She was holding together well during that part of the conversation.

Although... my mind was spinning.

Triplets.

The possibility had briefly crossed my mind at one point. Probably in the middle of one of my sleepless nights. But with all the information infiltrating my brain, I had a hard time keeping track. It had seemed so unlikely, which apparently it was.

Julia.

How could I figure out how to meet her?

23

"Have you told Julia about Rita?" I asked hesitantly, as if it weren't any of my business, and she was under no obligation to tell me. Technically, it was my business since my job was to notify the next of kin. Especially immediate family members.

For whatever reason, I felt out of place. Like I had manipulated my way into these people's lives. At the same time, I was hoping the answer was no. That Anna hadn't told Julia that Rita was dead. It might give me an excuse to meet her. Something I desperately wanted to do. Confirm what I suspected was true. Julia was the woman I met in the coffee shop. The one in *Champions* bar that night. If so, I had to know why she ran away from me and what her connection to the Strikers and the blonde woman was.

A sense of relief came over me when Anna answered my question by shaking her head no. She hadn't told Julia.

"I haven't had a chance," she said, soberly. Like she was dreading it, which I'm sure she was. "The FBI only left a few minutes before you arrived. It's not something you can do over the phone. You know what I mean? Rita and Julia were extremely close. All of us were. But especially those two. They were inseparable. Julia will be devastated."

I could tell Anna was as well, even though she was trying her best to hide the pain she felt inside.

"Would you like for me to go with you to tell her?" I asked, not trying to sound too anxious. Like I was desperate to meet Julia.

Which I was.

"That'd be great," Anna said without hesitation. "I don't know if I could hold it together long enough to tell her. Actually... she'll take one look at me and know."

The pain was written all over her face. Anyone would be able to tell something was wrong with Anna. Especially an identical sister.

I tried to be comforting and supportive. "I know it's hard. I've done it dozens of times. Tell family members they've lost a loved one. It comes with the territory for me; trust me, it doesn't ever get any easier. Of course, I'll go with you. Anything I can do to help. I can be moral support for you. And Julia."

"Didn't you say you know Julia?" Anna asked.

"I met her once at a coffee shop. We talked for about twenty minutes."

"She must've made quite an impression on you if you remember it."

You have no idea.

"It wasn't that long ago," I said instead. "The same day that Rita died."

"Oh."

"That's why I approached you at the grocery store," I explained almost defensively. "I thought you were Julia."

"A lot of people make that mistake."

"When you didn't recognize me, I was confused. And embarrassed."

Anna waved her hand dismissively.

"Don't worry about it. You didn't know. Can you go with me to talk to Julia right now?" Her voice shook as she said it.

I was hoping that's what she'd say.

"Where is she?" I asked, barely above a whisper matching Anna's soberness. I moved up in my chair, so my arms were resting on her desk.

"Let me find out. She's probably at work."

I wanted to ask where she worked, but it didn't seem like the appropriate time to drill Anna for information. And she'd already taken out her phone. Her head was down as she used her finger to swipe something. Probably scrolling through her contacts for the number.

When she put the phone to her ear, I presumed she was calling Julia.

I heard a woman's voice answer, although I couldn't hear what she said.

Suddenly, I felt uncomfortable. Like I was intruding on a personal conversation. I stood from my chair and turned my back to Anna, trying to give the appearance of giving her privacy. Stared at a framed picture on the wall. Some kind of poster actually. A person rock climbing, hanging upside down off a ledge. The caption read *Cliffhanger*. Underneath it said, *What the mind can conceive, it can achieve*.

I didn't know about that. I couldn't conceive hanging upside down on a ledge without a rope. In my mind, the cliffhanger person had achieved the prize for ultimate stupidity. I felt like I was on a similar ledge. Going to see Julia. Interjecting myself into her life when she clearly didn't want to talk to me. Manipulating the circumstances so she didn't have a choice.

I nonchalantly skulked over to another wall while Anna talked to Julia. There I perused Anna's diploma. An undergraduate degree from Northwestern in Psychology. A Masters from Loyola University in Education and a PHD from DePaul. I couldn't help but be impressed. I'd felt the same way when I met Julia. That she was exceptional. I didn't necessarily know why. I just got that impression.

Anna cleared her throat and I saw her dab at her eyes then I heard her get to the purpose of the call. "Hey Sis," Anna said. "Are you home?"

A clock in the corner of the room showed 1:30.

A momentary silence. A pin could've dropped, and I would've heard it although I couldn't hear Julia's answer to the question.

"Yes. I filed the police report," Anna said, out of the blue in an obvious response to Julia's question. "This morning. I'm with an investigator now. He'd like to meet you and ask you some questions."

I looked over at her and our eyes met. Anna held the phone away from her and shrugged. Like she was telling me that was the only thing she could think of. I thought she was doing great. This wasn't going to be easy.

I could feel myself starting to get nervous about the meeting. Julia probably wasn't going to like being blindsided by me either. I ignored the angst. Julia owed me an explanation. It might not be the right circumstances to demand one, but my very presence might make her feel obligated even with the horrible news I was about to deliver to her.

Anna hung up the phone.

"Julia's at work, but she's going to meet us at her house," she said, as I sat back down in the chair.

"It's better we tell her there than at her work," I said. Then I realized I was at Anna's work. It had to be awkward for her. No telling what I was interrupting.

"What does Julia do?" I asked.

"She runs a women's shelter. For women and young girls who have been abused."

More pieces were coming together. Their sister Rita worked in sex trafficking. The blonde-haired woman was looking for a young girl who'd been kidnapped by the Strikers and was being held in the basement of their house. Julia worked with abused girls. These correlations couldn't be a coincidence. There had to be a connection between them.

I was determined to find out what it was.

* * *

I followed Anna out of the high school, and we headed off in the same direction as Anna's house. Instead of turning on her street, we passed it, and traveled another couple of miles into another neighborhood. Then pulled into the driveway of a house that looked similar to Anna's. Parked in the driveway was a silver KIA SUV. Identical to Anna's.

Another mystery solved.

Julia and Anna drove the same vehicles.

I wondered whose idea that was. Did Rita have the same car? It made me chuckle, easing the tension somewhat. I could picture the three identical triplets, walking into a car dealership and purchasing three identical silver SUVs. I imagined that the three girls often made a game of using their likenesses to fool people. Anna had said as much in her office. They liked to play tricks on their boyfriends and parents. Having the same cars would make that easier.

That might've been why Julia said her name was Anna in the coffee shop. More games. She probably left the coffee shop amused. Which caused a hint of anger to rise up inside of me. I didn't like it when people lied to me.

We walked on a sidewalk and took several steps up to a porch with a couple of chairs. Before Anna could knock, the door opened, and Julia appeared. Dressed in black slacks and a red, short-sleeved T-shirt.

I pretended to be as surprised to see her as she was me.

"We meet again," Julia said. "Cliff Ford. Am I right?"

I wanted to say, *Anna is it? Guidance counselor?*

I'd be well within my rights to do so. Rub it in. Demand to know why she lied to me. Two could play games. I easily tamped that down. Truthfully, I was thrilled to see her. My racing heart confirmed it. My feelings for her, whatever they were, came rushing back like a flood.

"I wish it weren't under these circumstances," I said to her sincerely.

We stepped inside the house and followed Julia into a hallway.

She suddenly turned, causing Anna and me to stop in our tracks.

Julia and Anna were face to face. Tears had already welled up in Anna's eyes. Julia took one look at her and burst into tears.

Julia pointed at me.

I nodded as if I knew what she was thinking.

"You're a homicide... detective," Julia said, between sobs. "Is Rita dead?"

Anna had her arms around Julia. "Yes honey. I'm sorry."

Julia's knees started to buckle. Anna held her up and led her into the living room off the hallway. They made it over to the couch. Julia was doubled over as they walked. Anna helped her sit down.

The scene broke my heart. It felt like I'd known these girls all my life. I'd never met Rita, but I could feel the loss.

If she were anything like her sisters, I was sure she'd been an incredible woman. Rita rescued girls for a living. Even though Rita worked for the FBI, she was in law enforcement. Like me. We had a bond from that standpoint. I grieved every time we lost a police officer whether I knew him or not.

I felt like I knew Rita.

Strange, but the feelings were very real.

Julia just kept repeating the same words. "Oh my God. Oh my God. Oh my God."

Anna sat beside her on the couch.

Julia had her knees together and her elbows on her knees. She was bent forward, with her hands clutched in front of her. Rocking back and forth.

Anna had one arm on her sister's back and another on her arm. She looked over at me with a pained look.

No one said anything for a good minute. Other than Anna muttering words meant to comfort Julia.

"I'm here. It's going to be okay. We'll get through it together. I love you."

"How did Rita die?" Julia finally asked. She stared straight ahead not attempting to make eye contact with Anna or with me. Anna looked at me with a *please help me, I don't know what to say* kind of pleading look.

I was sitting in a side chair next to the couch. To Julia's left. Close enough to touch her but still at a professional distance. I leaned forward and said barely above a whisper, "Rita was murdered."

That caused Julia to begin sobbing and letting out painful moans.

"The men who did it are behind bars," I added, searching for anything that might make her feel better.

"Detective Ford is the one who solved the case," Anna said. "He found the killers."

Julia mouthed the words *thank you* to me. Or at least that's what I thought she did.

"I was afraid this would happen," Julia said, after she'd regained some composure.

I didn't know what she meant.

"Rita worked for the FBI," Julia said, looking up and into Anna's eyes. Then she looked at me. I nodded to let her know I already knew that fact.

"I know," Anna said. "The FBI came to the school to see me earlier today."

"Why did you say you were afraid this would happen?" I asked. The detective in me was coming out. The kind of statement I was trained to pursue.

Julia choked back more sobs then took a deep breath and sat up straight.

"Rita was into some dangerous stuff."

"My understanding was that she worked undercover for the FBI," I replied. "That is very dangerous work. Your sister was a brave woman. She died in the line of duty. Rita's a hero in my book."

"I had no idea that Rita worked for the FBI," Anna blurted out. "I thought she was in fashion sales."

Julia's tears had dried up, at least momentarily.

"I'm sorry I didn't tell you," Julia said to Anna. "She made me swear I wouldn't. She didn't want you to worry about her."

Anna pulled her sister into a hug.

"It's okay," she said.

"When did you learn, Julia, that Rita was with the FBI?" I asked.

"Not that long ago," Julia answered. "Only a couple of weeks. I run a women's shelter. Rita asked me to take in several young girls. They'd been caught up in sex trafficking. Rita rescued them from a local gang. I think."

"The Strikers," I said.

"Yes."

I moved in even closer. Close enough to smell Julia's flowery perfume I remembered from the coffeeshop. I had to ignore how it made me feel.

"What can you tell me about Rita's activities?" I asked. "It might be important to the investigation."

"A few days ago—the day before I met you at the coffee shop," Julia said, "Rita called me. Said she had a young girl. Wanted me to take her in. The girl was in danger."

The words were stilted. Julia was still struggling to get them out.

"Go on," I said, as my heart did a flip flop in my chest. Where was Julia going with this? I wasn't sure, but it seemed like I was about to learn something important.

"I said I would," Julia said with a stronger voice. Talking about work was giving her a newfound strength. "Of course, I would."

As if I could admire these three girls more. They were amazing.

"Don't keep her at the shelter, Rita told me. Keep her at your house."

"Why would she say that?" Anna asked.

"I think the Strikers would be looking for her at the shelter, but they'd never know to look here."

"That makes sense," I said. "Do you know the girl's name?"

"Of course. Bae. She's a North Korean girl."

I would've fallen out of my chair if the coffee table weren't in front of me so I could put my hand on it to brace myself.

24

I couldn't believe what I'd just heard.

The events over the last week were connected in ways I never thought imaginable. Julia was hiding Bae. The girl the blonde-haired woman was looking for. Rita had rescued her from sex trafficking. She probably lost her life because of it.

I almost did as well. The blonde-haired woman saved my life. In fact, if not for her, I'd never have even known about Rita or Anna or the connection. Something I couldn't disclose to the sisters. Even though I thought they had a right to know. I couldn't betray the blonde woman's trust. I'd go to jail before I'd break her cover.

Questions were coming into my mind like the waves of an ocean. One right after the other. Fortunately, Julia started to open up, and I didn't have to pry the information out of her.

"That's why I ran that night," Julia said to me. "At *Champions* bar. I saw the Strikers and I panicked."

That made sense. Julia thought they were after her because she was holding the girl.

"What happened in the alley?" I asked.

Julia's words started coming at a faster pace. Like she was feeling the same fear she felt that night. "I went to the restroom. As you know. I was going to come back. I really was. I swear," Julia said to me apologetically.

Anna looked at us like a deer in headlights. Clearly confused. Julia saw what I saw.

"I met Cliff at a coffee shop," Julia said to Anna.

"*Hipsters*," I added. "There was only one open seat by your sister. That's how we met."

"Cliff asked me for my number."

"I did not!"

Julia laughed. Out of place, considering how red her eyes were and tears soaked her cheeks and shirt.

"That's right," Julia said, flashing me an endearing smile. "I told you I never gave out my number. Which is not a lie!"

She said the last words strongly.

I smiled back at her.

"Anyway... I told Cliff I would be at *Champions* on Friday night. If he wanted to see me again, he could meet me there. From his response, I didn't think he'd come. But I had to know. So, I went there to see if he'd show up."

Julia suddenly put her hand over her mouth.

"Oh my gosh!" she said.

"What?" Anna asked.

"You must think I'm horrible," Julia said to me.

"What are you talking about?" Anna asked.

"I told him my name was Anna." Julia put her hands over her eyes in embarrassment.

"And that I was a... high school guidance counselor."

Anna didn't seem amused.

Julia looked into my eyes apologetically. "Oh my... I'm so embarrassed. I didn't know you. I figured you were just hitting on me."

Julia turned back toward Anna and clasped her hands. She looked back and forth between Anna and me like she was watching a ping pong match.

"You know how we pretend to be each other," Julia said to Anna. "I didn't want to tell him my real name. I didn't think I'd ever see him again."

"Sorry," she added. Looking over at me.

I waved my hand in the air. "Not important," I said. "I want to know what happened in the alley. To the three Strikers."

"Oh right... I was coming out of the bathroom, and I saw the three men heading toward me. They saw me and I took off out the back door. It opened into the alley. They followed me. I was so scared. I started running, but they caught me before I could even get out of the alley.

One of them grabbed me. I thought he was going to kill me. He shook me and said, 'Where's the girl?' I knew he was talking about Bae. I would never tell him where she was."

"You must've been so scared," Anna said.

"I was. I thought I was going to die."

"Then what happened?" I asked.

The story was fascinating to me. I think I knew what had happened next, but I wanted Julia to confirm it.

"This woman came out of nowhere. Whoosh. Like a flash. She started fighting the Strikers. I took off running. I didn't even look back. I don't know what happened to the woman. I wish I did so I could thank her. I think she saved my life. I got in my car and floored it out of the parking lot. I came back to my house and locked the doors."

"Did the woman have blonde hair?" I asked.

"Yes. How did you know?" Julia asked.

I ignored her question.

"Do the Strikers know about this house?" I said, as a sudden feeling of dread came over me.

"I don't think so," Julia answered. Her eyes were wide with concern and Anna's mouth had gaped open. I had obviously alarmed them by the tone of my question. I didn't care. This was important.

"Is the girl still staying here?" I asked.

Julia answered. "Yes. She's not here now though." Then asked a question. "Did the Strikers hurt the woman in the alley?"

I chuckled. "No. She put the three of them in the hospital."

"Thank God. That's what Bae said would happen. I told her about it when I got home that night. Bae said it was her friend Jamie. She works for the CIA, I guess. Something like that. Bae was kind of vague about the whole thing. But I got the impression that Jamie works in sex trafficking."

Julia's mouth gaped open as she blurted out, "Maybe Jamie and Rita worked together at the FBI."

I now had a name to go with the blonde hair.

Jamie.

"I'm not sure," I answered sincerely because I didn't know. Jamie was a mystery. "I haven't pieced that together yet. I don't think Rita and Jamie knew each other or worked together. But I do know that Jamie is looking for Bae. When will Bae be back?"

"Tonight. She goes out during the day but comes home at night."

"People are looking for her," I said.

Julia's face turned dead serious. Stone cold. Her brow furrowed and her eyebrows raised. Her jaw was clenched as tight as a vise. "You can't tell anyone she's here. I shouldn't have even said anything. I gave her my word."

"The girl is underage."

"She told me she's eighteen."

"She's seventeen."

"That makes her old enough to make her own decisions."

"Technically, she's still a minor. Her parents are worried sick about her. They need to know."

"You can't tell them! Especially Jamie. I promised Bae. My word is my bond. I have a patient/client confidentiality agreement. Bae doesn't want anyone to know. Especially Jamie."

"What is Bae running from?" I asked.

"I don't think she's running from anything. She's on a vendetta. She thinks she's a female Reeder Rich."

"Who's Reeder Rich?" I asked.

"He's a character in a book," Anna answered. For the last few minutes, she'd just been sitting there with a blank stare on her face. Trying to take it all in. She seemed as stunned by the conversation as I was.

"Reeder Rich is a vigilante," Anna answered. "The kids at school love his books. At least they're reading something. Anyway, Reeder

Rich travels around the country looking for bad guys. He's got this martial arts ninja thing going on."

"Bae has some of those same skills," Julia added. "Bae said Jamie taught her everything she knows. According to Bae, this Jamie girl is the best there is anywhere in the world. Like the number one female assassin in the world."

I could confirm that but didn't. I didn't know about the best in the world, but I'd never seen anyone with her skills.

"Cliff, I'm so sorry I said my name was Anna." Julia changed the subject back to something she obviously was feeling guilty about. "I really am. I thought you were just another guy. I'm sorry, Anna. That's just something we do. You know... we're triplets. That's rare... you know."

She was stammering around but continued, "Anyway. Sometimes... we tell people we are one of our sisters," Julia tried to explain to me even though I already knew the reason she had lied. I let her continue without interrupting anyway. It felt good to get the apology.

"I say I'm Anna. Or I'm Rita. Anna says she's me. We used to fool boys we dated by switching places. Until one of Rita's boyfriends kissed me. Then we stopped. Rita was so mad at me. I'm rambling."

"Anna told me about that," I said. "You didn't know me from Adam. You don't owe me an apology."

She did, and I'm glad I got one, but I honestly wanted to move on to more important things. I was concerned about the Strikers. Wondering if Julia's life was in danger as well.

"I'm sure she didn't mean anything by it," Anna said to me, clearly defending her sister.

"No. I didn't," Julia said. "I figured I'd never see you again. Then we got to talking. I thought you were cute. You know?"

My whole body suddenly felt warm. Like my heart heated it up from the kind words. One of the things I wondered in the dead of night was if the coffee shop girl even remembered me. I was obsessed with her, and my biggest fear was that she didn't even remember my name.

Now I knew that wasn't true, and I felt a great sense of relief. Julia remembered that my name was Cliff. Also remembered that I was a homicide detective. Although, I doubt she ever thought the next time we saw each other would be in my professional capacity.

I had to remind myself of that fact. Why I was there. The whole conversation was traversing back and forth between my investigation and our personal relationship. Which was the very reason why the Lieutenant would never let us get involved in an investigation involving someone we were close to.

I was torn. Part of me wanted to stop Julia from going down that rabbit hole. The other part of me was glad to finally get the answers to my questions that had haunted me at night. So, I let Julia continue with her internal cleansing of guilty feelings.

"That's why I invited you to *Champions*," Julia said, with a hint of defensiveness. Like she needed to explain her motivations.

"I wanted to see you again," she continued. "I was planning on telling you my real name. I swear. I just didn't get the chance. Then I didn't know how to get in touch with you. I've thought about you often since that night."

My heart felt like it was going to burst in my chest.

"I've thought about you too," I said.

Anna looked at both of us quizzically. She couldn't help but notice the romantic connection. If you could call it that. I didn't know what it was. It'd better not be flirting. That didn't seem appropriate, considering the circumstances.

"I'm sorry," Julia said to me again. I'd lost track of how many times she had apologized. More than enough.

She reached out and touched my hand, sending chills down my spine.

"Water under the bridge," I said in my most sincere tone. "I'm sorry about your sister."

Both of the sisters then clasped their hands together. I hadn't meant to bring up that painful reality, but it would've come back up eventually.

The girls were now back in an embrace. Consoling each other. Tears streaming down both of their faces. I could feel the tears well up in my eyes too.

It felt awkward. I didn't know how to share in their grief, even if I did feel it. The reality was that I was only an acquaintance. When the moment of grief passed, at least enough for me to interject a comment, I said, "Julia, have you seen anything suspicious around your house or work?"

The girls seemed more in control of their emotions when we talked about the threat. I was more comfortable as well.

Julia shook her head no.

"You mean, have I seen any Strikers?" she asked.

I nodded.

"Not since that night at *Champions*. I've been sleeping with one eye open though."

"Are we in danger?" Anna asked. Her face suddenly showed a combination of distress and terror.

"I don't know," I said honestly. "I don't think you are, Anna. The Strikers don't know who you are. But I think that as long as that girl is staying with Julia, then she may be."

"The Strikers don't know who I am either," Julia said.

"Yes, they do," I argued. "They obviously knew who you were at the bar. That's why they followed you into the restroom."

"They thought I was Rita."

"Rita was already dead. She was murdered the morning that you and I met. The Strikers killed her. So, they knew she was dead. They followed you anyway."

"Oh. I didn't know that."

"I'm going to arrange for the two of you to have protection," I said. "Until we sort all of this out. I'll arrange to have a police cruiser keep a presence outside of both of your houses."

"Thank you," Anna said.

"Until then, both of you be careful. I'm going to the office to arrange protection. I'll be back as soon as I can."

We all stood in unison.

As I was leaving, Julia threw her arms around me. Squeezed my neck tightly. I felt her lips brush against my neck.

For the first time, I realized that I was more than an acquaintance.

Or at least I wanted to be.

25

Outside of Julia's house

Shiv had barely escaped the explosion alive.

The warehouse at the docks had been one of the best-kept se-crets in Chicago. Shiv had been running his operations out of it for nearly six months. With the help of a dirty cop who warned him if a raid was coming. Expensive but worth it. The cost of doing business.

He limited the foot traffic at the warehouse for that reason. One of the ways he protected secrecy. Most in his gang didn't know that's where they manufactured their meth. Also warehoused other drugs. Distribution handoffs occurred in dark alleys. Automotive garages. Under a bridge somewhere. Shiv was extremely careful that the only ones who knew about the inner workings of his organization were men he could trust explicitly.

They didn't keep any of the girls there for that reason as well. Shiv didn't want to draw scrutiny to the area. Nothing drew atten-tion more than pretty girls coming in and out of a warehouse at all hours of the day or night.

Even with all of his precautions, somehow his operations were compromised. Someone infiltrated the warehouse, blew up his drugs, and killed his men. He attributed it to the Cuban woman. The one he'd ordered killed in front of the coffee shop.

He'd gotten word that she was with the Feds. Which infuriated him. One of his highest ranked soldiers brought her into the organi-zation to recruit women to work as prostitutes. Almost as soon as he did, women started disappearing. His men argued that the girls were running away. Then it became so frequent, it was apparent that something was amiss.

When the Korean girl escaped from the house over on Dexter Street, he knew the Cuban woman was behind it. Not that he cared that the girl was gone. She'd been a pain in the rear. They never got the chance to get her into the prostitution chain so she could service men. She kept trying to beat up his men. So, they locked her in a basement. Somehow, she escaped. Word on the street was that the Cuban woman took her.

The woman was a menace. She was stealing his profits. At first, he thought she was selling the girls herself. He could deal with the competition. He would've killed her over it, but at least he understood. He was a businessman as well. Ambitious. He liked that in his soldiers. He also demanded loyalty. The fastest way to die was to break his trust and betray him. The only thing worse than that was to work for the Feds.

He hated law enforcement with a passion. One of them getting close to him was his biggest fear. That's why Shiv went to great lengths to keep his inner circle small. The soldier that recruited the Cuban lady was at the bottom of Lake Michigan.

Now the Cuban woman was dead as well. Something very satisfying to Shiv.

The higher ups in his organization had said to let it go. Retribution might bring the Feds down on them. That wasn't how he rolled. He'd ordered the hit on the lady, and she was killed execution style. In broad daylight. At his insistence. To send a message.

That should've been the end of it.

But another threat emerged. A blonde-haired woman. She killed three of his men at the house on Dexter Street and put three more in the hospital. A dozen more of his men were now dead at the warehouse. Millions of dollars in drugs were destroyed. The blonde woman was at the scene right before the explosion.

She almost got him as well, but he got away.

He had to find her but didn't know where to begin. The blonde killer was like a puff of smoke in the wind.

Then Shiv got a tip.

The Cuban woman had a sister. Julia Navarez. She ran a women's shelter. She was hiding the Korean girl. They watched the shelter but never saw the Korean girl. So, they followed Julia to her home the day before. Identifying the woman as the sister hadn't been hard. They were identical twins.

Now Shiv sat in front of her house along with his right hand man, Lefty. His second in command. They'd been staking out the house the entire day, waiting for the Cuban lady's sister to get back home. Earlier in the day, the door to the house opened, the woman walked out, got in her silver KIA, and drove off. Presumably to work.

Still no sign of the Korean girl.

"Do you think blonde lady will show up here?" Lefty asked Shiv.

"Doesn't matter. We grab the Cuban lady's sister, and Blondie will find us. If we get lucky, the North Korean girl is in the house, and we can snatch her as well."

Actually, if the pain-in-the-ass Korean girl was ever in his possession again, he'd kill her. He was done messing around with that troublemaker.

"What makes you so sure Blondie will come to us again?" Lefty asked. "And do we even want that? The lady has skills."

Shiv rubbed his chin. Thinking. Searching for the words to reassure his good friend and trusty foot soldier.

"How do you find an alligator in a pond?" Shiv asked.

"How?" Lefty replied.

"You drain the swamp."

"How do you propose we do that?"

"Same way you find a snake in the weeds. You smoke him out. Set fire to the field, and he'll come slithering out."

"You're not making sense."

"You don't chase a bear into a cave. You force him out."

"I still don't know how you're going to do it. What are we going to do when the sister lady gets back?"

"We're going to grab her. We'll take her back to the Seger Street house. We can hold her there until I decide what to do with her. Somebody's got to pay for what Blondie did to my warehouse. And to my men. An eye for an eye."

"I don't know if it's a good idea. Blondie may come after us."

"That's what I'm counting on."

Lefty was one of the few people who could shoot straight with Shiv. He didn't always tell him what he wanted to hear. He told him what he thought. That's what made him valuable to Shiv. Annoying, but valuable.

Shiv reassured him. "Patience, my friend. Patience."

They waited another thirty minutes. Then a silver KIA pulled into the driveway.

Shiv backhanded Lefty on his shoulder.

"See I told you. Patience. Look at that."

A woman got out of the car. The same girl he'd seen the night before. Julia.

"Do you want me to snatch her now?" Lefty asked.

"Not yet," Shiv said. "Let's wait until it gets dark. Besides, we don't know if the Korean girl is here. Let's wait it out and see what happens."

As if on cue, another silver KIA SUV pulled into the driveway. Another Cuban woman got out of the car. The spitting image of the other one. She also looked identical to the woman who worked for the FBI. He wasn't sure what to make of it. Obviously, sisters. He had to do a double take. For a moment, he wondered if the Federal agent wasn't really dead.

She had to be. The execution was confirmed by multiple sources.

Then he considered it a stroke of luck. He now had two women he could snatch and hold as leverage to smoke out the blonde-haired woman.

When another car drove into the driveway, his mouth flew so far open it would've fallen off his face if not attached to his head.

He couldn't help but think that his luck had just flown right out the window.

A detective.

Chicago PD.

Ford was his name.

His face was etched in Shiv's memory.

As were the events of thirteen months ago.

Ford arrested one of his soldiers, Gunner Danielson. Second in command at the time. Lefty had taken Gunner's place in the organization. Necessary because Gunner was in jail. Ford was to blame.

Shiv had ordered a hit which Gunner carried out. Shouldn't have been a big deal. A rival gang member. Happened all the time. But Gunner made a mistake. When he left the scene, he got pulled over by a police cruiser for having a broken taillight. Shiv had told him to get that fixed. He had said he would but forgot.

Gunner was driving a car with stolen license plates. When the cop ran the plates, he called for backup. Gunner should've taken off in the car. Instead, he took off running. Dropped his gun in the process. The cops caught him a few minutes later and hauled him off to jail.

Not a problem from Shiv's perspective.

Resisting arrest. Stolen license plates. Carrying a gun with a serial number filed off. That was enough to get Gunner three or four years in prison. Especially since carrying the gun violated his probation. No big deal. They all did time in the big house at some point. Came with the territory.

Problem was that a witness saw Gunner's car as he was fleeing the murder scene. Wrote down the license plate number. Gunner hadn't had time to switch out the plates.

Ford was the investigator. An easy case to solve. He didn't have to go looking for the murderer. Gunner was already in jail. Ford ran the plates the witness gave him and discovered the car was in impound. Ford put two and two together. Ran ballistics on the gun. Found a match. The case was made. At least that's how Shiv figured the whole thing played out and that's how the evidence was presented at trial.

Gunner was charged with murder and found guilty. Fifteen years to life was the sentence. He'd likely end up doing closer to life.

Shiv had gotten his revenge.

Not against Ford, but against his wife. Same thing.

He ordered a hit on her when he found out Ford was married. The execution style murder was carried out by one of his soldiers. A drive by shooting. Random. One of his most trusted men carried it out. A man who'd been with him since the beginning. Not a leader type but a foot soldier. Someone he trusted. Who followed his orders—explicitly.

Chicago PD never solved the case.

The same man who killed the Cuban woman, the federal agent, also killed Ford's wife.

Unfortunately, that man was in jail now. Shiv didn't know exactly how everything went down or how he ended up in jail. But three of his men were killed over on Dexter Street a couple days before. Later that night three more were arrested.

Now he heard from his source inside Chicago PD, that his men had been transferred to the Feds. None of it made sense, but the Cuban woman had to be behind it. Which was why he was sitting in front of her sister's house. To exact revenge.

Cliff Ford complicated things. Shiv might have to rethink his plan.

Too many things were happening that were outside of his control. Unexplainable things.

Why was Ford there? What did he have to do with it? The scene unfolding before his eyes was giving him pause.

Then he came up with the only plausible explanation he could think of. Ford was probably investigating the Cuban woman's murder. But... he thought the Feds had the case. Maybe his source was wrong. It didn't make sense.

He'd lay low and watch the scene until he had some answers. Ford was inside for nearly an hour. Then he came out by himself, got in his car, and left. The two women were still in the house and the two identical silver KIAs were still in the driveway.

Shiv contemplated his next move.

When one of the Cuban women came out of the house and got in one of the silver SUVs the decision was made for him. He decided to follow her. Easier to kidnap someone on the street than in their house. The doors could be locked. The woman inside could have a weapon or an alarm system. A man could be inside.

Shiv started up his car and began following her. They went through several neighborhoods and pulled up in front of another similar-looking house. Shiv drove his car into position. So that it blocked the driveway. Her only possible escape route.

The woman didn't notice right away.

The hesitation was all Lefty needed. He was out of the car in a flash. With his gun drawn.

The woman screamed when she saw him and started to run toward her front door.

Lefty was on her in a flash.

She fell to the ground.

He jerked her to her feet by the hair. Then forced her toward the car with the gun in her side. She tried to pull away, but he threatened to shoot her.

Lefty opened the back door on the passenger's side and forced the woman into the backseat. Then got in. Keeping his gun on her at all times.

Shiv revved the engine and sped away.

He'd made the right decision.

Always easier to snatch someone on the road.

The blonde woman would have to come looking for her. Ford might as well.

His luck was improving. He could kill all of them at the same time.

26

T he Lieutenant violently shook his head no with exaggerated motions.

"Why not?" I asked roughly.

I was standing in his office. The anger inside me was so strong, the argument could lead to blows, except that he was my boss, and I couldn't let him see how angry I really was.

"I can't spare the men," he said.

I'd just asked permission to assign cops to protect Anna and Julia in case the Strikers intended to harm them.

"These women are in danger!" I argued.

"You don't know that."

I bit my lip. Almost to the point that I expected to taste blood. Controlling my anger was hard. This shouldn't even be an issue. He should rubberstamp the request. We had one dead FBI agent. More than a dozen dead Strikers. Not to mention the three Strikers who had chased Julia out of *Champions* bar. Clear intention that she was in their crosshairs.

I needed to make that argument without divulging all of my information. My volume increased so that he knew how serious I was about it.

"Their sister is dead. Rita. The FBI agent. Her sister, Julia, is the one who was chased by the Strikers out of *Champions* bar into the back alley. That means they are already looking for her. It's only a matter of time until they find her."

"That doesn't mean the Strikers know where she lives. That explosion decimated their operations. I doubt they are even in a position to launch an attack."

"You said yourself, that Shiv survived the bombing. Or at least we assume he did. His body was not recovered. He'll be looking for someone to blame. Maybe the girls."

"What do the girls have to do with the bombing?" the Lieutenant asked.

"Nothing. As far as I know. But their sister worked for the FBI. Undercover. That's what got her killed."

"How do you know she worked undercover?"

"The sister told me. She's known for a few weeks. The woman was working the sex-trafficking angle. She was taking their girls and hiding them at a woman's shelter that her sister ran. That makes the sister a target."

He already knew about the missing person's report and my investigation of it. Thankfully, he hadn't made an issue out of it. Just commended me for solving it so fast.

The Lieutenant maintained his stubborn stance. "Until you have a specific threat, I'm not pulling two people off the street for a potential threat."

I started to protest further, but he raised his hand to stop me. I'd already pushed him harder than I should've.

I stormed out of the office anyway to let him know I wasn't pleased. If he didn't always leave the door opened, I would've slammed it shut.

When I got to my desk, I found a note.

See me. Magnum. News.

I had a phone call to make first.

I dialed a number I had recently memorized.

The blonde woman answered.

"Hello Clifford," she said.

That caused me to smile. I looked around the bullpen to see if anyone was within earshot and could hear the conversation. I decided to stand up and walk out into the hallway anyway.

"I know where Bae is," I said, as I was walking.

"Where?"

I gave her the address. Julia's house. Julia would be mad at me, but it couldn't be helped. How would she feel if Rita had been kidnapped and was alive, but no one told her that information? Bae's relatives had a right to know that their daughter was alive and where she was. Once Jamie contacted Bae, the Korean girl could decide for herself if she wanted to go back home or not.

I explained, "Rita has a sister. Bae is staying at her house."

"I know about Anna. I'm the one who told you about her. Bae is not at her house."

I realized it was confusing. I was still having trouble keeping it straight in my head. The blonde lady didn't know about the third sister.

"Rita has two sisters. Anna and Julia. Julia is the name of the third sister. They are identical triplets. What are the odds?"

"Astronomical. I've never heard of it before."

"One in two hundred million is what I heard. Anyway, it doesn't matter. I think the sister's lives are in danger. Shiv is still alive."

Another pause.

"We never recovered his body at the explosion site. So, he's still on the loose. Probably looking for you as well. Keep your radar up."

"I'll be gone before he can find me. As soon as I get Bae, we're out of here."

"That's a good idea."

A good idea for Julia as well. She'll thank me after she has time to think about it. Getting Bae out of town would make things safer for Julia. The Strikers wouldn't have any reason to come after her. Revenge maybe. But like the Lieutenant said, they weren't really in a position to waste their time going after somebody's sister. They had bigger worries.

"Have you told your boss about me?" Jamie asked. She didn't know I knew her name. I'd hold that card close to my vest if I ever needed it.

"Your secret is safe with me."

"Thank you. Tell your boss you think the Lito gang is behind the bombing. That you have an anonymous source who fed you that information."

The Lito gang was out of Little Italy. Smaller than the Strikers and not as powerful, but a force to be reckoned with, nonetheless.

She added, "I'm already working behind the scenes to make Shiv think Lito is behind the warehouse bombing. Nothing like a little gang war. It's the best of both worlds when they are killing each other, as long as innocent civilians don't get caught up in it."

"That's a good idea. I'll tell my Lieutenant."

"Thanks for the intel on the girl."

"The Strikers will still be looking for you," I said for a second time.

"Hopefully, Bae will go with me. She's very stubborn."

"I heard she thinks she's a female Reeder Rich."

"Like I said, the girl is a little crazy. She means well, but she got in over her head with the Strikers. Hopefully, she learned a lesson. I'm glad to hear she's still alive."

"If I don't talk to you again, thanks for everything," I said sincerely.

"You're welcome."

"Good luck."

Before I could go see Magnum, the Lieutenant called me into his office.

To introduce me to my new partner.

* * *

The next morning

I went to see Magnum the first thing the next morning. After another restless night. One trying to rack my brains trying to figure out what he wanted. He was at his desk going through some papers.

"Have a seat," he said grimly.

I could feel the fear rising up inside of me again, though I had no idea if it was necessary.

"I have some news."

"Okay."

I shifted in my seat.

"About your wife's killing."

My heart did a somersault.

Just the mention of my wife's murder brought up all kinds of emotions. Magnum had been there for me through the whole thing. I'd leaned on him on more than one occasion. What kind of news could he possibly have about her killing?

"What about Gabby?" I asked.

"You know the gun that killed the woman at the coffeeshop? The one you brought to me the other day?"

"Yes."

"That's the same gun the killer used to shoot your wife."

My mind began to process that information. The department had put all kinds of resources and manpower into the investigation of Gabby's death. Every thread ended up being a dead end. The Strikers were suspects, but nothing ever stuck.

"How do you know?" I asked.

"I compared the bullets. A perfect match."

"What made you check that gun?"

"I check every gun that comes through here."

"What?"

"Since your wife's murder, every time I run a ballistics check on a gun, I always compare the bullet with the one taken from your wife. "I never found a match. Until this one."

"I can't believe you would do that for me."

Magnum shrugged his shoulders.

"Oh well. I want to find the killer. I think we did. Or at least we found the gun that killed Gabby. That's a first step."

I didn't know what else to do but to give him a man hug. I slapped him on the back several times. My heart was warmed to think of how good a friend he was. Going beyond the call of duty. Just for me. And for Gabby. Someone he didn't even know.

He handed me a copy of the ballistics report. I stared at it for several seconds. Then thanked him again and left his office.

My next step was for me to go see the investigator in charge of Gabby's case. This information would be huge. I considered keeping it a secret and doing my own investigation. Maybe paying the lowlife Striker a visit. Problem was that the FBI had him. I didn't know where they were keeping him. This information would eventually get him transferred back to our jurisdiction.

Going it alone wasn't a good idea. I needed to make sure this information got into the proper channels.

I had another idea.

Before I went to his office, I stepped into a private office and redialed the number to the blonde woman. She answered on the first ring.

"I didn't expect to ever hear from you again," she said.

"There's been a development."

"What kind of development?"

"My wife was murdered a little over a year ago. A drive-by shooting."

"I know. I'm sorry."

"How did you know?"

"I have my ways of gathering information."

I'd long since given up trying to figure out how she came about all these things. Not important for this conversation. What I really wanted was her to use her skills to help me find Shiv. He was clearly the one who ordered the hit on my wife.

"Anyway. It's gone unsolved all these months," I said. "Turns out. The Strikers killed her. The same gun that killed the FBI agent killed my wife thirteen months ago. The guy at the Dexter house, the one who was about to kill me... he was the one with the gun. He killed my wife."

My voice cracked as I said the last sentence.

"Doesn't necessarily mean the guy in jail is the shooter," she said in a business-like voice, but with warmth, so I knew she wasn't cold-hearted about it.

"I suppose."

"He could've pulled the gun off somebody. Stole it. Another Striker might've been carrying it at the time."

"I know. But... fifteen months ago, I nailed one of the Strikers for murder. A higher up in the organization. Put him away for life. I think Shiv put the hit out on my wife. To get back at me."

"Why are you telling me this?" she asked.

"I need your help. I want to kill Shiv."

"Sorry. But I'm getting out of Chicago. I've helped you all I can."

"You owe me. I gave you the location of the girl."

"And I appreciate it. I got the girl in the middle of the night. She's with me now. We're going home soon."

"Stay and help me. I can't do this alone. Like I said, you owe me."

"I saved your life. Let's call it even. I'm glad you found the gun. But I can't help you."

"You *can* help me. I can't take on the Strikers by myself. I have to get warrants. My Lieutenant's permission. Which he won't give me. You don't play by the same set of rules."

"I play by the same set of rules; I just have a little more cover than you. Some powerful people in our government have my back. They are more interested in my results than my methods. But this isn't my battle. My beef with the Strikers was because they took the girl. Now that I have her, I'm gone."

"You're the only one who can help me, Jamie." I was practically begging.

Dead silence on the other line. I hadn't intended to play that card. It popped out of my mouth like a hiccup.

"How do you know my name?" she asked.

"You're not the only one with sources."

"You got it from Bae. That little weasel. I thought I taught her better than that."

"Will you help me?"

"Are you going to turn me in if I don't?"

"No. I'd get in as much trouble as you. Maybe more. Anyway, I'm not a snitch. Your secret is safe with me. I'm asking for help. Not threatening you. I wouldn't do that."

"Let me get back with you."

"How do I know you won't bolt? That I'll actually hear from you?"

"Because I gave you my word. If I tell you I'm going to get back with you, then I will."

I had no choice but to trust her. In reality, she could ditch the phone and vanish into the wind. I'd never find out who she was or how to locate her.

So, I said, "I appreciate it. I think Julia and Anna... the two sisters are in danger. I can feel it. My gut tells me. I've always trusted my gut. Shiv is after them. He's after you. Probably me too if he thinks I'm involved. It's to all of our benefit to take him out."

"Tell your boss about Lito. Plant that seed. That'll take the focus off of both of us."

"I'm on it."

"I'll be in touch."

I hung up the phone, then practically ran into the bullpen to find Cameron Green. The detective assigned to Gabby's case.

We needed to question the man who shot Rita. The one who was carrying the gun that shot Rita. The same gun used to kill my wife.

I wanted to look him in the eye.

First, I had to convince Cameron to let me be in the same room.

Then convince him to give me five minutes alone with scumbag!

27

Cameron and I spent more than two hours going through the evidence he'd collected on Gabby's murder. Trying to build a case against the Strikers and the man in custody. We intended to take our evidence to the Lieutenant and put the wheels in motion to file state murder charges against them.

The ballistics report was the most compelling evidence. The gun was in the possession of the Striker and was the same gun used to kill Gabby. In addition, witnesses saw a black four-door sedan speed away from the shooting. The man in custody drove a black four door Lexus. At some point, we needed to go through security camera footage and see if we spotted the car.

Cameron's thorough investigation of my wife's murder was impressive. He was an experienced homicide detective, but as months passed and he still hadn't made an arrest, I began to question his skills. Mostly because I was in the dark. The agony of not knowing and the urge to investigate it on my own kept me second-guessing his resolve to solve the case. I put that concern out of my mind after having seen his attention to detail and grasp of the facts.

He was doing a good job. He didn't have much to go on. Until now. With cases, sometimes you come to a stopping point and have to put it aside and wait for a break. Having the murder weapon was a big break that would put momentum behind the case and move it back up to the front burner.

Going through the evidence brought up a lot of unresolved raw emotions in me. As Cameron and I painstakingly went through the evidence trying to piece things together, I'd been able to maintain my professionalism and approach it as a detective. At some point, I'd have to deal with the fact that Gabby was killed because of me. Because of my job. The Strikers killed her for revenge. I'd put one of their own away in prison for life. They took Gabby's life from her in a sick form of retribution. While Gabby and I both knew the risks of my job, that knowledge didn't lessen the guilt.

Regardless of what I was feeling, I couldn't let the Lieutenant see it. If he got any sense that I wasn't able to control my emotions, he'd pull me out of the loop and put me on the sidelines faster than a junkyard dog who'd just bit a neighbor. While he'd sideline me from the main investigation anyway, he might be willing to let me continue to investigate on the periphery. At least instruct Cameron to let me know what was happening.

I had no intention of staying on the sidelines. Shiv was behind my wife's murder. I was certain of it. He also ordered the hit on Rita. He'd already proven his thirst for revenge. Gabby. Rita.

Who was next?

Bae? Jamie, the blonde-haired woman? A likely target. Shiv killed Rita because she took one of his girls. He killed my wife because she was associated with me. What would he do to someone who blew up his warehouse? Destroyed millions of dollars-worth of drugs? Killed more than a dozen of his men?

I was certain Shiv was planning something. What though? Jamie would be hard to find. If not impossible. I was off his radar. He'd go for the easiest targets. Julia. Anna. Bae. That's why we needed the Lieutenant to give us permission to go after Shiv.

Cameron and I walked into the opened door of the Lieutenant's office and sat down. A breach in protocol. We were only supposed to sit when invited. A strategic move on our part. It'd let him know we were serious.

Cameron took the lead in the discussion for obvious reasons.

"What's up?" the Lieutenant asked, ignoring our deviation from his silly rules. He almost certainly knew we had some big news.

"We have a break in Gabby's murder," Cameron said.

The Lieutenant's eyes widened.

It seemed like my heart was skipping every other beat.

A break in Gabby's case would be welcomed news to the Lieutenant. He had a hard outer shell, but he was a detective above all else. A good one at that. He might treat me like a pig in a pigsty sometimes, but I was still one of his own. Gabby's murder had hit him hard as well. He would've moved heaven and earth to find her killer. That's why he put Cameron on the case. His best senior detective.

Cameron made the comment that the Lieutenant had been on his back since the beginning. Made him give daily updates for weeks. Chewed him out for the lack of progress.

I had no idea.

"Are you going to tell me what you got, or do you want me to guess?" the Lieutenant asked, clearly trying to keep the upper hand in the situation by maintaining his image as a jerk.

"We have the murder weapon," Cameron said.

"Spell it out."

"The gun used to kill the FBI agent, Rita Navarez, is the same weapon used to murder Gabby."

Cameron handed the Lieutenant a copy of the ballistics report.

That halted the conversation while the Lieutenant studied the report. A welcomed reprieve for me. The words, 'murder Gabby' were piercing. Like a knife had been thrust into my heart and then twisted several times. By a cruel attacker. I bit my lip to fight back all the emotion.

I shifted positions in my seat as if that would make me more comfortable. The best thing for me to do was to keep my mouth shut. Maintain professionalism. Treat it like another case. The Lieutenant would understand the personal nature of it, but he'd expect the conversation to be emotionless. He demanded it from his detectives.

"What else you got?" the Lieutenant asked, as he slid the report back across the table.

"The murderer was driving a black four door sedan. Ms. Navarez's killer drives a black four door Lexus."

Cameron paused to let that sink in.

I couldn't tell if the Lieutenant was skeptical or following the thread. Normally, he'd be playing devil's advocate. Shooting holes in whatever evidence we had no matter how good it was. I understood. His job was to make sure the charges stuck. The last thing he wanted was one of our cases falling apart because we didn't tie up all the loose ends.

Not that we could. Murder investigations were almost never airtight. The Lieutenant knew that. The reason he pressed us so hard was to squeeze every ounce of juice out of the lemon. At some point, we had to go with what we had.

As Cameron continued to speak, I realized we didn't have enough.

That's why I needed Jamie. She got me the information on Rita. The only reason we knew about the gun was because of her. She also extracted the information from the Striker. Shiv's whereabouts. The warehouse. If I were Shiv, I'd go into hiding. If anyone could find him, it'd be Jamie. I still hadn't heard from her and wondered if I would.

I could feel it coming. The Lieutenant was about to blow us out of the water. The reason our evidence was flimsy was obvious, which he was quick to point out.

"You don't know that the man in custody is the shooter."

"He had the gun in his possession," I blurted out. So much for me keeping my mouth shut.

Cameron glared at me.

"You know the drill," the Lieutenant said. "He bought the gun off somebody. He wasn't in Chicago at the time. He's never been anywhere near where she was killed. I can hear his defense attorney making the arguments now. Actually, it'll never get to trial. The DA will have the same concerns. The two of you already know that."

"We have a circumstantial case," Cameron argued. "We know that. The investigation isn't over. We're going to go back through video footage from that night. And see what we see. Maybe we'll catch a break and see the Lexus. Or see the man's face at a toll booth. Anything to tie him to the scene. I'll follow up on more leads. Interview the witnesses again."

"That may not be enough," the Lieutenant said.

I started to say something, but he raised his hand in the air to stop me.

"I want to nail this S.O. B. as well," the Lieutenant said. "Keep looking into it. We got time. The man's not going anywhere. The Feds have him. We all know that they're going to get the first crack at him. He's likely going to jail for the rest of his life. That doesn't bring Gabby back. I know. It's not justice. Cliff, you may just have to take satisfaction in knowing that Gabby's murderer is behind bars."

"I want to see him go to trial for her murder," I said, no longer willing to hide my emotion.

"Me too," the Lieutenant said. "And he will. But you don't have enough evidence against him. Go find some. I promise you this. We'll take it to the D.A. If you don't find anything else, we'll take what we have. It's probably not enough to file charges, but I'll take it. For you. But go get me more."

"We will," I said.

"Not you," the Lieutenant said to me. "You. Cameron. You go find me more. Ford, you stay as far away from this investigation as possible. Let Cameron do his job."

"I'm the one that found the murder weapon. I can help. I'm already up to my eyeballs in the Strikers. I believe Shiv is behind these murders. He had Rita killed. And Gabby. Who knows how many? Magnum's going through all of our unsolved cases to see if we can get matches on any of those bullets. If the guy in jail is Shiv's main enforcer, we might solve a lot of murders. I'm sure there's more."

"Like I said, let Cameron handle it. I'm warning you, Ford, go anywhere near this case, and I'll put you on extended leave."

I glared at him.

He glared back.

Really, he was cutting me some slack. Because of the nature of the case. My reaction was to be expected. The Lieutenant would probably be concerned about me if I didn't feel that way. Still, he was doing the right thing. That didn't make it better or easy to take, but at least I understood where he was coming from.

It still hurts.

I left the office feeling like a wounded prey.

Cameron must've felt it because he put his hand on my shoulder.

"I'm going to nail him," he said. "I promise. I'll do everything I know to do."

"I know and I appreciate it."

I didn't go directly to my desk. Instead, I went into the men's restroom and splashed water on my face. Then roughly pulled a paper towel from the dispenser and dried it.

In a full-blown battle with my emotions.

They all came flooding back. Like a wound had been opened. A scar that was suddenly bleeding. Not a scar. The wound had never healed. Wouldn't until Gabby's murderer was brought to justice.

My phone rang.

I fumbled as I tried to get it out of my pocket. My hand was still slightly wet and shaking from the anxiety that was pulsing from the top of my head to the end of my fingers.

Julia.

I'd entered her phone into my contacts the day before.

Why was she calling me?

Now wasn't a good time.

I needed to send it to voicemail. One day before, I'd have given anything to receive a call from Julia. Now it felt wrong. I'd worked hard to bury my feelings for Gabby which was why I thought I was starting to have feelings for Julia. Move on with my life, as my sister told me I should.

Now, those feelings for Gabby were back at the surface. Intense love. Missing her. Accompanied by even more powerful emotions. Anger. Guilt. Her death was my fault.

How could I possibly have a conversation with Julia with all those feelings swirling around inside like a washing machine in a laundry mat.

I let it go to voicemail and then waited for the ding which told me she had left a message.

My hand was still shaking as I played it.

"How could you?" Julia said angrily. "I told you about Bae in confidence. You told Jamie where Bae was. Now she's gone. I could lose my job because of you. I told you that I have patient confidentiality. Not that you care!"

I could tell that Julia had been crying. Or at least fighting back the tears.

"I thought you were a decent guy!" she added. "I guess I was wrong."

The voicemail ended.

I didn't know what to feel. Angry. Guilty again.

Indifferent.

That's the emotion I chose to embrace.

I barely knew this woman. Jamie had saved my life. Bae was acting irresponsibly. I'd do it again if I had to. A thousand times out of a thousand. If Julia didn't understand, that was her problem. Not mine.

My infatuation with her needed to be over, anyway.

Clearly, any hopes of a relationship were dashed.

One question remained.

Should I call her back?

28

Anna found herself in the basement of an older two-story house in one of the seediest neighborhoods in south Chicago. Except for the fact that she was in a makeshift prison, her surroundings were surprisingly adequate. The bed—mattress actually—was on the floor but had clean sheets on it. A couch was against one wall and a dresser against another. The chest of drawers was full of women's clothes as was the closet. Some of the articles of clothing still had the tags on them.

The room contained a small kitchenette including a microwave oven and a small refrigerator. A standalone cabinet contained plates, bowls, glasses, and eating utensils. Everything but knives. For obvious reasons.

A ceiling fan provided some ventilation.

Julia had said that the Strikers were into human trafficking. Anna wondered if this was where they kept some of their girls. If so, it'd explain the conditions. The Strikers would want the girls to be attractive to the men.

The thought made her shudder. Anna wondered if they made the girls turn tricks in that room. She dismissed the thought when the idea popped in her head that they might've kidnapped her for that purpose. This had to do with her sister. And that girl named Bae. Did they think she was Julia? Did they even know she had another sister? Do they think she knows where Bae is? She'd never even met the girl.

Anna put those thoughts out of her mind and focused on inventorying her surroundings. The bathroom had the basic necessities she might find in a five-star hotel. Soap, shampoo, toothbrush, toothpaste, deodorant, feminine products. She took advantage of the ones that were new and still unopened and used the opportunity to regain her bearings.

A splash of cold water on her face and freshening up made her feel normal, at least for a few minutes. She even considered taking a shower but didn't want to leave herself vulnerable should one of the kidnappers come back down to the basement again. Which they no doubt would.

That's when she'd make her move.

She was kicking herself for having not made it already.

Anna was trained in martial arts. As were her two sisters, Julia, and Rita. They'd taken a class together at Anna's gym. The instructor taught them the basics of self-defense and how to handle themselves when attacked. At the end of the class, Anna felt confident. Assured that she could handle herself. The instructor said all three girls were good. Rita was the best by far. Which made sense now. She was already trained by the FBI and, clearly, had only pretended not to be for their benefit.

At the thought of Rita, a heavy sadness came over her, but she fought it. Now wasn't the time to grieve. She was in extreme danger and needed to keep a clear head. These were probably the same men who killed Rita. Gunned her sister down on the street. Execution style, the detective had said.

They'd kidnapped her in broad daylight, brandishing guns. These men were either desperate or brash. Or both.

Her mind returned to questioning why she was now in that position. Why did they take her? She'd kept her mouth shut driving to the house. Now she wished she'd tried to engage them in conversation. To at least try to garner some information. It'd help if she knew their motives. As much as she tried, she couldn't figure out why they had grabbed her.

Regardless, Anna was on her own. No one knew where she was. It'd be tomorrow before anyone would even know she was gone.

The only consolation was that they hadn't killed her yet. For some reason, they wanted her alive.

A big mistake on their part.

She'd use her training to get out of there.

Actually, Anna was the one who made the big mistake. She never should've allowed them to put her in that basement. Or the car for that matter. Her instructor wouldn't be happy with how she'd handled the situation.

Don't ever get in a car or trunk. Once you do, the odds are, you're dead.

When she was in front of her house, in the open, she should've fought back. But when the gun was suddenly thrust in her side, she froze. All the training left her. Like a deer in headlights, she let him lead her away and pushed her into the car. They drove her to the house. Made her get out of the car at gunpoint and forced her into the basement. She had a second chance to run away but hadn't taken it.

Stupid.

Her instructor was right. The stark reality was clear. Now, she was their prisoner. In a confined space. With no windows. In a strange neighborhood. The door was bolted shut. She'd checked. The worst possible situation for fighting back.

To complicate things, the house had filled up with other Strikers. She heard stomping around and loud conversations.

Anna looked around the bathroom for something she could use as a weapon. Several sharp objects would work but weren't ideal. Tweezers. Nail clippers. A hot curling iron would do some damage. The cord to the hair dryer wrapped around the neck of one of her kidnappers would do the trick. She doubted her ability to make that happen.

Picturing it in her mind at least had the effect of strengthening her resolve. Empowering her to the fact that she wasn't totally helpless.

The hand mirror gave her an idea.

She wrapped it with a towel to mute the sound. Then banged it on the edge of the bathroom counter. Careful not to hit it so hard that the glass shattered. It worked. The glass was broken into several large pieces. Sizable enough to be used as shards.

Anna carefully took out several pieces of glass and gripped each one to see which one was easiest to hold and had the sharpest point. Once she decided on one, she hid the others in a drawer. Then looked in the mirror, studying her face to see if she had the courage to use it.

What she saw gave her pause. Anna still wore the same clothes she had on at work. A skirt, blouse, and pumps. Not ideal for when she made her move. The skirt was form fitting. She needed her legs free in case she had to execute a leg kick. If she had to run away, pumps would slow her down. If she took them off, her feet wouldn't be protected from gravel, rocks, or other unseen objects she could step on while trying to get away.

She needed to change clothes. Before she could, a loud noise startled her. Someone had opened the door to the basement.

Did they hear her break the glass?

Anna picked up the shard of glass and gripped it with her hand. Careful not to cut herself on the sharp edge.

She heard footsteps. Someone was coming down the stairs. The sound got louder as the person got closer to where she was hiding. Not hiding really. There were only two places she could be. The closet or bathroom. Whoever had entered the basement banged on the bathroom door. Even though she expected it, she still jumped.

"I'm busy," Anna said. "I'm going to the bathroom."

"Your pizza's here," the man said.

It sounded like Lefty. The one who forced her into the car at gunpoint. He'd come in an hour or so before and asked her what kind of pizza she wanted.

Mushroom.

At the time, she'd been confused. Why were they feeding her? Was she like a hog being led to slaughter? Like a prisoner on death row being served her last meal?

Then she doubted they'd actually bring her anything to eat. Apparently, they had.

"I'll be right out," Anna said.

She opened the door slowly and saw Lefty setting the pizza box down on the table in front of the couch along with a plastic bottle of Coke. She'd asked for Diet Coke but wasn't going to press the point.

His back was to her.

Anna gripped the shard. Envisioned herself plunging the glass into his back. Just to the right of the spine. Hopefully where it'd nick a vital organ. Preferably the heart.

Then she thought better of it.

What would she do then? The upstairs was filled with Strikers. Presumably armed. She hadn't had a chance to change clothes or shoes. They'd kill her before she got out the back door.

She froze again with sudden fear and indecision.

Her instructor's words resonated in her mind. Indecision *will get you killed*.

The next words gave her the rationalization to stand down. *Fight on your own terms. When you are ready. Unless you have no choice.*

"Don't get any stupid ideas," Lefty said to her, like he could read her mind. "Do what we say, and you might get out of this alive."

"I won't," Anna said, firmly, but not belligerently. She didn't want to provoke him. Her instructor was right. She wasn't ready to fight.

Anna walked around him, careful to keep the shard behind her back. She sat down on the couch and slipped the piece of glass between the cushions.

Then breathed a sigh of relief when he left the basement and went back upstairs.

Anna pulled the shard out of the cushions and took it into the bathroom and hid it. Then went back in the main room and opened the pizza box and smelled it. Her stomach responded with a growl. The pizza was still hot. Eating would have to wait though. She had to get changed in case the man came back.

Anna went into the closet and pulled out a pair of black leggings and a black T-shirt that came down below her waist. Neither had the store tags on them but were best suited for what she had in mind. The thought of wearing clothes that might've been worn by another woman creeped her out but couldn't be helped. At least they were clean.

She found a pair of sneakers that didn't fit perfectly but would have to do. A hoodie had a pocket in front where she could hide the shard. She slipped on the T-shirt.

Anna went back into the bathroom and looked at herself in the mirror. The only thing that gave her pause was the hoodie. It was hot in the basement. Any observant person would be suspicious.

Didn't matter. She was committed. If they questioned her about it, she'd make something up.

Anna went back in the main room and scarfed down two pieces of pizza and the coke. She needed sustenance. She wrapped up the rest of the pizza in a paper towel and put it in the refrigerator.

It might've been the sugar and caffeine from the soft drink, but she felt a sudden rush of energy. It could be because she felt empowered. Like she was more in control. She wouldn't just sit in the basement and let them decide her fate.

Then she paced around. Nervously. Considering her options.

Her mind flitted in different directions. Perhaps she should let things play out. They'd threatened to kill her several times but hadn't done so. Why were they feeding her? Treating her nicely? Were they going to hold her for ransom? If so, she should be patient.

That caused her to chuckle. She didn't make much money.

Anna thought of her fiancé. The wedding. He was out of town on business. He wouldn't be back for two days. So, he wouldn't know she was gone or in danger. He'd be beside himself when they all realized she'd gone missing. He'd move heaven and earth to come up with a ransom though.

Then reality hit her.

She wasn't being held for ransom.

They let her see their faces.

She knew their names. Shiv and Lefty.

They made no attempt to hide them from her.

She saw where they brought her. She had memorized the route in case she got the chance to tell the police where they had taken her. They didn't put a bag on her head. Put her in the trunk. Make her lie down on the floorboard of the back seat.

Why?

Anna could only come to one logical conclusion.

They intended to kill her.

29

I didn't call Julia back right away.

Not because I didn't know what to say. My arguments for doing what I did were solidified in my mind. Telling Bae's whereabouts to Jamie had been the right thing to do.

Julia had left me an angry voicemail. Her words had been sharp and accusatory. I tried to be understanding even though I thought she was overreacting. She wouldn't lose her job. She hadn't violated any patient client communications. I was a homicide detective. Investigating a murder. Along with a missing person's case. She was obligated to answer my questions.

Bae was the victim of a crime. She might want to go into hiding, but I had a right to question her. Gather evidence against her kidnappers. Force her to cooperate in the investigation if need be.

More importantly, loved ones were looking for Bae. If the shoe were on the other foot, wouldn't Julia want to know? In a way it was. Rita had been missing. Anna had filed a missing person's report. How would Julia feel if Rita had been in hiding and I knew where she was but refused to tell her that her sister was okay?

She wouldn't like it at all.

Add to the fact that Julia had lied to me in the coffee shop. Then ran away from me at *Champions* with no explanation. Even put my life in danger. Unknowingly. But if I'd had more information, I could've helped her sooner. In some ways, she had obstructed my investigation.

In my head it all made sense. I wanted to call Julia and make my arguments to her. From her tone, I doubt she'd understand.

Maybe I dodged a bullet not getting involved with her if she was that irrational.

But I kept putting off the call. I didn't want to say something I might regret. Julia had just lost her sister. I'd no doubt scared her with all my talk about the Strikers coming after them. Of course, she was on edge. We all were. Emotions were running high. Julia could not have known that mine were about to erupt like a volcano.

Julia seemed like a good person. If she knew what I was going through perhaps she would've been more careful with her words.

I'd just learned that the man who killed Gabby was in custody. That we had the murder weapon. That Shiv probably ordered the hit. That Gabby died because of one of my cases. The range of emotions set off inside of me were set to explode. Anger had turned to rage. Guilt to despondency.

I'd be no good to anyone if I didn't snap out of it soon.

Fortunately, my new partner had some vacation days coming, and took them before he started his new job with me. That only gave me a few more days to find Shiv without having my partner looking over my shoulders.

That gave me time to consider my options. Not calling Julia back was not one of them. I'd practically promised her police protection. I couldn't provide it. I had to break the news to her and Anna and suggest they go into hiding for a few days. Stay with a friend or another family member.

With Bae out of the picture, Julia might be out of the crosshairs. Anna probably already was. I had no reason to believe Shiv would come after her. She had nothing to do with the situation.

I couldn't guarantee that though.

Julia, on the other hand, needed to know, and I needed to call her. Sooner rather than later.

I thought of every excuse not to.

I didn't trust myself. I'd feel worse if I took my frustrations out on her. This wasn't her fault. I understood how she felt.

Would she think I lied to her about the police protection?

The fact I even had to make the call and tell her none was coming infuriated me. The Lieutenant had made the wrong call. If anything happened to Anna or Julia, I might just walk into his office and slam his smug face on his desk and shatter his tobacco stain teeth.

Then spend ten years in jail.

Maybe deflecting my anger at the Lieutenant instead of Julia wasn't the best idea.

All these conflicting thoughts were why I hadn't called her.

Then I got a different idea. I'd call Anna first. Feel her out. She'd know how mad Julia really was. I could get Anna to call Julia back and give her the message. Save me from having to do it.

He dialed her cell phone, but it went to voicemail. I left a generic message.

"Anna, this is Detective Ford. Could you call me at your first convenience?"

I left her my number and hung up.

Then realized Anna would already be at work, so I dialed the high school.

"South Skyline High. How may I help you?" the familiar voice said. The same lady who I met when I had visited the high school answered the phone.

"This is Detective Cliff Ford with Chicago PD. I'm calling for Anna Navarez. Could you connect us please?"

"I'm glad you called. I was about to call you."

What did that mean?

"Ms. Navarez didn't show up for work today."

My heart skipped a beat.

"Have you tried calling her?"

"Of course. All I get is her voicemail. I'm worried."

I'd gotten her voicemail as well.

"Could she have taken a personal day?" I asked, trying to grasp hold of anything other than my biggest fear.

"She would've called. Ms. Navarez has parent teacher conferences this week. She's already missed several appointments with parents. This is very unlike her."

"Did you call her sister?"

"Yes. She's Anna's emergency contact. Rita didn't answer either."

The lady didn't know that Rita was dead.

That made sense. Anna said she was closer to Rita than to Julia. Rita was the one invited to help her pick out her wedding dress.

I suddenly wondered why Julia wasn't invited.

"I'll check into this," I said. "Please call me if you hear from her."

I gave her my number even though she already had it. I'd given her my card when I went to the school.

"I will," she replied. "Will you call me when you talk to her?"

"Of course."

Some detective's said things meant to be reassuring. "I'm sure she's fine. Don't worry. She's okay."

I knew better.

Anna struck me as someone who was as dependable as the morning sun. If she had a responsibility, I had no doubt she'd fulfill it. No way she'd miss something as important as parent conferences. Not unless she couldn't be there.

I got in my car and drove over to Anna's house. Her silver KIA SUV was sitting in the driveway. One thing I noticed when I drove up were tire marks in front of the house. A car had burned rubber. Perhaps making a quick getaway.

A black Lexus? I had no proof of that but filed it away in the back of my mind.

I walked up to Anna's vehicle and looked inside. I didn't see anything unusual. Tested the doors and they were locked.

Then I walked up to the front door and rang the doorbell. Knocked sharply when no one answered right away. I looked in the window and everything was dark inside. It didn't appear like anyone was at home. I didn't see any signs of a struggle.

At that point, I had a decision to make. Normal procedure would be to call for backup. Or leave. That wasn't happening. I was going to search the house. I could enter a premise if I thought someone's life might be in danger. In this instance, I felt like I had probable cause. Anna didn't show up for work. Her sister was just murdered. I'd already asked the Lieutenant for around the clock protection. When he turned it down, he wouldn't say anything about me checking on them myself. He might even be expecting it.

With the information I had from the school, I could make a strong case that Anna could be inside. Hurt or dead. The proper procedure would be to call Julia and see if she had a key. A family member letting me in covered all my bases. That was a call I didn't want to make. Not yet anyway.

The decision was made. I was going in.

I tried the door.

Locked.

I went around to the back door which was locked as well.

No sign of activity in the back part of the house either.

The lock to the back door was flimsy. The next time I talked to Anna, I'd mention it to her. I pulled a credit card out of my wallet and was able to open it with little trouble. If I could get in that easily, so could the Strikers. Although, they'd just bust the door down. Which wouldn't be hard either. A strong shoulder would shatter the lock.

The door creaked open. I didn't enter right away.

A weird feeling came over me. Like I was in a Hitchcock movie.

I called out Anna's name. Identified myself.

"Cliff Ford. Chicago PD. I'm coming in."

No response.

Was I going to find a dead body?

I didn't think so. Why would someone break into the house, kill Anna, leave her body there, and then lock the doors on the way out?

I called out Anna's name several more times.

Then pulled my gun and entered the premises. I went from room to room to clear them.

No sign of Anna. No sign she'd even been there recently. In at least twelve hours.

The house was full of clues, though. No dishes in the sink spoke volumes. Anna's bed was still made. I touched her toothbrush to see if it was wet. Then her towel. Everything was dry. The shower hadn't been used that morning.

Of course, she could've stayed at her fiancé's house. I didn't know how to reach him. It occurred to me that I didn't even know his name. If Anna had mentioned it, I didn't remember.

Maybe Anna stayed with Julia. So they could protect each other.

I hoped that one of those scenarios was true but feared the worst.

If she was safe, why didn't Anna show up at work today?

The thought occurred to me to call the morgue. Then I decided not to overreact.

My first instinct was that Shiv had kidnapped her. For whatever reason. To get the girl. Maybe thinking she was Julia.

I pulled out my phone to make a call. Jamie answered on the first ring.

"Anna is missing," I said. "I think Shiv has her. Tell me you're still in town."

"I am. Was just going to call you in fact. Your ears must've been burning."

"Why were you going to call me?"

"I've been working on finding Shiv."

"Do you know where he is?"

"No luck so far. He's clearly gone into hiding. That gives me an idea. Do you know Anna's cell phone number?"

"I do."

I scrolled through my contacts and read it to her.

"Let me call you back," Jamie said.

It felt like an invasion of privacy, but I looked around Anna's house searching for clues. I didn't find anything out of the ordinary. If she was kidnapped, it happened outside the house. Of course, she might not be kidnapped at all. There might be a logical explanation for her disappearance.

I couldn't think of one but could only hope.

A half an hour later, my phone rang. Unknown caller.

"I found Anna's cell phone."

"How did you do that?"

I immediately regretted asking the question. It was the least important information I needed at the moment.

Thankfully, Jamie ignored the question.

"She's in South Chicago."

"What's the address?"

"No... Not so fast. It's not the part of town you want to go charging into."

"Tell me the number! If she's in a bad part of town, then I was right. Shiv kidnapped her."

"Ask yourself this question? Why would Shiv leave her cell phone on?"

"So we would know where she is."

"Exactly. He wants you to come there. It's a setup. Shiv doesn't want Anna. She's the bait. He wants you."

"Then I'll oblige him."

"It's too dangerous."

"I can handle myself."

"I'll get back with you. Go back to your office and wait for my call. Don't tell anyone about this. Not yet."

"Jamie! Give me the address."

The line went dead.

30

J amie lied to me about the cell phone.

After I hung up with her, it took me all of about a minute to realize it. Shiv wouldn't use the cell phone to set me up. The first thing I'd do in a missing person's case was track the cell phone. What Jamie implied was that Shiv purposefully left Anna's cell phone on, so that I could track the location of the phone. Thinking that I'd come there myself to try and rescue her.

Shiv would know that I wouldn't come by myself. If I knew where he was hiding Anna, I'd bring a small army with me. A SWAT team. A dozen police cruisers. A hostage negotiator. The house would be surrounded by armed men in less than ten minutes.

Blonde-haired girl was an enigma. Half the time she was helping me, the other half she was impeding my investigations. I honestly didn't know whether we should give her a medal or throw her in jail.

I immediately called her back. The number had been disconnected. That quickly. Or probably she destroyed the SIM card and threw the phone in a lake somewhere.

The realization sent me into an annoyed fit. I began pacing Anna's house. Contemplating my next move. The detective in me couldn't stop thinking about the mysterious blonde-headed lady.

Jamie, if that was her real name, had an agenda. At first, I thought it was the Bae girl. If that was really the girl's name. Now I wasn't so sure. Perhaps Jamie had motives beyond finding the Korean girl. Then I realized how pointless it was to go down that rabbit hole.

Regardless, I was back to square one. Anna was missing and I had no idea where she was. Not even sure where to begin to find her. That certainly had priority over discovering the identity or motives of the blonde lady, even if the cases were related.

I drove back to my office. Determined that, from that point on, things had to be done by the book.

I walked into the Lieutenant's office to fill him in on the details. As sketchy as they were.

"One of the sister's is missing," I said to him.

His eyes widened.

That statement clearly got his attention. He was the one who'd turned down protection. One of our worst fears was when it turned out to be the wrong decision. Like when we went to a domestic disturbance. A battered wife might warn us that her husband or boyfriend was going to kill her and that we should do something. We might want to, but we can't have a policeman outside the home of every woman in Chicago who was in danger.

Most of the time, nothing happens. It's heartbreaking when something does. Comes with the territory.

Anna was foreseeable, though. The Lieutenant knew that now. That didn't prevent him from trying to find a different explanation for her disappearance.

"How do you know she's gone?" he asked.

"Didn't show up for work today. Doesn't answer her cell phone. I went by her house. Her car's there, but she doesn't answer the door."

I didn't mention that I went inside. I did mention the tire tracks out front. I even took a picture of them and showed him on my phone.

"I want to get a warrant and track her cell phone and search her house."

"Go," he said. My cue to do whatever it took.

A couple of hours later, I had a warrant. Shortly after that, I had the last known location of Anna's cell phone.

One street over from her residence.

I drove to the location and scoured the street. I found the phone laying in the grass. Still working. I put on gloves and lifted it off the ground and put it into an evidence bag. More than likely, Shiv or one of his accomplices threw it out of the car as they were making their getaway. More conclusive evidence in my mind that Anna was kidnapped.

I looked for any other evidence around where the phone had landed but didn't see anything. Didn't put up police tape but made a note in my mind to remember where I had found it.

The search team had arrived at Anna's house, but I had the warrant, and they were waiting for me. When I arrived, I suggested they try the backdoor which I had left unlocked so they wouldn't have to bust the door down to enter the premises.

Then I drove back to my office and took Anna's cell phone out of the evidence bag. She had four missed calls from Julia. Not unexpected. By that time, I figured Julia would've begun to suspect something was up. I was halfway surprised she hadn't called me. It reminded me that I hadn't called her back. She was probably fuming mad at me.

I listened to the messages. Each one increasingly filled with anxiety. The last, full-blown panic.

Hearing Julia's voice sent a pang of regret through my heart. If it had been under any other circumstances, maybe we might've had a chance. This was too complicated.

I needed to call her back though. I could imagine the pain she was going through. She'd already lost one of her sisters. She was no doubt wondering if she'd lost the other.

Before I could dial the number, Anna's phone rang.

Julia.

I answered it. "Detective Ford."

Stunned silence on the other end. I could picture Julia's face. Mine was undoubtedly the last voice she expected to hear on the line.

"Why are you answering my sister's phone?" Julia said roughly. "Is Anna there with you? Has something bad happened to her?"

"She's not with me. I think Anna has been taken. I don't know that for a fact. But I'm fairly certain the Strikers have her."

"She didn't show up to work today."

"I know."

"I called the school. They said she missed her meetings."

"I know. I talked to the school earlier as well. That's why I'm investigating her disappearance. Any chance she's staying with her fiancé."

The question made no sense. I was holding Anna's phone.

"He's out of the country on business."

"I think you should come down here and answer some questions."

"What are you doing to find my sister?"

Julia sounded surprisingly calm.

"We're doing everything possible. I have someone at her house searching for clues now."

"Is that how you got her cell phone? Did she leave it at home? Anna would not leave her house without her cell phone."

"I found her phone along the side of the road. About a block from her home."

"Oh my..." Julia began to cry. "My sister's dead, isn't she?"

"We don't know that. At this point, we're treating it as a missing person's case. I can assure you I'm going to do everything in my power to bring your sister back alive."

"I thought you were going to provide us with protection."

I'd been waiting for that to come up.

"I put in the request to my supervisor. These things take time." I wasn't going to throw the Lieutenant under the bus. Even if he deserved it.

Before she could respond, I added, "That's a good point though. I don't think you should stay at your house. It's not safe. The Strikers might be after you as well. We need to get you to a safe place. Like I said, come to the station. You'll be safe here for the time being. We'll figure something out later."

I was sure I could get her around the clock protection now. Although, it'd be better if she stayed somewhere besides her house.

Maybe a hotel for a few days. Until we could get more information about what happened to Anna.

"Do you want me to send a cruiser to pick you up?" I asked.

"No. I'm leaving now. I want to have my car."

Julia hung up without saying goodbye. She arrived at the station within the half hour and was led into a room for questioning.

I had informed the Lieutenant she was coming.

"I think someone else should question her," I said to him. "I doubt she has any information. I'd rather spend my time focused on finding her sister."

Truthfully, I didn't want to face her at that moment. I could imagine how angry she was.

"That's a good idea," the Lieutenant said. "I'll have Carson question her. He was in charge of her sister's case back when we had it so he's already familiar with it."

Why did it have to be him?

I was suddenly sorry I had suggested another detective question Julia. He wasn't familiar with the case. I don't think he even picked up the file.

Now I wished my partner was on the job. I'd have him do it. I wouldn't put it past Carson to flirt with Julia. Then hit on her after the investigation was over. He'd have her phone number in the file.

Was I jealous?

No! I was only thinking of Julia. Trying to save her from having to deal with the biggest cad in our office. Although Julia might put that label on me at the moment. I was probably the last person she wanted to see or talk to. Our eyes met when she walked through the bullpen back to the questioning room. If looks could kill, I'd be like a cat. Dead. I'd need more than nine lives to save me.

My mind turned back to the investigation. Where did I begin? I didn't have a clue. While I was certain Shiv took Anna, I had no idea where he was. He could be anywhere. It had become apparent that he had a series of gang houses throughout south Chicago. Like the one on Dexter Street. The Striker's enterprise was larger than I had even imagined.

I decided to call Scully. The FBI agent. Maybe he could lean on the two suspects in custody and get an address. He might have another undercover agent deep in the Striker's organization who would have some inside information. At the very least, he should be apprised of the new developments.

I was grasping at straws but had no other ideas.

"Scully," he answered.

"Detective Ford, Chicago PD."

"What can I do for you?"

"Rita Navarez's sister is missing. I believe she's been kidnapped. Probably by the Strikers. I think Shiv is behind it."

"How long has she been missing?"

"I'm not sure. At least seven hours. She didn't show up for work this morning. They might've grabbed her yesterday afternoon. Or last night. The last time anyone saw her was yesterday afternoon. At her sister Julia's house. I was there. Anna and I went there to tell her about Rita's passing."

"This isn't our jurisdiction."

"I know that. I'm leading the investigation. I just wanted to keep you in the loop. Since it's related to Agent Navarez's death."

"How is it related?"

"Shiv had Rita killed because she was infiltrating his organization."

"Why would Shiv target the sisters?"

"For revenge."

I explained the circumstances surrounding Gabby's death. How Shiv murdered my wife to get back at me. Because I had arrested one of his men.

"Shiv is irrational," I explained. "For whatever reason, he has a thirst to avenge his men. We arrest some of his gang members and he retaliates. It's almost like he sees law enforcement like a rival gang. He's fearless. Not afraid to take on the entire police force."

"Keep me posted. I wish you luck in your investigation."

"If you can think of anything that will help me, let me know. Maybe the two men in your custody might have some information."

"Maybe."

"Can you ask them? Maybe they'd know where Shiv would take Anna. They must know where his hideouts are. I have evidence that the Strikers have been trafficking girls. They have to keep them somewhere. That might be where they took Anna."

"Maybe. I'll let you know if I find out anything."

"Thank you."

I hung up, not saying what I wanted to say. Why did he play things so close to the vest? We were on the same team. He was treating me like a pariah. Even though he got credit for a bust I made. A crime I solved. With the help of the blonde-haired lady.

But still.

That thought made me think of Jamie. I still hadn't told anyone about her. She was my best hope. She said she had an address. In south Chicago. She made up some bogus story about the cell phone so I wouldn't go down there. I could only hope she was hot on Shiv's trail. If I had read her right, she would help me. On her terms. I had to be patient.

As if on cue, my cell phone dinged. I had a text message.

7401 Seger Drive.

I stared at the message.

It had to be from Jamie. Who else could it be from?

Is that where Shiv is holding Anna?

It had to be.

I was up from my desk and on the move within seconds.

Once I got to my car, I paused. I needed to think about what I might be facing. Going to the address alone was impulsive.

What if Shiv was the one behind the message? Was it a trap? Did he want me to go there?

I didn't know who sent the message. Maybe Jamie. Maybe Shiv.

I had to know.

A debate raged in my mind. Should I call in the Calvary or go there myself?

I decided to go alone.

31

Darkness had fallen on the Windy City and Seger Street was in a part of Chicago that no cop went to alone in the daytime, much less at night. My trepidation was compounded by the fact that I was in my government issued detective's car. Obviously, a police vehicle. If I spray painted the word *Cop* on the driver's side door with an arrow pointed at me, it wouldn't have been more obvious. Might as well have a bullseye on the side as well.

On any given weekend in Chicago, anywhere from twenty to fifty people were shot and killed in similar neighborhoods. While it wasn't the weekend, I half expected the last thing I'd see on this earth was a flash of light out of the corner of my eye. The last thing I'd hear was the glass shatter in the windshield or one of the car door windows. From a bullet. That splattered my brain all over the car.

For now, I was still alive and one block from Seger Street. I wouldn't make the same mistake the Strikers had made over on Dexter Street and drive by the house. That'd only telegraph the fact that I was in the neighborhood and coming for them.

Coming for who? Or is it whom?

I didn't know who was in the house or which pronoun was proper in the thought.

I could only hope and pray the intel had come from Jamie. I half expected her to pop up in the back seat of my car at any moment. Even though I had checked when I got in it. The woman was spooky in how she operated so stealthily and so smoothly. With such efficiency. Almost like a ghost. More like a guardian angel.

I did say a prayer. A couple of them on the drive over. For Anna. And for me. For Jamie if she indeed planned on taking on Shiv by herself. Even prayed for Julia. That she'd forgive me. Though I didn't think I'd done anything to be forgiven for.

I parked the car. Intentionally trying not to park it under a lamppost. So it wouldn't be illuminated under a spotlight. Didn't matter. The light bulbs in all of the lampposts in the neighborhood had been shot out. The streets were as dark as a black lab. No porch lights were on either. Occasionally, I saw a dim light inside a house.

That made it easier for me to skulk around once I got the courage to leave my car. I breathed a sigh of relief when I made it to the cover of the houses. The biggest worry was when I hopped over the fences. Not knowing if a Doberman or pit bull was in the yard.

My gun was drawn just in case. My senses were on high alert.

I gave up trying to slow my heartbeat.

Once over the last fence, I settled in behind what I thought was the right house. I couldn't tell because the address would be in the front. Although, another thing I had noticed was that most houses didn't have numbers in front of them. I wondered how ambulances found the houses in an emergency. Probably the same way I had found this one. With the GPS on my phone.

I'd taken up a spot behind a bush in the backyard. As close as I dared get. About twenty paces from the back door. A light was on inside, but the porch light was either off, burned out, or shot out. The moon was behind the clouds, so all I could see was the outline of the house.

At some point, I had to make my move. One of the things that gave me pause was that I didn't see a Striker guarding the back door. If Anna was in the house, I suspected armed men to be guarding the entrances. Not that I wanted them to be there. It made my job easier if they weren't. But still it made me question myself.

What if this wasn't the house?

What if the intel was bad?

I didn't even know who sent me the address.

I certainly had no proof that Anna was being held there.

Could I go in with my gun drawn?

Was my career over in about ten minutes if I had the wrong house?

Was my life over less than two minutes if I had the right one?

I wasn't getting any younger. That's what I told myself in moments of indecision. Not going in wasn't an option. I had to know. Somebody sent me this address. Curiosity overrode my desire for self-preservation. Hopefully, I didn't have to choose between the two.

I crept toward the back door. As I got closer, I saw an object near the back entrance.

Not an object. A body.

I knelt down beside it. Beside him. Felt for a pulse. The man was dead. I turned him over carefully. This explained why I didn't see someone guarding the door. It also told me I was at the right place and that Jamie had been the one who sent me the text.

How did I know it was Jamie? Her signature was on the dead man's forehead. One bullet wound, just above the bridge of the nose. Her calling card. A gun lay next to the body. Missing a cartridge. Presumably, Jamie had separated the bullets from the gun. We'd probably find them later somewhere in the yard where she threw them.

Emboldened, I opened the back door. Not bothering to identify myself. More than likely, all the Strikers were dead. If not, I didn't want to give them a warning that I was coming in.

The back door opened into the kitchen. To the right of the kitchen was a door. With huge locks on it. The door was slightly ajar. I'd seen the same configuration before at the house on Dexter Street. I was certain it led to a basement.

Was that where they kept Anna? As much as I wanted to know, I had to make sure the house was clear.

I heard a noise in another room.

A grunting sound.

I came around the corner carefully.

A lamp cast my shadow over the room. In the corner were two men. Lying on the floor, hogtied. Their back feet were tied to their wrists in a most uncomfortable position. Their mouths were gagged. They appeared to be Strikers. One of them fit Shiv's description.

"Anyone else in the house?" I whispered.

They didn't answer, but I figured if anyone else was in the house, they were dead. These two men probably wished they were. Each had a twisted grimace on his face. Their mouths were contorted to the side and their eyebrows went up and down as they squeezed their eyes shut in pain and then opened them again.

I checked the house anyway. The house was only one story, and it took less than a minute to clear it.

I made a beeline for the basement.

With my gun still drawn I crept down the stairs. When I got to the bottom, I identified myself.

The lights were on.

The room was empty.

Anna wasn't there.

* * *

The Lieutenant showed up about thirty minutes later, with a small army in tow. Several police cruisers. A van to haul the two Strikers out of there. ASAP. A forensics' team. Even the coroner arrived. The Lieutenant probably wanted to get the dead Striker out of there as fast as possible as well.

We walked through the scene. Starting with the basement.

"This is where I think they were keeping Anna," I said.

"Why do you think that?"

"That's where they kept the girls on Dexter Street. Those locks on the door at the top of the stairs are there for a reason. The bathroom looks like it's been used recently. There's an empty pizza box on the table. I think she was definitely here."

"Doesn't matter what you think."

"That's true," I said. "Forensics will be able to tell. There should be DNA on that empty coke bottle." I pointed to it. Then led him into the bathroom.

"There's a wet toothbrush and towel in this room. There's hair in the hairbrush."

"Sure looks like someone was here recently. Probably a woman."

We went to the closet. I turned on the light.

Then I saw it.

A skirt and blouse.

The same ones Anna had been wearing yesterday at school. And at Julia's house.

My speech increased and matched my level of excitement.

I walked over to the clothes but didn't pick them up.

"This is what Anna was wearing yesterday. When I saw her at school. These are definitely her clothes."

"Okay. I'm with you. So where is she."

"Is Anna's sister still at the station?" I asked. "We should get a DNA sample while she's there. Then compare it to what we have here."

The Lieutenant nodded.

"I ask again. Where's the girl?"

"I don't know. I thought she'd be here."

"How did you know about this place?" he asked.

I knew that question was coming. I showed him the text on my phone.

"Did the blonde-haired lady send it?" the Lieutenant asked.

I nodded.

"I think so anyway," I said. "She was giving me a heads up that this was where the girl was being held."

"The bullet wound to the head of the dead Striker would certainly lead me to believe it was her."

"I'm hoping she took the girl," I said, almost to myself.

"Where would she take her?"

"I don't know."

"You don't know much."

"You don't like for me to make assumptions. If I told you what I thought, you'd say I was spitting in the wind, and it'd be all over my face soon."

He chuckled. "The woman could be dead for all we know."

I could feel my heart wince. If that was even possible.

"Let's assume she's not for now."

"What did the two low-lifes upstairs say?" he asked. "I assume you questioned them."

"The Strikers aren't talking. I took their gags off, but they clammed up. I even offered to take the hogties off them if they'd give me some information. I could see in his eyes that one of them was tempted... but they didn't say anything."

"Are you any closer to finding out the identity of the blonde-haired woman?"

"Nope."

I hoped he couldn't tell I was lying. He was trained to spot a lie. If he noticed, he didn't say anything.

"Why didn't you call for backup?" he asked. Typical Lieutenant. Grilling me instead of the Strikers.

"I didn't know what I had. I got a text. Like you said, we don't have extra men to spare. My partner doesn't start until next week. If he'd been here, we wouldn't have called for backup. We would investigate. See what we see. I followed the book on this one."

The Lieutenant let out a grunt and slightly nodded. As if to let me know he agreed with me.

"It seems like you're in the clear," he said. "You didn't fire your gun. You didn't hogtie the suspects. With the dead guy on the doorstep, you had probable cause to enter. Not how I would've played it, but it worked out. Lucky you weren't killed. Not a place to be alone at night."

"If the girl was here, I'm sure she was thinking the same thing. She was probably scared out of her wits. That's why I came. For her."

The Lieutenant's phone rang before we could get out of the basement.

"Does she need a doctor?" I heard the Lieutenant say to the caller.

"Have one check her out anyway? Then have Carson talk to her?"

He hung up the phone.

"What was that?" I asked, as if it was any of my business. He'd tell me if it wasn't.

"Good news," the Lieutenant said with a rare smile on his face. "The girl showed up at the station."

"Anna?"

"Yep."

"Is she okay?"

32

Ten days later

The church that held Rita's funeral was packed.

I stood off at a distance while everyone filed in, and I was one of the last ones to enter and stood in the back since all the seats were taken.

A few days before, Anna had called to thank me for everything I'd done to rescue her and also to invite me to the funeral. I felt obligated to go. Truthfully, it was the last place I wanted to be. I was there because Anna wanted me to be there.

I still hadn't talked to Julia.

Anna had been in the basement on Seger Street. She left shortly before I got there. She filled in a lot of the details at the station that night. The Lieutenant had rushed back to the station to supervise her questioning. Carson asked the questions, and the Lieutenant filled me in later.

As I suspected, Anna was kidnapped in front of her house. By the two Strikers. Shiv and Lefty were their names. Anna wasn't harmed or assaulted in any way. Which was a relief.

That's when the details became vague.

Anna heard a gunshot. Then shouting and a scuffle upstairs. When the door to the basement opened, she saw a woman wearing a black hoodie. Brandishing a gun. The woman rushed her out of the house. Into a waiting car. Drove her to the police station. Another younger girl was with her. She didn't get a good look at their faces.

"No." She didn't know their names.

I got the feeling that the Lieutenant believed Anna knew more than she was letting on. Of course, so did I. The woman in the hoodie was Jamie, the blonde-haired woman. For whatever reason, Anna didn't want to give too many details. Jamie had that effect on people. She didn't want her identity known. Anna wasn't going to give it away, and I sure wasn't going to add what I knew.

The Lieutenant didn't press the point. We were all just thankful Anna was safe, and the two Strikers were in custody with enough evidence to put them away for life.

Those trials would have to wait. Two days after Anna's rescue, Scully showed up. Said the FBI was taking jurisdiction. They had the men dead to rights on murder, conspiracy to commit murder, racketeering, making terroristic threats, and any number of other charges in the book they intended to throw at them.

The Lieutenant put up some resistance, but eventually caved, and the men were whisked away in a van to some unknown location. We'd get our chance to file state charges, the Lieutenant assured me. But he figured that'd be two to four years down the line.

It pained me that the FBI had taken jurisdiction. I wanted a chance to prove Shiv ordered my wife's murder. Scully assured me they were pursuing that investigation.

There must've been a hundred FBI personnel present in the church. Including Scully. I expected the FBI would be there in force since Rita worked for them, but I didn't expect that many.

The Lieutenant was there. As was Carson. Which fried my behind. Made me so angry I could barely see straight.

What was he doing there?

I knew he'd try to worm his way into Julia's life if given the chance.

Why did I care?

For Julia's sake. Not for mine.

What feelings I once had for Julia were buried deep in the cavernous abyss which were my emotions. I knew I'd never have Julia. But it was driving me crazy that Carson might. I wanted to somehow warn her.

I remembered the conversation like it was yesterday. The day this whole nightmare started. Carson was assigned to Rita's murder. At the time, it was just a Jane Doe case. I asked him how it was going.

"She's the prettiest stiff I've seen in a long time," Carson had said to me.

I wanted to hit him then, and my fist was in a ball now. Even several weeks later. Probably more so now that I actually knew Anna and Julia. I felt like I knew Rita. He was disrespecting her. How could he have the gall to show up at her funeral? Did he still think she was a 'stiff'?

"Maybe she's got a pretty sister I can meet," Carson said that day.

I was seething inside. I wanted to scream at the top of my lungs. Warn everyone there that Carson couldn't be trusted. I wanted to find Julia afterward and tell her what Carson had said about her sister.

Surely Julia was smart enough to see through someone like Carson. I wasn't sure. I didn't actually know her that well. She was probably vulnerable. Her sister just died. She needed someone to comfort her. A shoulder to cry on.

It should've been me.

The service started. They played a song. A couple people got up to speak. Julia wasn't one of them. Anna did speak. She gave an emotional and heartfelt tribute to her sister. We made eye contact. She spotted me standing in the back. In the middle of her eulogy. As much as I was trying to be inconspicuous, she could clearly see me.

I noticed her smile slightly when she saw me. It warmed my heart. She saw me again at the end when the family exited the church following the casket out to the waiting hearse. To my knowledge, Julia didn't see me.

At the cemetery, I stood off at a distance again. Somehow feeling like I was intruding if I got closer. The preacher's message was brief but moving.

When the graveside service ended, Anna made a beeline toward me. Before I could leave. Actually, I wanted to leave, but my car was blocked in.

"Thank you for coming," Anna said.

I suddenly was glad I did stay. Her words warmed my heart. Just hearing her voice made me feel better. She wasn't Julia but was the next best thing in a weird sort of way. The only connection to Julia I had left.

"You're welcome," I said warmly. "It was a beautiful service. You did good. I didn't know your sister, but I'm sure she would've appreciated your words. I'm very sorry for your loss."

I was rocking back and forth on my feet, nervously. My head was down. For whatever reason, I didn't want to make eye contact. My hand was firmly in my pocket. Anna didn't know that I was the first person to see her sister in the morgue. I'd never disclosed that fact to them. Rita's face was seared into my memory.

"We didn't expect that many people," Anna said. "I had no idea Rita had that many friends and colleagues."

"I doubt that church has ever had that many guns in it at any one time," I said, with a slight and forced grin.

Anna laughed politely.

"How's Julia holding up?" I blurted. Before I could stop myself.

Anna turned and looked back behind her. Toward Julia. She was walking toward a car. Julia looked our way. Saw us and then kept walking toward the car. Carson had hold of her arm and was escorting her.

I could feel my jaw clench!

I gritted my teeth to keep from saying something.

"Julia's taking it hard," Anna said. "As you can imagine."

I couldn't help myself.

"Julia needs to be careful. Is she dating Carson?"

Anna waved her hand dismissively.

"They went out once. Not really a date. He wanted to talk about the investigation over dinner. I think. It's not anything serious."

As if I could be any angrier.

Carson was using the investigation to manipulate his way into a date with Julia. Taking advantage of her. Totally against protocol.

I had a good mind to tell the Lieutenant. Better yet, when I saw Carson at the office, I'd take him out back and beat the daylights out of him.

Then get thrown in jail and off the force. Carson would love that.

"I gotta go," Anna said. "You're welcome to come by my house. We're having a reception for friends and family. Julia would like to see you, I'm sure."

I wasn't sure about that.

"I'm sorry. I can't. But give Julia my deepest sympathies."

I didn't know if Carson was going to be there, but I assumed he would be. I didn't trust myself to be in the same room with him. To see him with Julia. Just the thought was driving me crazy.

Anna held out her hand. I shook it. She didn't let go right away. Tears had welled up in her eyes.

"I can't thank you enough for what you did for us. You saved my life. I know Julia appreciates it too. We both do."

Was it that obvious? Could Anna tell that I had feelings for her sister?

"You're welcome," I muttered barely above a whisper. Suddenly finding myself fighting back my own emotions.

Then she abruptly turned and walked away. I watched her all the way to the car. Her fiancé took her arm, looked over at me, and opened the door for her. Then got in behind her and they drove away.

I stood there stunned. Unable to move. Not sure what I felt. I guess because I was incapable of feeling anything.

Later that night, I sank into a deep depression. Didn't even try to get out of it. Plopped down on the couch with a soda and turned on the TV and just stared at it. My mind was elsewhere. Eventually, I grabbed the remote and turned it off. Roughly. Tossed the remote aside and sank deeper into the couch and deeper into my thoughts.

It had all happened so fast. One day I met a pretty girl in a coffee shop. Two weeks later my world was turned upside down, and she was out of my life forever. I presumed. Before I even had a chance to process any of it.

My sister, Shay, called and tried to talk me out of the funk. She was the one person who could usually do so. I told her everything that had happened. About the girl at the morgue. *Champions* bar. The Strikers. Anna's kidnapping. The blonde-haired woman. Discovering the gun that killed Gabby. My feelings for Julia.

I unloaded it all. Dumped all my feelings on the table at once. Shay listened supportively and let me ramble on, even though it was getting late.

"I don't think I'll ever feel anything for a woman again," I said, in my most feeling-sorry-for-myself voice.

"Honey. It feels that way now," Shay said. "It'll pass. Do you want me to come over?"

"Nah. I'll be okay."

"The sun'll come up tomorrow."

"If you start singing, I'm going to hang up the phone."

Whenever either of us was feeling blue, we mentioned the song. Both of us had been known to sing it occasionally. When the other needed a good laugh. Neither of us could sing.

Shay did start singing.

"Stop it!"

Then I joined in. We both sang the entire verse. I felt a little bit better.

"What are you going to do tomorrow?" Shay said. "You want to have lunch?"

"Sure. I'll meet you right after I go to the morgue."

I was kidding.

"You are a sick man, Cliff."

"Nothing like a good murder mystery to take my mind off my problems." I yawned as I said it. I was tired and starting to fall asleep.

"I'm hanging up now," Shay said.

A ding on my phone startled me.

I'd gotten a text.

"I should go too," I said, wondering who would be texting me at that hour.

After I hung up with Shay, I pulled it up.

Carson is behind your wife's murder. And Rita's.

Whatever happens tomorrow, go with it.

I was fully awake now.

33

When I arrived the next morning at the station, I had no idea what to expect. I hadn't slept a wink, and my thoughts were running as wild as a loose stallion. What did the text mean?

I assumed Jamie sent it. The mysterious blonde-haired lady who never ceased to amaze me. I thought she was long gone from Chicago, and I'd never hear from her again.

Who else could it be from?

The message was from an unknown number. It certainly seemed like something she'd do.

The message was almost beyond my comprehension. Carson was behind Gabby's murder?

Why?

What did it mean?

What was going down today that I needed to go with?

Carson was sitting at his desk doing busywork. It took all of my willpower not to glare at him. I couldn't give anything away. If something was going down, I wanted him to be as shocked as me if and when it did.

It didn't take long for events to start to unfold.

Scully walked through the doors. With purpose.

Two agents trailed him. One was carrying a large satchel.

They went straight to the Lieutenant's office and closed the door. I'd worked in that office for several years, and that was the first time I'd seen the door closed.

The Lieutenant's office had a big picture window, and I could see

Scully standing in front of the Lieutenant's desk talking to him. The conversation went on for a good half an hour. The longest thirty minutes of my life.

The door opened and the Lieutenant summoned me into his office.

I could feel a hundred eyes follow me into it. The Lieutenant closed the door behind me.

"What's going on?" I asked.

"Have a seat," the Lieutenant said.

"I prefer to stand."

"Have a seat," he said again, in a stronger tone.

Scully was sitting in the other seat. His two cohorts were standing against the wall. A stack of papers sat in front of the Lieutenant. He motioned to Scully with his hand. Like he was giving him the floor to lead the conversation.

My ears were ringing from the pounding of my heart pulsing through my neck and head.

"There have been some developments," Scully said. "We have evidence that one of the detectives in this department is affiliated with the Strikers."

"Carson," I said.

Scully nodded. I could see the Lieutenant grimace out of the corner of my eye.

The Lieutenant handed me some of the papers that were on his desk.

"Carson's a mole?" I asked, as I took them from him.

"More than a mole," the Lieutenant said. "He's running their operations."

"What?"

I knew Carson was dirty, but that information was hard to process.

"Carson is the brains behind the Strikers," the Lieutenant said. "That's why we could never nail them. He was covering for them. Warning them if we were ever going to raid them. Eliminating witnesses when necessary. He even led some of the investigations against them which is why they never led to any arrests."

The Lieutenant shook his head in disbelief. His lips were twisted in disgust. I could only imagine the blowback he was going to get from his bosses. All of this happened right under his nose.

I looked through the papers. Bank statements. A list of phone numbers.

"What am I looking at?" I asked.

"Some of those bank accounts are owned by Carson. Some by the Strikers. By Shiv. There are dozens of transfers between the accounts. Carson got a piece of everything. Drug money. Prostitution. Money laundering."

One of the bank statements had seven-figure numbers on it. In the name of some corporation. I assumed a shell corporation that they'd traced back to Carson.

"There's more," Scully said. "Smitty, the man we have in custody —the one you arrested—he's the one who killed your wife."

"I knew it," I said soberly. "How do you know?"

"He's talking. He cut a deal."

That caused an adrenaline rush. That he'd made a deal was the last thing I wanted to hear.

"Is he getting out?" I had visions of Smitty going into the witness-protection program and never truly paying for killing my wife. Shiv and Carson were bigger fish. They might let the smaller fish go for the bigger bust.

"No," Scully said emphatically. "He's pleading guilty to your wife's murder and is willing to implicate Shiv."

"What's the deal?"

"We take the death penalty off the table. He'll spend life in prison without parole."

"I can live with that."

Scully added. "He's tied to a dozen other murders. So is Shiv."

"We can close a lot of unsolved cases with his testimony," the Lieutenant said.

"Where does Carson fit into my wife's murder?" I asked. That's the thing I was most dying to know.

"Carson ordered the hit on your wife," Scully said.

"How do you know?"

"We have text messages and phone calls between Shiv and Carson. On the day Gabby was killed. And texts and calls with Smitty. Between all three of them."

I slumped back in my chair.

"Do we know why Carson would kill my wife?" I asked.

"Because you nailed their man. Put him in jail." The Lieutenant's tone was angry.

Then almost apologetic. "You were right about the Strikers. You just fingered the wrong man. Turns out he was one of our own. There's nothing I hate more than a dirty cop."

"We can tie Carson to Rita's . . Agent Navarez's killing as well. He called Shiv on the day she was killed. We think Carson ordered that killing as well."

"Do you have the phone?" I asked, knowing that was the best evidence they could get to prove their theory.

"Carson has it on him," the Lieutenant said. "We're going to nail him. Right here and now. All we have to do is call the number, and the phone'll ring. We'll have him dead to rights. He'll never be able to explain it."

A burst of adrenaline pulsed through me. The *Hipsters* coffee was kicking in. So was the thought of seeing Carson's face when we busted him.

"I'll go get him," the Lieutenant said. He opened the door and called for Carson to come into his office.

Instead of coming in, Carson bolted out of the bullpen and ran out the door.

Scully didn't give chase, which surprised me.

A few seconds later, I knew why.

Two FBI agents brought Carson back into the bullpen. Handcuffed. Carson looked like he'd been in a tussle.

They led him into the Lieutenant's office.

"What's this all about?" Carson asked roughly.

"You know. Why did you run, you piece of scum?" the Lieutenant said, getting right in his face.

"You're under arrest for murder," Scully said. "Conspiracy to commit murder. Money laundering. Too many things to name. You have the right to remain silent. Anything you say can and will be used against you in the court of law. You know the drill."

Carson didn't say anything. By the look on his face, he looked resigned. Like he knew he'd been caught. The proverbial kid with his hand in the cookie jar. Except Carson was the worst of the worst. A crooked cop using his power to kill people, then covering it up.

I despised the man.

It took every ounce of strength not to attack him.

Scully pulled out his phone and dialed a number.

A phone rang in the bullpen. Coming from the direction of Carson's desk.

Scully walked out of the office toward the sound. The Lieutenant followed him. So did I. The men holding Carson stayed behind.

The ringing was clearly coming from Carson's desk. Then it stopped.

Scully pulled on the desk drawer. It was locked.

"Do I need a warrant?" Scully asked the Lieutenant.

"Hell no. This is government property. You have my permission to break the lock. Actually, move over."

The Lieutenant grabbed the handle and jerked it hard. The lock shattered, and the door opened.

A phone was inside the desk. Scully dialed the number again, and it started ringing. Scully took out a pair of gloves, put them on, then removed the phone from the drawer and put it in an evidence bag.

We all walked back into the Lieutenant's office. Now Carson had a look of sheer terror on his face. His eyes were wide as a plug nickel.

"Get the scum out of my office!" the Lieutenant said angrily.

Scully directed his men to take Carson out of there.

He glared at me as they dragged him away. I glared back.

"We'd like to ask Detective Ford some questions," Scully said to the Lieutenant. "Can we use one of your rooms?"

"Of course. Ford will show you the way."

I led them to an interrogation room. Sat down in one of the seats. Scully sat across from me. Then directed his men to wait outside.

It felt weird being on the other side of the table.

"Thank you," I said to him after he sat down across from me. "Where did you get all the information? How did you know Carson was behind things?"

"Anonymous tip," Scully said with a sly grin. "Came into our office a couple of days ago. It took a minute to verify it. We already had the testimony of Smitty, the man in custody. The one you arrested. We were getting close to nailing Shiv. We didn't know about Carson. Not until you sent us that information."

"Excuse me."

"Don't worry. Your secret's safe with me."

"I don't know what you're talking about."

"We know you sent the anonymous tip."

"I didn't send it."

"Right."

"Seriously, I didn't send it."

"You don't have to keep up the ruse with me. We tracked it to your computer. I know you tried to send it through a server in Korea, but you can't fool the FBI. We have ways to track the information."

Jamie.

She obviously sent them the anonymous tip and made it look like it came from me. How did she do it? Not my biggest concern at the moment.

"Am I in trouble?" I asked.

"No. On the contrary. You're a hero. You single-handedly brought down the biggest gang in Chicago. The Strikers are out of business. You helped us nail a dirty cop. He killed one of our agents. We found her killers because of you."

"Thank you."

"I should be thanking you."

"Carson killed my wife."

The reality was just starting to hit me. Even though I'd received the text message, it didn't seem real. Now it seemed as real as a train barreling down on me.

"I know," Scully said. "I'm sorry for your loss. This won't bring your wife back. But it helps to know the men responsible will pay for their crimes and are off the streets so they can't do it to someone else. It's what we do. You know that as well as anyone."

"I hope you have enough evidence to nail him to the wall."

"Carson's going to jail for a long time. Hopefully, not a long time. We'll go after the death penalty. For sure. For him and Shiv. Killing a federal agent was not a smart thing to do. There are a lot of people who want a shot at him. We've got everything we need. A money trail. Phone records. The testimony of the Striker. Thanks to you."

"I'm glad I could help."

"Is there anything we can do for you?" Scully asked.

"There's one thing," I said, hesitantly.

"Name it."

"Can you call Rita's sisters? Julia and Anna. Tell them about Carson. They should know that he was the one behind their sister's murder."

"I'll do that today."

I wish I were a fly on the wall.

34

Two months later

My morning routine still hadn't changed. *Hipsters* was still my go to place for my coffee fix. I ordered the same coffee smoothie every morning. Except on Sundays. Katy was still behind the counter. Jed still called out names when the orders were ready.

If there were such a thing, Jed would be the face of *Hipsters*. A throwback from the days of hippies. Long hair in dreadlocks. Unshaven. He wore a tight, form-fitting red jacket with sleeves halfway down his arms and a white tee-shirt underneath, tucked into skintight jeans. He gave me no more than a glance as he bustled to keep up with the demand and didn't even bother to call out my name written on the side of the large to-go cup. He didn't have to. I already knew my drink was ready.

I took a big sip and scanned the crowd for a place to sit.

As usual, *Hipsters* was hopping, and the line was out the door. Only one seat was available. Facing the wall. Not ideal. I liked to have my back facing the wall. Looking out. In case someone tried to sneak up on me. As if that could happen in a coffee shop. I touched my gun on my hip as I walked over to the seat.

The man sitting across from the empty seat was deep in thought.

"Is this seat taken?" I asked.

"Yes," he said.

I looked around and didn't see anyone.

"She went to the restroom."

"Okay."

I turned to walk away. I was on my motorcycle, so I'd have to stand and drink my smoothie.

I suddenly felt a presence behind me.

"Are you trying to steal my seat?" a familiar voice said from that direction.

Julia.

I turned and faced her.

"Steal is a strong word. I didn't know you owned it."

"I actually do. I own this whole bar. I bought it."

"What?"

"I'm joking."

Julia gave me a wide grin. I could feel my heart melt, and my shoulders suddenly relaxed. It'd been a couple of months since I'd felt it.

"It's good to see you," I said, not knowing any other comeback.

"I was hoping you'd be here," Julia said sheepishly.

"Is everything okay?" I asked, suddenly concerned. "Is Anna okay?"

The man sitting in the seat facing the wall stood and left. Someone else started to grab the seats.

"These are ours," I said, then moved my suit jacket to the side so they could see my badge and the gun on my hip.

We sat down. It felt like déjà vu. A flashback to two months ago. The day my life was turned upside down by the mysterious woman who now sat in front of me. It felt like a dream. It felt good.

Julia seemed nervous. "You should know that I don't give my phone number out to strangers," she said with a grin to know she was kidding.

"I already have your phone number," I quipped.

"I figured you deleted it off your phone. After the way I treated you."

Julia turned her head to the side so she wasn't looking at me.

She couldn't know how many times I'd looked at my phone and wanted to dial her number, but didn't. I think I still had her nasty message on my phone. I hadn't had the resolve to delete it. I was saving it in case I wanted to hear her voice one more time. My sister, Shay, said that was masochistic. I didn't disagree with her.

"You were going through a hard time," I said.

I saw her wipe away a tear that had escaped her eye.

"You said you were hoping I'd be here," I said, in a soft tone to match her mood. "Were you looking for me?"

"I wondered... if maybe... you'd like to." Julia was stammering like she was struggling to get out the words.

She took a deep breath.

"My sister's getting married. You know. Anna. I was wondering if you'd be my date to the wedding."

I couldn't believe what I was hearing.

"How do I know you are really Julia?" I joked.

"What do you mean?" she asked, as her eyes suddenly widened and the tears dissipated.

"How do I know you aren't Anna?" I asked. "Trying to pull a fast one on me. Like you used to do to all your boyfriends."

"I don't think Anna's fiancé would be too happy about that."

"How do I know you don't have four sisters?" I added.

Julia laughed.

Then I said, "Is that even possible? Four identical... what *quadtuplets*? Is that even a word?"

"It's quadruplets," Julia corrected me.

"That's what I mean! How do I know you're not identical sister number four?"

"Do you want to go or not?" she asked roughly.

"Of course. When's the wedding?"

"Actually. It's four months from now."

I laughed this time.

"Can I see you between now and then?"

She reached out her hand and took mine. A tingle went down my spine and didn't stop until it reached my toes.

"It's may," Julia said.

"I don't understand. The wedding is in May? I thought you said it was in four months."

"No, silly. Not May the month. *May* I see you between now and then is the proper way to structure the sentence. Not *can* I see you."

"Do you want to see me or not?" I asked strongly.

"Absolutely!" Julia smiled warmly.

"When?

"How about tonight? Dinner."

"Perfect."

"Where do you want to go?" Julia asked.

Anyplace but *Champions* bar.

Not The End

SNEAK PEEK
BOOK TWO OF CLIFF HANGERS SERIES

Mr. & Mrs. Platt

A CLIFF FORD MYSTERY

THE CLIFF HANGERS
MR. & MRS.
PLATT
TERRY TOLER

1

Two Years Later

M r. and Mrs. Robert S. Platt walked into the Regency luxury, five-star hotel in downtown Chicago coming up on their sixth hour as husband and wife. The girl at the front desk was friendly and accommodating.

"We have you booked in the honeymoon suite," she said with a smile. "Congratulations on your nuptials."

Sylvia, the beaming bride, flashed her rings which cost just under a hundred thousand dollars for the set. Robert could never afford such extravagance. His wife came from old Jewish money from the North Shore. A source of angst between Sylvia and her parents who weren't particularly pleased with her choice of husband. Once they realized they couldn't convince her otherwise, they spoiled the pair with gifts and money.

Including an extravagant wedding by anyone's standards. In addition, Sylvia's parents provided an all-expenses paid honeymoon to the British Virgin Islands along with a wedding night in the honeymoon suite at the prestigious Regency hotel in downtown Chicago.

"Would you like some champagne brought to your room?" the clerk asked.

In sync, Robert and Sylvia answered at the exact same time except with different answers.

"Yes please," Robert said.

"No thank you," Sylvia answered.

She thought Robert had a drinking problem and, now that they were married, was already trying to change him.

"It's on the house," the girl behind the counter said. "Compliments of the manager."

Robert caught the clerk's eye and gave her a nod of the head. "Since it's free, go ahead and bring it up," he said tersely.

Sylvia let out a huge sigh but didn't protest further.

The clerk handed them the keys and called for the bellman who was standing to the side. She gave him the room number, and he directed the couple to follow him.

"You're on the top floor," he said.

"How many floors are there?" Sylvia asked hesitantly. She was afraid of heights.

"Forty-three."

Robert took her hand and squeezed it reassuringly.

When they arrived at the room, Sylvia seemed to lose her concern. She ran from room to room like a silly schoolgirl.

"Robert, come look at the bedroom," he heard her say from the other room.

"Just leave the bags here," Robert said. "We'll take care of them."

Robert slipped a five-dollar bill out of his pocket and handed it to the bellman who was unable to hide the disappointment on his face. Probably used to big spenders in this suite. Once the bellman was gone, Robert hurried into the bedroom as his wife called for him a second time.

The master suite was as big as a small house. A large king-sized bed seemed dwarfed by the size of the room and the three separate areas. A sitting room off to the side had a huge plate glass window overlooking Lake Michigan.

Sylvia was in the bathroom and called for Robert a third time. His mouth almost flew open when he entered it. Everything was marble. The floors. The countertop. The large, walk-in shower with at least a dozen spray faucets. The large jacuzzi tub had tints of off white and red marble on the sides and walls.

Lush towels and two bathrobes that said *His* and *Hers* hung on hooks on the walls.

Robert didn't remember seeing Sylvia so happy. She gushed like you'd expect from a new bride. She threw her arms around Robert's neck and gave him a big kiss.

Before he could comment, she was off exploring the other rooms.

Robert went back into the living room, gathered up the bags, and brought them to the bedroom. He didn't dare open them. Sylvia was particular about her things and would want to unpack them herself.

When he heard his name and another squeal of delight, he made his way to the kitchen and dining room area. In the room was a massive dining room table that would seat at least a dozen people. That struck him as odd since a honeymoon suite would only be for two people. Perhaps couples held after wedding receptions there for special guests and family.

A knock on the door interrupted his thoughts.

Probably the champagne.

The bellman sat the large bucket filled with the bottle and ice on the dining room table and then stood waiting for a tip. Robert pulled out another five-dollar bill and handed it to him.

This could get expensive, he thought. Good thing her parents were paying for it.

Sylvia came out of the kitchen area with what looked to be a menu in her hand.

"I'm famished," she said. "Let's order room service."

"That's a good idea," Robert said.

Sylvia ordered a Gluten-Free Penne with pappardelle pasta. No chicken or shrimp but with wild mushrooms and edamame on top. Robert ordered Cigar City braised bone-in short ribs in a red wine sauce, with onion soup, steamed asparagus, and whipped Yukon potatoes.

When the food arrived, and for the first time in what seemed like several months, Sylvia actually looked relaxed. While waiting, she had taken a shower and changed to more casual clothes. Robert had taken his suit jacket off, loosened his tie, and unbuttoned his collar as well though he didn't expect the tension to leave his shoulders anytime soon.

He opened the bottle of champagne and poured two glasses. Sylvia even took one sip, much to his surprise. They then allowed themselves to think about the activities of the day. Which seemed like a blur to Robert.

"I can't believe the Rabbi forgot the rings," Sylvia said, almost giggling like she'd had a full glass of champagne even though she'd only had a sip.

"I didn't even notice," Robert said, letting out his own still-tense laugh.

"He pronounced us man and wife, and we just stood there," Sylvia said. "I was, like, something's wrong. Did we forget something? Then I remembered we hadn't exchanged rings or said our vows!"

"How old is that Rabbi?" he asked.

"I don't know. But he's been there since I was a little girl. Bless his heart. He's forgetful in his old age."

"Something always goes wrong at a wedding. If that's the worst of it, then it's not so bad."

"Forgetting the rings is a pretty big deal. Daddy didn't look very happy."

"You know how he is. If everything's not perfect..." Robert said it almost bitterly.

"I'm going to get changed." She gave him a seductive look as she stood to leave the room. "I have a surprise for you." She disappeared into the bathroom and closed the door.

Robert went into the bedroom and got out of his suit and into shorts and a tee shirt. Then went back into the dining room and downed another glass of champagne. He set the glass down and opened a set of double doors that led out onto a balcony and stepped out onto it. The height caused him to almost lose his balance and took a second to get used to it.

A heavily secured steel railing ran around the outside of the balcony and came up to his chest. The bellman had said the honeymoon suite and presidential suite were the only two rooms in the entire hotel with balconies.

Two chairs and a table were in the small area and Robert sat down in one of them and took in the view. By that time, darkness had set in, but the moon provided enough light to still see the waves of Lake Michigan beating against the shoreline. The city lights in both directions delivered spectacular views in all directions.

After a few minutes, Sylvia called for him.

"I'm ready, Robert," she said.

He stood and went back inside.

"What do you think?" She was wearing a white nightgown with a train, and she twirled around in a circle.

"Beautiful," Robert said as he walked over to her and took her in his arms. He kissed her hard and deep.

"Let's go into the bedroom," she said.

"In a second. I want to show you something."

Robert took her by the hand and led her toward the balcony.

Sylvia resisted.

"Trust me. It'll be okay," he said. "I've got you. You have to see the view."

"I don't like heights."

"I know. It has a railing all around it. You'll be fine."

Sylvia was hesitant but finally agreed. She stepped out onto the balcony gingerly, with trepidation like she was scared to death. Which he knew she was.

"Okay. I've seen enough," Sylvia said, as she started back into the safety of the room.

"Just a second! We forgot something."

"What?" she asked.

"I never carried you over the threshold."

Before she could say anything, Robert had Sylvia in his arms. He played linebacker in high school and was a bigger than average guy. He hadn't lost all his muscles and was able to pick up his petite wife with little trouble.

She let out a nervous laugh and looked back at the railing. Her head was precariously close to it.

"You're fine. I have you," Robert said. "Just relax."

He swung around so they were facing the doors that led into the room and started to walk forward like he was going to carry her over the threshold of the two double doors.

Suddenly, Robert took two steps back and in one motion flung Sylvia backward over the railing.

He leaned over to watch her fall the forty-three stories.

By the end, she was barely a blip. Robert had to squint to even see her hit the concrete sidewalk below.

Without emotion, Robert took the glass of champagne off the balcony table and took another sip. Then dropped it on the balcony floor.

The crystal shattered.

Careful not to step on any glass, Robert went back into the room, left the double doors slightly ajar, and turned out all the lights.

He went into the bedroom, pulled back the covers on Sylvia's side of the bed, and mussed the sheets.

He walked around the bed to the other side. Pulled back the covers. Got under them and went to sleep.

2

C liff Ford arrived at the Regency hotel within thirty minutes of being awakened from a deep sleep. He hadn't expected to get a call. Technically, at midnight, he was off the clock. Tomorrow was his wife's birthday and he'd taken the day off. Now that he was at the scene of an apparent homicide, his day off wouldn't start until he finished whatever preliminary investigation was required.

"What have you got?" Cliff asked the beat cop in charge of the scene who had requested a homicide detective.

Cliff could see a body lying on the sidewalk behind yellow police tape. A crowd had gathered. He didn't see any reporters which caused him to breathe an undetectable sigh of relief.

"Female," the cop said in his most serious tone. "Deceased. Looks to be in her early thirties. Wearing a nightgown. Severe trauma to several parts of her body."

That immediately didn't make sense. Why would a woman be wearing a nightgown outside the hotel? He didn't bother to ask if she had identification on her. He'd have said so if she did.

"Any witnesses?" Cliff asked.

"None that we know of."

"Did anybody touch my crime scene?"

The cop hesitated.

A jolt of concern flashed through Cliff.

"I was the first on the scene," he said. "When I arrived, I checked for a pulse. When I didn't find one, I called it in and secured the scene."

"Good work," Cliff said. The first on the scene had to tend to the victim first. Even if it potentially contaminated the evidence.

"Thank you, sir."

The beat cop looked wet behind the ears, but it seemed like he'd done everything by the book. Cliff walked toward the body and lowered his shoulder to go under the tape. He squatted down beside the lifeless figure, careful not to touch anything. Just observe. The beat cop stood over his shoulder.

After a good minute, Cliff checked for a pulse even though he didn't expect to find one. The visual was confusing and not just because of the nightgown. The woman had severe injuries and a number of obvious broken bones. Her right leg was contorted and lay in an unnatural position—sticking out and to the left with broken bones visible. Her arms and legs looked to have multiple fractures.

Her head was turned to the right in the opposite direction of her leg. It had sustained severe trauma, and the side of her face that lay against the sidewalk was basically caved in on the one side.

The cause of death could be any number of things.

Strange.

Cliff stood and turned his attention to the surroundings. His first thought was that the woman was attacked right where she lay. Not an ideal place to murder someone, if there was such a thing, but doable. The area was well lit, but the lobby was around the corner. As was the parking lot. Unless someone had been looking out the window or happened to be walking on the sidewalk at the time of the attack, they might not see or hear anything.

If anyone had, they would've come forward by now.

The injuries didn't seem consistent with blunt force trauma. They were too severe. Something you'd be more likely to see in a torture chamber than in a public place.

No obvious gunshot wounds. Someone in the hotel would've heard a shot ring out, so Cliff had already moved that down the list of possibilities.

Did she fall?

Cliff looked up in the night sky at the building and scanned each floor as far as he could. The top of the building wasn't clearly visible, but he could see the occasional light on in a room which gave him some depth perspective. From what he could tell, none of the windows opened.

A man suddenly approached, ducked under the tape, and walked up to where Cliff and the beat cop were standing.

"Hey!" the cop said. "You're not allowed in here."

"I'm the manager of the hotel."

Cliff motioned to the cop that it was okay. He needed answers, and the manager might be the person to provide them.

"What's your name, sir?" Cliff asked.

"Gil Hildebrand."

Cliff motioned for the man to follow him. He led him away from the body, still inside the yellow tape but out of earshot from the crowd which had grown in size.

"Does this hotel have a roof?" Cliff asked.

The manager chuckled slightly. "Of course."

Cliff realized how foolish the question must've sounded.

"What I mean is, can guests of the hotel access it?"

"There's an observation deck at the top and a bar."

"Was it open tonight?"

"Yes. It closed at ten. On the weekend, it's open until two in the morning."

"Was it crowded?"

"Not like the weekends, but there would've been a dozen or so people up there along with the staff."

The woman wasn't dressed for a party. The white silky nightgown had a slight train. That made her noticeable. No way she walked through a crowded bar without being noticed. For that matter, it was just as unlikely that she walked through the lobby without anyone noticing her.

Was she a prostitute?

Cliff began to consider the possibility that the body had been dumped.

Out of the corner of his eye, Cliff saw that a forensic team had arrived. One of the women on the team walked straight to the body and began to examine it. He had to cut short his conversation with the manager to talk to her.

She was already taking the woman's temperature.

"I'm Cliff Ford," he said after she finished.

"Roz," the woman replied without bothering to look up at him.

"Do you have a time of death?" Cliff asked. He knew that's why she was taking the woman's temp. When circulation stops, the body cools by one to two degrees per hour until it reaches ambient temperature. She examined the woman's pupils and the bottom of her feet before she answered.

The woman was barefoot. Another inconsistency in the crime scene. A woman wouldn't be walking around late at night with no shoes on.

"From the looks of it, I'd say... more than an hour, but less than two hours."

Cliff looked at his watch. 11:33

That ruled out the party on the roof. It seemed unlikely that a woman wearing a nightgown could jump off the roof without anyone seeing her. Cliff stared in the sky and strained again to see the top of the building.

As if he had read his mind, the manager approached and said, "There's no way she jumped off the roof, if that's what you're thinking. There's a high railing and a landing net that goes around the entire building to prevent that from happening."

Cliff looked at his watch again.

He'd been there thirty minutes and was no closer to piecing together what had happened than when he had gotten there.

Clearly, he wasn't going to be finished by midnight.

If he didn't get answers fast, he might not even be home in time to fix his wife's breakfast in bed for her birthday.

3

Cliff took out his phone and dialed his wife, Julia. She answered on the first ring, which meant she was still up.

"I wanted to be the first to wish you a happy birthday," Cliff said.

"Thank you," she said through a noticeable yawn. Midnight was about the latest she ever went to bed.

"I'm sorry I'm not there to wish you happy birthday in person."

"If you were here, you'd be asleep!" Julia said.

"That's true enough," he said with a chuckle.

Cliff shifted his weight from one leg to the other. He was standing outside the Regency hotel several yards away from the crime scene. Since he wasn't going to make it home before Julia went to bed, he wanted to call her before she fell asleep. At this rate, he might not be home before she woke up in the morning.

Normally he went to bed between eight and nine and was an early riser. This was way past his bedtime. Surprisingly, he was wide awake. The adrenaline of the murder case and the second cup of coffee contributed to that.

"Are you coming home soon?" Julia asked.

"I don't think so. I'm going to be tied up at the crime scene for a while."

He looked over and saw the coroner loading the woman's body into a body bag, preparing to take it to the morgue where they'd do an autopsy. For him, the real work was just beginning. Canvassing. He needed to find a witness. And an identity. It'd help if he knew who she was.

"I thought you were off duty at midnight," Julia said with a slight groan like she missed him.

"Technically I am. But you know how it works. If I get a case, I have to work it until I'm finished. Then I can take off. I don't have to solve it, but I do have to take care of the preliminary work."

"Sounds like you have a tough one," Julia said sweetly.

He could hear the sound of what he thought was ruffling bedding in the background. Cliff could picture his wife tucking herself in. A strong desire to be in that bed with her shot through his heart. Even though she was right. He'd be asleep. Always was when she went to bed.

"It's shaping up to be a tough case," Cliff said. "It's a mystery. I've got a dead woman."

"How old?"

"Thirty-five or so."

"Is she pretty?"

"Hard to say. One side of her face is caved in."

"Ouch."

"But I would assume she is. She's wearing a nightgown. On the expensive side. White satin with a train. What's weird about it is that she's laying on the sidewalk. Outside the Regency hotel. No witnesses. No ID. No clue if she was killed on the spot or the body was moved to that location."

"Is she wearing a wedding ring?"

Cliff often ran the specifics of cases by Julia. She had a knack for asking the right questions and seeing things he hadn't seen.

"Yes. An expensive set. Her hair's all dolled up too. Like she had been somewhere special that day or something."

"She's on her honeymoon," Julia stated emphatically.

"What?"

"Ten to one she got married today."

"Why do you say that?"

"The white nightgown. Remember the one I wore on our honeymoon?"

"How could I forget?" Cliff said. The image firmly in his mind.

"Have you seen me wear it since?"

"No. I don't think I've seen you wear any nightgowns since our wedding night. You like that old T-shirt and pajama bottoms."

"My point exactly. The woman's on her honeymoon. And they're staying at that hotel."

"Who killed her though?"

"Her husband." Julia seemed certain.

"Why do you say that?"

"Because most women are murdered by a husband or by someone's lover. Either the husband or hers. Am I right?"

Cliff paused for a moment to let the question sink in. "Unless it's random. It's not quite as simple as that. But... you're right. Most people are murdered by someone they know."

"You said her face is smashed in. She was killed by a man. A woman doesn't have that kind of strength."

"She also might've fallen. Off the roof of the hotel or something." Cliff still hadn't ruled that out. Even though it seemed unlikely that she was on the roof. Someone would've seen her at the bar which was filled with people.

"Yep. It has to be the husband," Julia stated again.

"Oh, that's what you think, huh. You solved that awfully fast," Cliff quipped.

"Take my word for it. Find the husband, and you'll find the killer."

"How did she get on the sidewalk?"

"Do I have to do everything for you?"

"I gotta go," Cliff said as he suddenly thought of something.

"Find the husband," Julia said as he was about to hang up.

"I'm on it. Love you. Happy birthday."

Julia made the sound of a kiss as he hung up the phone. Cliff looked around and spotted the manager. He was still hanging around the scene. The deceased woman had been loaded into the coroner's vehicle.

The manager and the crowd watched as it drove away.

"Do you have a honeymoon suite?" Cliff asked the manager.

"Of course."

"Does it have a balcony?"

"It does. The Presidential Suite and the Honeymoon Suite both have balconies."

"Is it occupied?"

"I believe so. Yes."

"I need to see it."

"The guests are probably asleep at this time of night."

"I need to see it. Right now," Cliff said more forcefully as he started walking toward the hotel lobby. He looked back to see if the manager was following him.

He was.

Cliff quickened the pace.

To read more:
https://cutt.ly/ZE8s6vX

SAVE ME TWICE

FROM THE AUTHOR

Save Me Twice is the same story as Anna, just from Bae and Jamie's perspective. Bae was first introduced to my readers in book two of the Jamie Austen thrillers, *The Ingenue*. My readers have been clamoring for more of Bae. I took the opportunity to introduce Cliff Ford as a new character. In the future, there'll be more of Cliff and more of Bae in their own spin off series'.

THE JAMIE AUSTEN THRILLERS

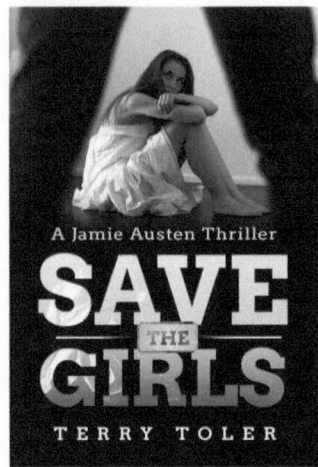
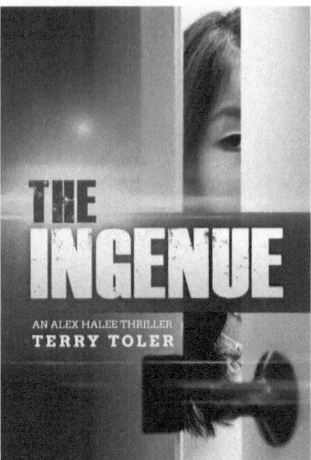

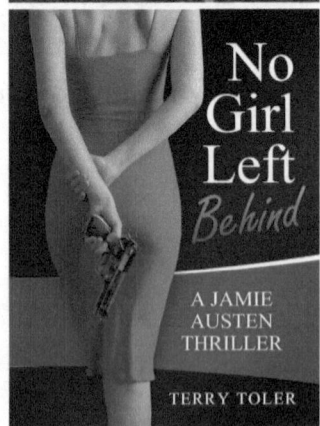

Thank you for purchasing this novel from best-selling author, Terry Toler. As an additional thank you, Terry wants to give you a free gift.

Sign up for:

Updates

New Releases

Announcements

At terrytoler.com

We'll send you the first three chapters of *The Launch*, a Jamie Austen novella, free of charge. The one that started the Spy Stories and Eden Stories Franchises.

Terrytoler.com

About the Author

TERRY TOLER is the author of the Jamie Austen and Alex Halee book series along with *The Eden Stories*. He is a minister, public speaker, counselor, and retired entrepreneur. Impacting the lives of people worldwide through storytelling has become one of his passions in life. He can be followed at terrytoler.com.

www.ingramcontent.com/pod-product-compliance
Lightning Source LLC
Chambersburg PA
CBHW050411260626
47156CB00003B/959